Killer's Craft

(A DI Shona McKenzie Mystery)

Wendy H. Jones

Published by Scott and Lawson

Cover Design by Cathy Helms of Avalon Graphics LLC

ISBN: 978-0-9930677-3-0

DEDICATION

To the memory of my mother, Catherine Jones who fostered my love of reading

To the people of Dundee without whom I would not be able to write these stories.

To the children of Liff Primary School who made me so welcome as their visiting author. I believe some of them will be writers one day.

ACKNOWLEDGMENTS

I would like to thank the following people who have helped me every step of the way.

Megan Appleton, Liz Strachan and Betty Doe for their tireless work with editing.

Fellow crime author Chris Longmuir, for all her help and support throughout the process of bringing the book to completion.

Karen Wilson of Ginger Snap Images, Dundee for the professional author photograph.

Nathan Gevers for all his hard work and enthusiasm building the website for my books.

Police Scotland for their patience in answering myriad questions about the nuts and bolts of policing. Particular thanks must go to my local police sergeant who has never failed to answer any of my questions with good humour and has supported me in my endeavor.

The members of the Angus Writers Circle for their valuable advice, feedback and support
.

1

The bodies lie, quiet and still, in a perfect black and white tableau, no longer able to sing their praise to the heavens. A thick, malevolent silence cloaks the scene. Not a word is uttered, not a sound made. One deadly twist, had introduced them to Charon, the aged ferryman who waits to carry the dead to the other side. That is if you believe such myths. Killer, of course, does not.

The faint glow of a nightlight provides just enough illumination to a monochrome image portrayed in its purest form. Killer, seeming nothing but a shadow, gazes in wonder before slipping from the room. Gliding along the dark, wood panelled, corridors, with a practiced familiarity, he makes no sound. The outer door shuts. The night encloses his figure in its wintery grasp as he leaves the building. Fat, heavy, flakes of snow conceal footsteps, obliterating any sign of human presence. The mournful hoot of a lonely owl echoes in the eerie stillness. Majestic snow-covered, trees conceal killer's fleeing form. Inside the building, the occupants sleep, knowing nothing of the presence of evil under these ancient eaves. This small part of the world has been changed forever.

2

"Nuns! Why would anybody want to kill a nun?"

Detective Inspector Shona McKenzie is pondering this very thought as she trudges down a long path, through deep snow, to the front door of St Winifred's Convent. Who indeed would even want to kill one, far less three, nuns? Why do these things always happen in the middle of the night? A five am call to a winter crime scene is not getting her day off to the best start. Shona is the head of the best CID Team in Dundee. Actually they're the only CID team.

Detective Sergeant Peter Johnston, who uttered the original words, continues "I mean there were a couple of nuns at my school who were terrible wifies, but that disnae mean I'd want tae murder them."

Having had a rare night out with Nina Chakrabarti Shona is not in the mood for Peter's ramblings.

"Give it a rest Peter. I'm trying to think."

"Feeling a bit precious are we Ma'am? Good night was it?"

"You'll be feeling precious in a minute if you don't shut up. Do you fancy moving to crowd control at Tannadice Park?"

They walk on, in silence, Peter, having got the message. Not only is the convent in the middle of nowhere it also has acres of grounds making it inaccessible by car in these conditions. As they reach the front door snow still falls in blizzard like proportions blanketing the area in an eerie silence despite the bustling scene ahead. As is usual, at a murder scene, there are people everywhere. Shona thinks there should be fewer willing bodies around at this hour, but no, everyone still turns up. It's like the circus has come to town. For once no one outside is worrying about where they are stepping or moving. The relentless snow renders any footsteps invisible. Shona and Peter put covers over their shoes, open the scarred, yet imposing, oak door, and step inside the convent. The tiled hallway is slick with melted snow despite the best efforts of Sergeant Muir, the Police Official Licensed Search Advisor.

"Better watch your step, Ma'am. We've enough problems withoot an accident," says Peter.

Glaring at him Shona approaches the POLSA.

"Have you got anything to report yet?" she asks.

"Not a thing, Ma'am. All we've done is seal off the area. Not that we need have bothered with all this snow." Sergeant Muir is a man of few words.

"Can we go up to the crime scene?"

"Of course. I've been waiting for you."

"When the rest of my team bother to show up send them along."

Shona turns to a distraught nun who is standing next to a priest.

"DI Shona McKenzie," then adds, "and my colleague DS Peter Johnston."

The priest responds, "Father MacIntyre and this is the Reverend Mother Mary Joseph."

"I have to ask you a few questions, but could you show me the bodies first." Blinking rapidly, the Reverend Mother moves off. They follow her through numerous corridors, and up steep stairs. The threadbare carpet spells looming disaster so Shona treads warily. The Mother Superior leads them to an open door. "In there." Tears, trickle down her cheeks.

Shona has already gathered the whereabouts of the

bodies from the crime scene tape, but keeps her counsel. The nun obviously feels that she has to help. "Thank you. Would you mind waiting here," says Shona as she turns into the room.

A bizarre sight greets her. In the dim overhead light she can just about see the scene. Inside the tiny cell three nuns are arranged, feet together, bodies forming a neat fan. Each has the rope from her habit tied tight around her neck. Gaffer tape covers their mouths. What is this, Shona wonders? Firstly, the perennial question, why kill a nun, and then why arrange them so?

"Peter, what the heck are we looking at here? Ever seen anything like this?"

"Nope. I can't say it means anything to me. This is a new one for sure."

"Do you think it might be some sort of religious symbol?"

"Haven't a clue. It's not my area of expertise."

"Aren't you a Catholic?"

"I am. That disnae mean I know anything about murdered nuns."

"Good point. Well, standing gazing at them isn't going to help us figure it out. We need to take a better look. Why isn't there any decent lighting in here?" Her breath steams out and freezes in the glacial air as she speaks. There doesn't appear to be any heating either, despite Antarctic level temperatures outside.

"It's a convent. No money, and they're meant to live frugally. We're probably still waiting for the council to turn up with the lights. Seeing as it's still the middle o' the night they would have had to chap them up."

"What on earth are you talking about?"

"Chap. Knock. In the old days a man who knocked on the doors to get people up for work."

4

"Peter, never mind the history lesson." She turns and says to the lone PC who is guarding the area, "Go and hurry them up." He scurries to do her bidding.

As he disappears down the long, narrow corridor, Shona moves towards the cell. "How in God's name are we supposed to process anything in here?" she says, trying to squeeze further into the cell. This proves to be damn near impossible, so she stops. "My bathroom's bigger than this and that's saying something."

"I wouldnae blaspheme in here Ma'am," Peter says, eyes looking to the heavens. "You might get struck by lightning or something."

"Good grief man. Get a grip. I'm sure God has better things to do than strike down the police in the course of their duty." Peter doesn't look any more cheery.

Closer inspection does little to improve their knowledge. Two of the nuns appear to be in their sixties and the other one about thirty. Shona looks again at the cords tied tight around their necks. "Looks like they've been strangled to me but I don't want to speculate. This is a single bedroom so a couple of them at least must have been carried in here."

"Seems like a lot of effort to me, Ma'am."

"Yep. Why would anyone go to this amount of effort to kill a few nuns and why these particular nuns?"

The PC returns with the man from the council in tow.

"What time of the night is this to be chappin a man up oot o' his bed? In this weather as well. This is nae life for a man my age."

Shona smiles. He must be Peter's twin. Leaving them to moan companionably, in a dialect she would never understand, Shona takes the opportunity to speak to the Mother Superior.

"I'm sorry for your loss, Reverend Mother. I know

this must be difficult for you but could you talk me through events here this morning?"

"Sister Mary Claire, Sister Mary Elizabeth and Sister Mary Josephine didn't turn up at morning prayers. It's extraordinary for one person to be late far less three. I sent Sister Mary Martha to look for them. She found them just as you saw them. We're all in shock. I rang the police and Father MacIntyre."

How will she ever keep these names straight Shona wonders?

"What time did Sister Mary..." glancing at her notes, "...Martha find them?"

"It must have been about 3.40 am as we start prayers at 3.30."

Why on earth would anyone want to get up at that time every day? Shona would never last in here. Pulling her mind back to the investigation she asks, "Has anyone touched anything?"

"Not as far as I know. Sister Mary Martha might. I stopped anyone going near the area after she told me."

"We'll have to interview all the occupants of the convent. Who lives here?"

"We're a small order these days. There are only ten nuns." Tears fill her eyes. "I suppose we are seven now." This isn't the usual grief fuelled, uncontrollable, sobbing, but a silent sorrow. It pierces Shona's heart.

Shona gives the nun a moment to collect herself, then, "Have you noticed anything different about them in the past few weeks or days? Any change in their behaviour?"

"No, they went about their job as always. No difference in what they did or said. Who would ever imagine something like this?"

"Were these three nuns particularly close?"

"No more close than anyone else. We spend a lot of time together in here so we all know each other well.

That's it."

"Did they work outside the convent?"

"Yes. Sister Mary Claire and Sister Mary Josephine were teachers. Sister Mary Elizabeth was a nurse."

"Thank you. Can you arrange somewhere quiet for me to speak to Sister Mary..." looking at the notes on her iPhone again, "Martha?"

"Of course. I will sort it out for you now."

Shona heads back to the murder scene where Peter is peering in at the door of the cell. "I'm frightened to go in. There's not much room and I dinnae want to disturb things."

"Where's Iain? He needs to take photographs and do fingerprints before we do anything." Looking around she adds, "Come to that where's the rest of the team?"

"Probably takin' their time tae get here seeing as it's the middle o' the night and sna'ing."

"What did you just say? I didn't understand a word of it."

"Do you no' speak English lassie? I said It's early morning and snowing," Peter says in a mock English accent.

"I speak English perfectly well thank you. It's your Scottish I seem to be having difficulty with. Your mastery of the English language, as always, leaves me speechless. Now - the others - get hold of them and tell them I want them here now. No excuses. How am I expected to process a crime scene with half the team missing?"

Peter whips out his brand new iPhone to give the missing coppers a stern talking to but they all come hurtling up the corridor.

"Sorry Ma'am."

"Had to park at the train station - couldn't get any closer."

"My dad couldn't dig the car out of the garage."

"Keep your voices down this is a convent not a night club. We've three dead nuns to focus on. Iain, get on with the photographs."

"Why would anyone want to kill a nun?"

"We might be able to answer that if you get on with your job instead of idle chit chat Iain."

Seeing Iain's look of puzzlement Peter mouths, "The DI's no' feeling quite herself."

She turns to Nina Chakrabarti, one of her sergeants, who is particularly energetic considering she partied on after Shona left. There's no justice in this world Shona thinks. "The three nuns were found at 0340 by a Sister Mary Martha. Could you go and interview her?"

"0340? Are you having a laugh? No one gets up at that time. I went to bed about half an hour before that."

"Whatever your views on a decent time for an alarm, that's when nuns get up so, go and interview her."

Nina turns and walks away, shaking her head.

"Do a decent job with these photos Iain. Once people get in that cell there's no chance with evidence."

"You're right there. A' these coppers with their muckle great feet will soon have it wiped away," Peter adds.

"I will be the only one going in there, apart from the police surgeon that is. I wish he'd get a move on. I'm fed up of all this hurry up and wait."

"I'll do you a grade A job Ma'am. You'll feel you're at the scene itself when you see these photos."

"Hi, Shona." Shona hears a warm voice behind her. The sound makes her come over all warm.

"Douglas." She turns and smiles. She has a soft spot for the procurator fiscal, Douglas Lawson, and is always glad to see him. They've had several dates but are taking things slowly.

"We must stop meeting over dead bodies. It's not natural. How did you manage to get here so quickly? Don't tell me you've brought your kids?" In her last case she couldn't seem to move around a crime scene without his son Rory turning up beside the body.

Holding up his hands Douglas says, "Stop with the questions. No. They were staying with their gran last night so I came straight here. What have you got for me?"

She shows him to the door of the small cell.

"Why would anyone want to kill a nun?"

"Good question but none of us can answer it yet. Have you heard of anything like this before?"

"Never. It's a first as far as I know."

The Police Surgeon, Larry Briar ambles along the corridor. "Shona, Douglas. Sorry had to come in from Monifieth at a crawl. Filthy weather." He squeezes his lanky frame into the small space, making Shona glad they'd already finished the photography and fingerprints. He returns to join them a short time later. "I can certify them all dead. From the condition of the bodies I would say they died somewhere around midnight. It's freezing in here so rigor mortis would take a bit longer. Mary, the pathologist, will give you a better idea after she's had a chance to open them up."

"Thanks Larry," but he is already on his way, leaving Shona speaking to the air. Situation normal. Shona often wonders why everyone feels that the most appropriate way to finish a conversation with her is to ignore her?

"He must be getting shedloads of overtime to be coming out in this weather. He could have got a nearby GP to come," she says.

"I agree. I've seen everything I need. I'll let you carry on. I'll ring you later for an update." With a smile

9

that lights up his eyes, and does a tap dance on Shona's heart, Douglas leaves. She is already looking forward to his call.

"Are ye sure you're not killing these people off so you can see your fella?" says Peter.

Shona blushes. "There would be many more dead bodies if that were the case. Come on, let's see what we can find in that cell."

Snapping on a pair of rubber gloves Shona squeezes into the cell to have a look. Closer inspection shows that one of the nuns is very red around the area of the tape. The Pathologist will have to decide whether this is from the tape or a chemical. The placing of the bodies seems very precise.

"I'm sure the way the bodies are lying is significant. We need to look into that," she says to Peter, who is hovering in the doorway. He pulls out his iPhone and attempts to make a note.

"Friggin thing is useless. No point tae us having them." He pulls out a notebook and pen.

Shona smiles. Since the reorganisation of the force into Scottish Police they have gone all high tech and Peter is having difficulty keeping up. "I'll send you on a computer course," she says. "That'll teach you to moan."

Peter groans. "Dinnae fash yersel, maam. I'll learn it just fine."

"Relax Peter. You're safe. I'm more worried about three dead nuns than your computer skills. There's a piece of black wool here caught in the young nuns watch. Get me a pair of tweezers and an evidence bag."

Shona finishes and says, "I'm off to speak to Father MacIntyre and the Reverend Mother. Find the rest of the team and search the convent."

The priest and the Mother Superior are drinking tea in a large kitchen.

"I need to ask you both a few more questions," says Shona.

"Of course. Would you like a hot drink?"

She accepts a coffee and cups her hands around the mug. Nectar from the gods or manna from heaven she supposes, despite its obviously being very cheap instant. The convent is freezing. Shona thinks she wouldn't last a minute in here.

"Thank you. Do either of you know why this could have happened. Has anyone got a grudge against the convent?"

"I can't see how. We do good works. Work with the poor. Run a large soup kitchen and give food parcels away. We've never done anything to draw that much attention to ourselves."

"Do you know where the murderer may have got in?"

"It could have been anywhere. This building is over a hundred years old and we haven't got the money to look after the place. I don't think it would take a lot to break in." Embarrassment is evident in the Reverend Mother's voice. "If someone opened a window round the back then no one would hear."

"Who has keys to the convent?"

"The Diocese would have some, as would the Bishop and all the nuns living in the convent. Various cleaners have had keys as well. We never thought it would be a problem. We've got nothing to steal, not even a television."

"Father MacIntyre what time did you arrive?"

"About 4.45. I had to walk most of the way from St. Monica's Church."

"Was the door locked when you arrived?"

"Yes, I had to ring the bell."

"How well did you know the nuns who were killed?"

"Not well at all. I've only been in the area six months. I was transferred here as there was a problem when the previous priest left suddenly."

"Why?"

"I don't know." The ecclesiastical fraternity like to keep things brief thinks Shona. She makes a note to follow that up.

"Thank you. I may need to speak to you again. Someone should be here soon to remove the bodies. I am sorry it has taken so long but the snow is holding everything up. Do you mind if I take a look around the convent?"

"Please do. Feel free to look anywhere you want. We've nothing to hide."

The team are gazing into a small back porch, which holds boots, wellies and coats.

"Have you lot got nothing better to do than stand around peering at footwear? Is this some sort of fetish?"

"Looks like we may have found our method of entry Ma'am. The lock's been broken," says Nina Chakrabarti.

"Any footprints?"

"I've taken photos of everything but it's not looking good. There are loads of footprints. We need to eliminate all the shoes in here. Also I think the killer may have covered his shoes. You can get a box of a hundred shoe covers like ours for a couple of quid on Amazon these days. Any idiot who watches CSI knows you need to cover your feet."

Shona sighs. The Internet should make their job so much easier but all it seems to do is make it harder. That and stupid crime programmes. "Nina, have you finished interviewing the nuns?"

"Yes. Not much to report."

"Debrief us back at the station. Iain, you stay with me and take more photographs Also fingerprint the remaining nuns and the priest. We might as well eliminate them, or catch them, as the case may be. I want to take a better look around. The rest of you get back to Bell Street and set up the incident room. I'll stay till the bodies are gone."

As everyone departs an eerie quiet descends. This place would give Shona the creeps even without dead bodies. Walking down corridors, and peering in rooms, she avoids the chapel where the priest and a superfluity of nuns are praying. She doesn't want the wrath of God falling on her head. It's funny the effect a convent has on a level-headed individual she thinks. She looks in a few cells, which are empty - evidence of the shrinking numbers. The ones which are occupied, don't hold much more - a bed, narrow wardrobe, chest of drawers. A Bible, dressing gown and towel. A few paperback books on shelves are the only adornment. Not much to show for a lifetime of devotion. She peers at the paperbacks. What do nuns read? There is a lot of catholic literature and two or three Rosamunde Pilcher and Ian Rankin. Much the same novels as anyone else she thinks. The sitting room isn't much better. Like the Mother Superior said not even a television. It's evident to her that this isn't a robbery gone wrong. There is nothing to steal.

After the bodies have been removed she goes to find Iain.

"It might be easier for you to get prints now. I'm off back to the station. I'll see you there." With that she steps into a bleak white world. Not sure how she will find her car, far less dig it out, she puts one weary foot in front of another, and goes to find out.

3

The blizzard does nothing to improve the concrete monstrosity that is Bell Street station. Its grey edifice, reminiscent of the Russian Gulags, does not inspire confidence in Shona as a copper, never mind the fine upstanding citizens of Dundee City. She finds the Chief to break the news to him that there has been a triple murder. Better get it over with.

"Nuns? Why would anyone want to kill a nun?"

She is a tad fed up of this. "I really don't know sir but my team and I will be doing our very best to find out."

"Don't you get sharp with me, Inspector. That tone is unnecessary."

"Sorry Sir, it's been a long night and everyone has asked me the same question."

"As your boss I can ask you any damn question I like and I expect a civil answer."

"Yes Sir. I'll report back to you when we have more news." She's talking to the Chief's bald head. She leaves wondering how she can help him shuffle of this mortal coil and bury him in the snow. Nobody would find him till Easter. She entertains herself with thoughts of how she can do this without being caught.

The squad room is empty apart from Peter who is reading *The Courier*.

"Where is everyone?"

"Most haven't managed to get back yet. Iain's off doing exciting things with fingerprints and Nina's gone down the canteen. Malnourished apparently."

"What about the rest of us? Is she getting anything for us?"

"Haven't a clue. She's too malnourished to care."

"The ungrateful little..." She is interrupted by Nina's backside crashing through the door, followed by the rest of her body and a tray of bacon rolls. "I take it all back. Give the girl a promotion."

"Thought we needed these, and thanks for the promotion. I accept. Can I be Chief Inspector?" Nina says, with a grin the size of India.

"Don't push your luck. Pass the nosh over." Shona grabs a huge roll, filled with several fat rashers of bacon, and dripping with butter and grease.

Peter has a look of ecstasy on his face as he chews. "Nobody can dae a bacon roll like us Dundonians."

A few minutes later the others turn up and fall on the rolls like characters from one of Dickens's bleaker novels. One thing Tayside's finest can do extraordinarily well is devour food.

As they are chewing, grease running down most chins, the Duty Sergeant enters with three people in tow.

Swallowing, Shona says, "Good to see you all. Grab a roll and we'll do introductions after that."

Everyone munches companionably for a few minutes before heading into the incident room.

"As you all know, when they reorganised the Scottish Police they decided our team needed to be bigger," says Shona.

"Aye, I couldn't believe it. Must be the only time reorganisation has worked in our favour," says Peter.

Shona waits for the choruses of agreement to die down. "You all know Jason Roberts, and Burns MacIntosh who helped us temporarily with our big case last year. They will be joining us on a permanent basis from today."

"Soldier boy, have you come to cause more havoc with rifles?" asks Iain.

Jason Roberts grins. He did a stint in the TA before joining the Police, hence his nickname. "If you need somebody who's a dab hand with a rifle I'm your man."

"What sort of name is Burns for a man?" asks Roy. "Did your mother have a love affair with the Bard or something?"

Burns grins. "You've just about got it right. She teaches poetry at the university. I think I got off lightly. My brothers are McGonagall, and Byron."

"McGonagall MacIntosh. I'd bet the family spaniel that he got some stick at school," Roy replies.

"Good to see you both again. Welcome to our crazy little world. Prepare to say goodbye to normal, but, of course, you know that already," says Nina.

Indicating a beautiful young Asian woman, Shona says, "I would also like to welcome our newest DS, Abigail Lai, who is joining us from The Highlands and Islands."

"Great to meet you all. I can't wait to get started," says Abigail in a lilting Scottish accent.

"You don't sound very Chinese," says Peter.

"I was born and bred in Skye. My dad is a GP there. I can speak Cantonese if it makes me seem more authentic." Abigail grins.

"Don't bother, you've a lovely accent."

Shona interrupts. "Take a seat everyone. Much as I would like to spend the day socialising, we have three murders to solve. You're going to be thrown in at the deep end I'm afraid."

"That's an understatement," says Peter. "We've three dead nuns on our hands."

Shona gives an overview of the situation so far whilst Nina writes notes on a pristine whiteboard. Little does she know it won't stay that way very long.

"Why would anyone want to kill a nun?"

The next person to say that will find themselves in the role of the body parts in Tayside Amateur Dramatic Society's production of Sweeny Todd, thinks Shona. Hangovers and stupid questions don't go well together in her world. She manages to rein her irritation in for the sake of team unity. "That's the question we'll have to answer if we want to solve this case. Any thoughts?"

"We need tae get a bit more info on the dead nuns," says Peter.

Nina chips in, "And on everyone else in the convent."

"The last priest from St Monica's disappeared under a cloud. Add that to the list of further enquiries," says Shona. "Unless of course anyone here knows what happened?"

"Nothing rings a bell with me," says Peter.

"What about researching suspicious deaths related to religions, or religious icons?" says Abigail.

Shona likes her already. She is quick on the uptake and keen to contribute.

"Might be worth enquiring into whether the nuns were well insured. Someone said the convent is bit run down. Maybe they're in financial difficulty," says Jason.

"I can't see members of the Church getting up to anything like that Soldier Boy."

"Roy, we can't assume. It's as good a point as any. You know yourself the Catholic Church is always in the news at the moment. Let's split up into pairs and start. Peter can you take Abigail and go back to the convent, then St Monica's. Dig up as much as you can."

"I don't think that's going to be possible Ma'am. You might think I've the skills of Jackie Stewart but even I cannae drive in this."

Moving to the window Shona peers out onto a

17

fierce blizzard. "Looks like we're stuck here for the duration. Do as much as you can by phone. Also get all your notes onto the computer and into Home Office Large Major Enquiry System, otherwise known as our friend HOLMES. We can see what it comes up with. Report back here at 1500 and we'll share what we've got. Peter, allocate teams and tasks."

She takes a mug of the strong black muck the station calls coffee, back to her office. At least it has copious amounts of caffeine in it. The late night and early morning are knocking her off her stride. There's something I'm missing, she thinks. What is it? It laps at the edges of her mind, but she can't grasp hold of it. Sighing she turns to a huge pile of paperwork that has accumulated over the festive period. Where does all this crap come from? She was only off for a few days. Sometimes she thinks becoming a DI is one of her more stupid moves. Picking up the first page she starts reading about the force wide plans for new office furniture. That is the most exciting of the bunch. Be still my beating heart, she thinks.

After about an hour the duty sergeant interrupts her. During her last big case she saw more of him than she did most of her friends.

"Don't tell me there's been another murder."

"No Ma'am, Auld Jocks come in to see you. I've popped him in an interview room."

"I'll be right down." Auld Jock, a local tramp, sleeps out in all weathers. Several times a month he drops in to say hello and get a feed. Something hot would be on his radar today. Sure enough, when Shona arrives he is tucking into a full cooked breakfast and a mug of strong tea. His dog, Maggie, is wolfing down a plate of bacon and sausages, on the floor beside him. She is an honorary police dog so she can come into the station as often as she likes. She even has her own ID card.

"Hi Jock. How are you?"

"To be honest with you Shona, I'm struggling with this weather. I'm finding it difficult tae sleep out."

"Have you been to the shelters?"

"I have. Even the Sally Army can't squeeze me in. I thought I'd come here and get warmed up a bit." Shona deciphers the local name for the Salvation Army, who do a sterling job of running a homeless shelter in town.

"You should get in there earlier Jock."

"Aye, I know."

Jock unbuttons his coat and a small wooden cross catches Shona's eye.

"Jock, thank you. You always manage to help me somehow."

"What?"

"I have to go and do something but wait here. I'll ask uniform if they have space in the cells. You can stay there for a night or two until the worst of the weather is over. Maggie too. We'll even throw in hot showers and clean clothes."

"Thank you Shona. You're a kind lassie. It'll be nice to be in the warm."

Shona looks at the photos in the incident room. That is what has been pricking at her brain. None of the nuns were wearing a cross. Moving to the squad room she finds Peter making a phone call.

"I need to speak to you now."

"Thanks for your help. I'll be in touch if there's anything else." Peter ends the conversation.

"Peter. Do nuns wear a cross around their neck?"

"Aye they do. It's called a crucifix because it has Jesus on it."

"Were any of the dead nuns wearing them?"

He looks up at the ceiling. "I dinnae remember seeing them."

"We need to look at Iain's photos."

They hurry to the incident room. "No crosses," she says.

"Crucifixes Ma'am."

"Whatever they're called, the nuns aren't wearing them. I'm off to ring the Mother Superior." She leaves Peter gazing at her retreating back.

"I swear the DI gets more nutty by the day."

"What's that you're saying about the DI?" asks Nina.

"Nothing. Ye weren't meant to hear that. How come you always seem to peel your lugs back at the wrong time?"

After a brief conversation with The Reverend Mother, Shona confirms no one had removed the crucifixes. Her next call is to Mary, the Pathologist.

"Shona. I haven't had time to get around to your dead nuns yet."

"That's fine. I just wanted to ask if any of the nuns had a crucifix around her neck?"

"Hang on Shona. I'll take a look."

Mary continues chatting as she walks to the drawers. "What is it with you and dead bodies? We had nary a one before you turned up and now the place seems to be crawling with them. Was it as bad as this when you were in Oxford?"

"Now that you mention it. Yes."

"I've had a look and the only thing around their necks are their habits. Oh, and the cords of course."

"Thanks Mary. I'll speak to you soon."

"I'll start on your nuns later today. In the meantime try to keep the body count down."

Shona puts the phone down. What does the killer want with three crucifixes?

At 1500 everyone gathers in the incident room, tea and coffee in hand.

"Anything to report?" Shona asks. "Peter, you start."

"I've spoken to the Reverend Mother and Father McIntyre. They both swear there's nothing in any o' the nuns' lives which would warrant murder. I get the feeling she's hiding something though. It might be worth bringing the other nuns in and speaking to them individually."

"Fair enough. The council seems to have cleared the roads so go and fetch them."

"The previous priest left following allegations of alleged child abuse. The three dead nuns reported him."

"Nice one Peter. Roy, what have you got?"

"I've been looking into the finances of the convent. It's about a prayer book's breadth away from being bankrupt. Couldn't find anything about life insurance policies on the dead nuns but I'll keep digging." In the bowels of a computer Roy is a whizz. He can go where no other man has ever gone before. One small step for Roy usually means one giant leap for crime fighting. However, that is only where computers are concerned. He is Shona's number one headache in all other areas.

"Thanks. Keep on it. Abigail, did you find any deaths associated with Catholic icons?"

"Not much that would help us. The Soviets used to murder Catholics and burn their Icons. It doesn't appear to have much bearing on our case though."

"It might not, but at this stage we can't rule anything out. Did any of the nuns come from Russia originally?"

Everyone looks blank. "Do we know the nuns real names?" asks Shona. More blank looks. No one does.

"We need to get a move on. Peter, Abigail, bring the remaining nuns and the Mother Superior in. The weather seems to have broken."

Shona waits until they leave the room.

"The rest of you see if you can come up with another angle."

She rubs her temples in a vain attempt to still the throbbing. It's your own stupid fault so stop whinging, she thinks. That's the last time she is going partying with Nina Chakrabarti. No good ever came of it. Grabbing a double strength coffee she hurries back to the office and slugs it down like a dehydrated marathon runner. Phoning the Mother Superior she soon has details for next of kin. Her counterparts in other towns agree to inform, and interview, the NOK. She hopes the convent hasn't told them already. How has she managed to screw up this investigation at this stage? Not letting NOK know immediately isn't the brightest of moves. They will be lumping her in with her predecessor. Not that she knows what he'd been fired for. That is Britain's best kept secret.

Paperwork just makes her headache worse but she ploughs on. As she gives in and riffles through her bag for Paracetamol, Abigail peers around the door.

"The nuns are here Ma'am and we've given them a hot drink. They're ready to be interviewed."

"You're with me. Peter can take Jason, and Nina, Burns. It'll do them good to get more interview experience. We'll do the Mother Superior and split the rest up between us." Swallowing the painkillers she stands up.

Shona switches on the recording equipment. "Interview

with The Reverend Mother Mary Joseph, Mother Superior of St Winifred's Convent. DI Shona McKenzie and DS Abigail Lai in attendance." How she managed to get all those mothers, Marys and reverends in the right order is a miracle she thinks. What a mouthful. "Thank you for coming in Reverend Mother. As DS Lai will have told you we have a few more questions. Are you happy for us to proceed?"

"Yes."

"Earlier today I asked you if you could think of any reason why these nuns may have been killed. Now you've had time to think about it, have you anything to add?"

"No. Nothing. There were no problems."

"It has come to our attention that the previous Priest at St Monica's was removed from his duties following allegations of child abuse. The three dead nuns were instrumental in bringing this to the attention of the diocese. Is that correct?"

The Mother Superiors eyes narrow. "Yes, but that has nothing to do with the death of my sisters."

"With all due respect, Reverend Mother, I'll decide what's relevant. We require every piece of information you have about your dead sisters. Nothing is to be kept back. Now have you anything to add?"

"No."

"We heard the nuns went to the diocese behind your back. How did it make you feel?"

"I didn't feel anything. They're entitled to speak to anyone they please."

"You mean to tell me you've no problem with the nuns under your charge doing things without your knowledge or consent? Shouldn't they report to you?"

"They should, but they decided not to."

"Why would they do that?"

The Mother Superior wipes sweat from her brow.

"I don't know."

"You must have some idea, Reverend Mother. Why would they avoid bringing this to you?"

"I told you I don't know. Asking me over and over isn't going to change the answer."

She has spunk for a nun who took a vow of humility.

"How is the convent's financial situation?"

A slight lowering of the head accompanies the silence.

"Answer the question."

"Like all convents we haven't got much money. We get by with help from the diocese."

"Has that changed now? Were the nuns insured?"

"Yes... Yes they were."

"How much for?"

"Is that important? It doesn't seem pertinent to me."

Gripping the paperwork tightly, Shona musters up the effort to stay calm.

"I've told you before, I decide what's important. How much for?"

"One hundred thousand pounds."

"Together, or each."

"Each."

"And you didn't think to bring this up before now?"

"I'd forgotten about it."

"Forgotten? Forgotten about three hundred thousand pounds? I find that hard to believe. It seems somewhat excessive to me for nuns who took vows of poverty. How could you afford the premiums for a policy like that? They must have been exorbitant."

"They were taken out when the convent had more money. The dioceses paid for the premiums. Anyway they were paid off years ago."

"You seem to know a lot about this for someone who'd forgotten."

"I'm not saying anything else until I get in touch with the Diocesan lawyer."

"Interview ended at 1630 at the request of the Reverend Mother Mary Joseph."

"DS Lai will take you to phone your lawyer. We'll come back to this when he arrives."

Peter and Jason are interviewing Sister Mary Martha.

"I know my colleague has asked you some questions this morning. I have a few more. Are you happy with that?" asks Peter.

The young nun is still looking a little green about the gills but answers, "Yes."

"Thank you. I believe you found the sisters this morning?"

"Yes. I never thought, in my worst nightmares, that God would expect me to deal with something like that."

"Aye, it must have upset you. But if we're going to find out who did this, we need to know everything we can about your fellow nuns. Did you notice anything out of the ordinary?"

Sister Mary Martha opens her mouth, and then hesitates.

"No matter what it is, it's important you tell us. Keeping things from us won't help."

The nun says, "Sister Mary Claire was having an affair."

Peter, a staunch Catholic, thinks he's misheard. "Could you repeat that a bit louder for the recording please?"

The nun obliges. Peter is lost for words. When he recovers he says, "Having an affair? Do you know who with?"

"The new gardener. He arrived about 6 months ago."

Peter, stunned, can't formulate another question. Jason steps in.

"What is the gardener's name? Do you know anything about him that might help us?"

"John Staples. I'm ashamed to say he is married with a new baby."

"How long have you known about this affair?"

"Only a week. I told her to stop but she wouldn't. She said she was ready to give up her vows for him." Tears roll down her cheeks.

Peter finds his voice. "Thank you. You've done the right thing. We'll finish there." His faith is so battered he can't find the energy to muster up another question.

Interviews finished, the team meet back in the briefing room.

"By the looks on your faces can I assume you all had a similar experience as Abigail and me?"

"I didn't know Convents were such a hotbed of intrigue," says Burns. "I've had my eyes opened today."

"You might as well start then. What have you got?"

"Sister Mary Claire wasn't exactly the perfect example of contemplation and humility."

"You got the same as us then," says Peter.

"Probably. Sister Mary Margaret said, and I quote, "The filthy little slut was having an affair with a married gardener." She seemed more put out by the fact he is a gardener than anything else."

After the interview with the Mother Superior Shona is past shock. "It looks like the convent has quite a story to tell. I've had an interesting time with the Reverend Mother."

"Dinnae tell me she's having an affair," is Peter's response. "I can't take much more."

"I'm pleased to say she's not. That's the best part. It would seem she is a bit of a control freak. She runs the place more like an Army barracks than a convent. Jason you were right. The nuns were well insured. There will be a tidy sum dropping in to the Convent's coffers. Good catch soldier boy."

Jason grins, as Roy hisses in is ear. "Brown noser. You'll do anything to get on the DI's good side."

"Shut up. You're just jealous."

"Anything we should know about boys?" asks Shona.

"I said it brings a whole new meaning to the term naughty nuns Ma'am."

"No one's laughing Roy. Keep your sordid thoughts to yourself. You're skating on thin ice."

"I was just saying."

"Well don't say. Does anyone in here look interested?"

"What about the strand of wool Iain. Anything significant about it?" she continues.

"Nothing. It's standard wool. Could have come from anywhere. Most likely the habits, but I'll need to get it under a microscope to say for sure."

"Thanks Iain. I think we can let the nuns go. Make it clear they're not to leave Dundee, especially the Mother Superior. She could have had them killed for the insurance money. We'll need to bring her back for more questions."

"Peter, you and Iain go and speak to John Staples. We need to find out his whereabouts on the night of the murder. The rest of you, I think we've done as much as we can do here. Go home."

Shona heads to the Chief's office. She feels dealing with problematic nuns is above her pay packet. Given the lateness of the hour, he has already headed in the direction of his slippers and pipe. She pulls out her mobile.

"Sir, I need advice."

"Make it quick. I'm just about to sit down to dinner. My wife won't be impressed if it's ruined."

For someone who's been married to a copper for so long, his wife isn't half intolerant.

Shona updates him. "I'm suspicious about the size of those life insurance policies. They're way OTT for nuns who are supposed to be humble and poor. I'd say she had them killed for the money but there's no evidence. Do we have enough for an arrest?"

The line goes quiet. She says a tentative "Hello."

"I'm thinking. Give me a minute... At the moment I'd say no. Keep on digging. Wait until after you've interviewed the gardener and then make a decision. I'll see you tomorrow."

"Thank you..." As usual Shona is left listening to the dialling tone. I'd like to meet his wife and shake her hand. She seems to have the Chief firmly under control. Maybe she could give me a few tips. With this thought cheering up her evening, she heads home. Shakespeare, her cat, will be waiting. A large measure of rather nice Glenmorangie single malt has her name on it.

4

Leaving the pub they chat like old pals as they stagger drunkenly up the road. Two men, who are instant friends over a pint at the local.

"It's no half good o' ye to make sure I get home okay."

"No bother pal. Us men have got tae look out for each other."

Shuttered windows and discarded chip papers provide an eerie background to their stumbling walk. The killer says, "There's a shortcut up here."

"It's a bit dark up there. No' very safe. Anything could happen tae us."

"Should be okay with two of us."

Once inside the total darkness of the alley the killer makes his move. Tripping the man is easy in his drunken state.

"Sorry, Pal."

Whilst the man struggles to get up, the killer prepares for his first move. He makes as though to help him, then slaps gaffer tape on his mouth. Pulling the short bar from his coat the killer strikes. Each blow is deliberate. The blows are carried out with a craftsman's precision. The solid darkness hides the terror in his victim's eyes. No sound comes from sealed lips but this does not matter. In this place, clutched in the grip of winter, no one will hear. No one will care. Even in daylight decent people do not come here. Graffiti covered walls, broken windows and general squalor see to that. On a night such as this it is desolate. The darkness swallows the blows until, at last, the killer's victim takes his final anguished breath. His death brings the relief for which he has, no doubt, been praying. It's funny how every man's thoughts turn to God at such a time. The killer stands and contemplates the scene before him. Once satisfied the man is truly dead, he turns, and walks away, confident and calm in what he has achieved. The killer is the master of his own destiny. In control of a world of his own creating, he is preparing he stage for what is yet to come. A shadow protected by the darkness of the night. There is no one to see or stop him. At one with the night he disappears on his way. He does not look back.

5

The sharp ring tone of the phone wakens Shona at 0400. "Rats." She drops the phone, fumbles, then, "Hello."

"Hello, Ma'am," says a far too cheery duty sergeant. "Sorry to wake you but we've got another suspicious death. Body of a man found in Reids Lane, Lochee. Anonymous call."

Shona thinks he doesn't sound very sorry. "That's four suspicious deaths in as many days."

"Aye, Ma'am. There seems to be a right plague o' them."

"Okay. Tell them I'm on my way."

Stumbling from the bed she finds the warmest clothing she has and pulls it on. Captain Scott would have felt right at home here. Shona thinks he should have foregone his visit to the Antarctic and stayed in Dundee.

Driving slowly she peers through a snow covered windscreen, until she steps from the car in Lochee high street. Broken streetlamps result in an eerie darkness. The glow of her torch the only light, she stumbles up the narrow lane. The torchlight sends muted shadows dancing against graffiti clad walls. Unkempt bushes spill into the footpath, forming natural traps for the unwary. Why would anyone walk up here in the middle of the night? This God forsaken wasteland is devoid of life and hope. What a place to gasp your final breath. Steps guarded she approaches the crime scene. The usual crew are gathered, huddled against the cold and biting wind. Everyone is staying well back. Her reputation precedes her. Most of them had received a tongue lashing from her at some point if she thought they were contaminating her crime scene.

Peter's muffled form presses against the wall in a useless attempt at shelter. "Morning Ma'am. This one's not looking good. I'd say he's taken a real beating."

Shona yawns. "Your definition of morning doesn't seem to match mine in any way whatsoever."

Her gaze focuses on the dead man. She doesn't want to assume anything but, is willing to stake this month's pay that Peter is right. Any part of the victim's anatomy that can be seen through the snow is swollen and bruised. This is apparent even in torchlight.

"He looks like he's been hit by the largest articulated lorry in Scotland. Of course that's impossible unless that's what happened and he was dumped here."

"There's not many lorries come down Lochee high street. It's a bit narrow."

"Good point. Well argued. If he'd been hit by a truck elsewhere then I'm sure this would be the last place anyone would think of dumping a body."

As she wonders what to do next the lights arrive, as do Larry and Douglas. A smile transforms her face as she says, "Here we are again, whispering sweet nothings over a body."

"If there were ever a silver cloud in a murder then you're it," says Douglas.

"Thanks. I think."

Larry pronounces the man dead. "No way I can give you even an estimated time of death as he's been lying out in an arctic wasteland. Difficult to tell whether it's rigor mortis or he's frozen solid. Mary should be able to help you with that when she's thawed him out a bit. I've no doubt I'll be seeing you soon the way you attract bodies. Do you think you could keep the next one to a more decent hour?"

Shona is beginning to get a bit hacked off with these quips. Why does everyone think that dead bodies follow her around? It's not as if she's the one going around slaughtering them. The police side of her knows she would make a great suspect.

"I'll do my best Larry, although I do love meeting up with you in the middle of the night in winter, so I can't promise."

She pulls her wandering thoughts back to the job. Things are much brighter due to the efforts of the council's finest workman, aka Eddie.

"Eddie, have you thought about joining the police? You seem to spend as much time around crimes as we do," says Nina. She can always be counted on to lighten the mood no matter how dire the situation.

"Well, lassie, I would but I'm no sure they'd have me at my advanced age."

"You can't be more than twenty-one Eddie." Shona joins in.

"Ach away with the both of you, I was sixty-two last week."

"Jocularity is all well and good but we've a body needing our attention. Iain have you finished?"

"I've done everything I can at the moment. Once the snow's brushed away I'll get clicking again. That's if my fingers are still working."

Stepping forward, Shona enters the temporary tent, which the POLSA's team has now erected.

"The snow's tinged with pink so I am assuming there's a lot of blood. Iain we need a sample." Taking the bottle from him she fills it, with the blood tinged snow, and passes it back. She uses a soft brush to clear away the snow from on top of the body.

"The face is beaten to a pulp. I'm not sure if it's a man or a woman. From the clothing I would say a man but who knows these days."

She searches his pockets. "He has a wallet with a few pounds but no ID. Get it into evidence. He isn't wearing a wedding ring but again that might not mean anything. The clothes look old and frayed and his shoes have seen better days. He looks a bit scruffy and could do with a shave."

Continuing her search she says, "His hands and ankles also look like they've been beaten." She hitches the trousers up a couple of inches. "I'm sure the pathologist will find similar bruising and abrasions all over his body. The agony this poor soul must have gone through. He must have been terrified."

"You're affy soft, Ma'am, if you don't mind me saying. For a copper that is."

"Tell anyone and your pension's in jeopardy."

Backing out of the tent she says, "Roy, you stay with the victim until our friends from the mortuary arrive to pick him up. Peter, Nina, and Abigail, split the team up and search the area. Anything and everything you find goes into evidence. If you need more warm bodies I am sure the POLSA would be happy to provide them."

She catches a movement and swivels. It is a brace of journalists from *The Courier* and the *Evening Telegraph*. One is the size of a person who has to heed the warnings about low bridges, and the other could fit in a mini with plenty room to spare. Her brow furrows as she throws them a look that could curdle yogurt. "How did you pair find out about this so quickly?"

"That's got nothing to do with you. What's happening? The public have a right to know."

"The public will find out when I decide to tell them. Now move. You're cluttering up my crime scene."

"We're not inside the tape." That is a debatable point as they are so close they could meld with the crime tape.

"I've just enlarged the search area and any minute now I'm going to arrest the pair of you."

"That's outrageous. What about freedom of speech."

"I'm using my freedom of speech to tell you to wrack off. Now get moving or the next act in this little play will involve handcuffs."

Heading back to the station she detours via Rough and Fraser bakery. Ten minutes later she is clutching three huge bags of filled rolls and a tray of cakes. These will keep the troops happy. They need something healthier than Doreen's heart attack on a roll. Plus Rough and Fraser make the best melt in your mouth rolls in the whole of Tayside.

6

She is right about the food. The whole team come in complaining.

"It's cold enough tae freeze the nuts aff the Tay Road Bridge," says Peter.

"I had fingers and toes when I left home this morning, but I'm not convinced I still do," Nina adds.

"You're all a bunch of wooses. You should see how cold it gets in the highlands and islands." Abigail laughs.

Shona diverts the threatening Scottish civil war by enticing them with the rolls and cakes. Quietness descends. The only time there's any peace in the office is when the team's jaws are wrapped around food thinks Shona.

Carrying the food they congregate in the incident room.

"What did you...? Peter, where are you going? We only just got here. You're up and down like a whore's knickers."

"Does a whore wear any, Ma'am?" Hilarious laughter ensures.

"Very witty Roy. Keep your remarks to yourself."

"I'm a man of a certain age. I could pee for Scotland," says Peter.

"That's more information about your nether regions than we want or need. Hurry up. I'll wait until you get back."

Settled again, she restarts. "I've spoken to the duty sergeant. Our latest victim's demise was reported anonymously. Roy, when we're finished here, track the phone."

"I'll pinpoint it so precisely I'll be able to tell you what colour they've painted the bathroom in their house. If they, and the phone, are in their house that is."

Waiting until the laughter dies down she continues, "Peter and Iain did you have any joy yesterday with John Staples, the gardener?"

"He couldn't have done it as he was playing cards with 8 other people. He fleeced them so I'm sure they're telling the truth. Not only that he's as thick as my wife's dumpling so he wouldn't have the nonce to plan anything on that scale. It's a shame as I thought he might have killed his bit on the side and two of her friends just to cover it up."

"Thanks Peter. What did the rest of you find at the scene of the latest murder?"

Nina took the lead. "Not a lot. We did what we could, given the snow, but it's not a high traffic area. Not many folk use the lane. A few cigarette ends and one coke can but that's about it."

"Let's hope the killer was smoking a post murder Marlboro and conveniently left it there for us to find," says Iain.

"Can anybody think of any leads?"

"Kenny McGuire just got out of Castle Huntly. He was there to be rehabilitated after serving ten years for beating his sister's fiancé to death. He has a history of violent assault. His motto is, why speak when fists will do."

"Nice one Roy. Bears looking into. However, it still doesn't give us any idea as to who the victim is. Burns could you see if any missing persons reports have come in?"

"I'm on it."

"Peter. Pin down Kenny McGuire's whereabouts

since he left prison. He must have a parole officer. We might need to bring him in for a chat."

"I'll see if HOLMES comes up with anything as well," says Peter.

"Get to work then and keep me posted."

Sheer willpower and strong coffee keeps her going for the next couple of hours. A harried desk sergeant interrupts her.

"I've a woman downstairs who says her husband didn't come home last night. You need to deal with this one Ma'am."

"Can't you take the details?"

"Not in this case, Ma'am. No. I'm not paid enough to deal with her. She's in interview room two. I'd advise you to take a couple of strong coppers with you."

She frowns but takes his word for it and goes to the squad room. "I need a couple of Scotland's strongest. Burns and Roy, come with me. The desk sergeant thinks I need bodyguards." She is somewhat incredulous but soon changes her tune on seeing the size of the woman. The Incredible Hulk would be quaking in his boots faced with this.

"I believe your husband hasn't come home Mrs..." stealing a glance at the notes the desk sergeant has provided, "...Green?"

The gargantuan woman rises to her feet. Blimey, no wonder the desk sergeant had insisted on reinforcements, thinks Shona.

"What am eh doing in here? Eh only came to report my man missing and I'm treated like a criminal," says Mrs Green in a broad Dundonian accent.

"What did she just say?"

Roy interprets. "She came to report her husband missing and she's being treated like a criminal."

"Mrs Green can you please speak English."

"What for."

"So my constables don't have to translate everything you say. We'll be here all day."

Shona switches on the recording equipment. "I realise you're upset Mrs Green but I can assure you we will do everything we can to help you. Please sit down. Can we get you a cup of tea?"

"Aye. Strong, with two sugars. It's all the polis are good for."

She gives Burns the nod and he leaves to order the tea. She feels unsure about that. A cup of tea could be classed as a lethal weapon in this woman's hands.

"Can you tell us what happened?" she asks.

"I've already said. My, man went to the pub last night and never came home. Not that he's much o' a loss the worthless bag o' sh…"

Shona interrupts, "What time did you last see him?"

"Six o'clock last night. He had his tea and then went out. That's what I've been telling you."

"Could you give us a few details about your husband. Name, age, height, what he looks like, shoe size, any thing that can help identify him. Do you have a picture of him?"

"What would I want a picture o' him for? He's effin useless. His name's Archie. He's fifty eight. Five foot and weighs nothing. He's a skinny little runt. What you want his shoe size for I dinnae know but it's a six."

"Anything else you can tell us?" asks Shona.

"He's going bald and his eyes are broon."

"Does he wear a wedding ring?"

"Aye. Since the day we were wed."

Her heart sinks. The victim doesn't have a wedding ring on so it looks likely it's not Archie Green. Everything else seems to fit though. She thinks she'd better keep an open mind. Then she feels bad for wishing the victim is this woman's husband.

"Thank you Mrs Green. You've been really helpful. Would you mind waiting here for a little while? We may have more questions."

"I've no' got time tae be sitting around waiting for the polis tae get their act together."

"It's important Mrs Green. I won't be long." She makes her escape, followed by Burns and Iain. "Keep an eye on her and make sure she doesn't go walkabout."

Despite saying, "Yes, Ma'am" they both look a bit worried.

"For goodness sake you're grown men. I thought you did weight lifting, Roy. What can she do to you?"

She goes to ring the mortuary. "Mary, can you tell if our latest victim is male and going bald."

"You're in luck, Shona, I've just started on him. I can confirm he's male and at first glance I'd say he could have a bald patch. He does have a little bit of hair but it's plastered to his head with blood. I can't give you a definite on that yet."

"Thanks Mary. I think we might have his wife in the station. Is he in any state for her to see him for identification?"

"No way. It's difficult enough to tell he's human."

"Thanks. I'll ask the wife to provide something for DNA. I'll have to go. There seems to be some sort of ruckus going on here."

She can hear shouts and crashing coming from the squad room. Entering she finds Roy and Jason having a fistfight.

"What the hell is going on here? Stop this right now." Silence descends as everyone in the room freezes, more in shock at the DI swearing than her strident tone. "You two. My office now."

As the offending parties leave the squad room Peter and Nina look at each other.

"They're for the high jump," says Peter.

Nina adds, "I think the DI's a bit miffed."

"A Bit miffed? That's the art of the great British understatement. I wouldn't like to get on the wrong side of her. Is she always like this?" Abigail's eyebrows have risen up to meet her hair.

"Nah. The DI's an old softie. As long as you do your job right that is."

Slamming the door fit to burst the frame, Shona says, "What is going on between you two?"

"He's a racist pig."

"He kicked me in the nuts."

"One at a time. DC Roberts you start." Her glare leaves Roy in no doubt that he should keep his mouth shut.

Jason says, "Roy made racist comments about the female sergeants. He said the only way to get promotion around here is to be a bitch, a paki or a chinky."

"That didn't give him any right to kick me in the nuts."

Shona's face turns even stonier, if that were possible. "Shut up. Both of you. DC Roberts whatever you feel about the way DC MacGregor talks, that does not give you free rein to assault him. The Army might have thought it was okay for you to solve problems by kicking the crap out of each other but that's not how we do it here. Out of my office now. I will deal with you in a minute."

The full measure of her wrath turns on Roy. "DC MacGregor if there is a boundary you seem to go at it like an armoured division. You have no regard for anyone but yourself. One more racist comment from you and you will be out of CID so fast you'll break the sound barrier. Consider this your first and only warning. If I even see a racist thought flicker across your face, you are out. Do I make myself clear?"

"But, Ma'am, it's obvious…"

"Do I make myself clear?" Her tone would make an Inuit feel right at home.

Roy mutters, "Yes Ma'am,"

"Go and find some ice to put on your prized possessions and keep out of my way."

He stomps from the room, indignation apparent in every tensed muscle.

She calls Jason in. "This will go on your record. You're still on probation in CID and this is not a good start. I am going to give you another chance but I want no repeat of such behaviour, do you hear."

"Yes Ma'am. I'm sorry." At least one of them seems repentant.

"That will be all."

Neither Abigail nor Nina wants to take it further. "He's just a jealous twat. Not worth losing sleep over," says Nina. Abigail is in complete agreement.

"Very magnanimous of you both. I want you to know they're not going unpunished. It's going in their permanent record."

"Okay Ma'am. No bother," Nina replies for them both.

"However, this doesn't excuse the fact that as sergeants you should have dealt with this before I got there."

"We only arrived a couple of minutes before you. We'll make sure it doesn't happen again."

"Make sure it doesn't. I haven't got time for this sort of behaviour from grown men."

Honestly. Everyone else gets a well-oiled team and I get a bunch of idiotic scrapping nitwits, thinks Shona.

The Chief is not impressed. "You need to take control, Shona. Firstly you've got bodies strewn along the highways and byways of Dundee and now your team's rioting. Get it sorted."

Thinking it would be a good idea to add his dead body to the total Shona says, "Yes Sir, " and goes to see Peter.

"What can we do about the rivalry between that pair?" she asks. "I've not got the energy to deal with tall dark and angry versus tall blond and emotional. I think it's time to return them both to the place whence they came."

"I'll take them under my wing and straighten them out. Don't you worry." His confidence is comforting. Shona has no doubt it will be sorted. In his time in the force he's had a lot of experience with lively, young Bobbies. A large whisky would go down a treat right about now Shona thinks. If she had any in her desk drawers she'd turn into one of those detectives in crime fiction who are almost permanently sozzled. She is beginning to think that might not be a bad thing.

Peter waits until Shona leaves and then turns on the pair. "Dumb and Dumber listen tae me. Any fighting done around here has tae be done in your underwear like they did in the auld days. Outside. The snow should give it that extra little something. Are you still keen tae fight?" Silence. "No I didnae think so. Get out of my sight before I do something I regret."

Forgoing thoughts of a stiff drink, Shona returns to the interview room and the formidable Mrs Green. The long wait has not restored her good humour.

"I'm sorry to have kept you waiting so long. We don't have any leads on your husband at the moment.

However, it would be useful to have something of his we could use for DNA testing. One of my officers will take you home and would you mind giving him something of your husband's like a comb? You said he had some hair left."

"I'm no' going home in a polis car. What will the neighbours say?"

"I'll make sure it's an unmarked vehicle and one of my female DC's will take you."

"Aye, okay then. At least I'll get a lift hame. It's the least you can do after keeping me here like a criminal."

When Shona returns, the squad room it is quiet and everyone busy.

"I hear you've been dealing with the not so jolly Green Giant," says Peter.

Shona shudders. "If our victim hadn't been beaten to death, I'd say he killed himself to get away from her. What a woman. She's about six foot and at a guess weighs about thirty stone. By the sounds of it her husband's five foot and weighs about a hundred pounds soaking wet."

"I wouldn't like to see them in bed."

"For goodness sake Peter. That's a dreadful picture to put in my head."

She turns, "Anyone for coffee and cake?"

There is a subdued chorus of agreement.

"Abigail and Burns, you escort Mrs, Green home. Everyone else meet in the incident room after you've got your rations."

Once they gather she says, "With two murder enquiries on the go we need to keep things organised. All information is to be added to the board and HOLMES immediately. We think the latest victim is a Mr Archie Green but we need DNA to confirm. Nina, I want you, Peter, and Jason, on this one. You take the lead. Abigail, Iain and Roy are on the dead nuns' case. I'm still suspicious of the Mother Superior. See if you can come up with another angle. Work your magic with the computer, Roy."

"I'll see what I can do."

"Peter, did you manage to get hold of Kenny McGuire's parole officer?"

"Aye, I did. He's living with his auld mother in Whitfield. It would seem he's doing everything he's told."

"At least we know where he is. Take a look and see if there could be any connection between him and Archie Green."

"Roy, did you track down the phone call?"

"Yep. Tracked it to a flat in the Hilltown. I listened to the call. It's a young lass who sounded as drunk as a Scotsman at Hogmany. Do you want me to go and chase it up?"

"No. Nina, you take Burns when he reappears. Oh, talk of the Devil. How did you get back here so quickly? I hope you weren't speeding?"

"Nah. We were as good as gold. The roads are quiet, and it's not that far," says Burns

Shona isn't convinced but says only, "Did you manage to get the DNA?"

"Yep, his greasy comb is with the lab as we speak. I think it's a biohazard," says Abigail.

"We'll let the lab worry about that. Right, into your teams and crack on."

Wandering back to her office Shona wonders if the cases are connected? Could it be another spree killer? Calling in on Peter she says, "See if there are any links between the nuns and Archie Green? We need to rule out a spree or serial killer."

"Surely that couldn't happen again in a wee city like Dundee."

"I agree it's unlikely but we'll look into it anyway."

A couple of hours later Nina knocks at her door. "I checked up on the phone call. There were three young women with monumental hangovers in the flat. They tripped over the body when they were walking home from clubbing in town. They did their civic duty and phoned it in. They can't remember much else. They said there was no one else around."

"Okay. Thanks."

"One more thing. It seems our Mrs Green isn't as innocent as she looks."

"As innocent as she looks?" Shona thinks the woman looks as innocent as a drunk in an off licence.

"She's known to us, as is Archie. It seems there was a lot of spousal abuse going on."

"How on earth could Archie beat up that woman mountain? I can't even begin to imagine her letting him away with it."

Nina bursts out laughing. "It was the other way round. She was beating him. Several assault charges were brought by him but then dropped when he changed his story. A&E up at Ninewells have confirmed him as a regular visitor. They won't give us any more information though."

"That's restored my faith in the natural balance of things. Well done. I'll see if we can get the DNA results and get a positive ID on Archie. Then we'll bring Mrs Green in for questioning."

Picking up the phone she speaks to the lab.

"Morning Inspector. You've just saved us the trouble of phoning you. Turns out your corpse and Mr Green are one and the same."

"Thanks for getting it done so quickly. I could kiss

you."

"Anything to help Ma'am. We aim to please. I'll collect the kiss at the summer barbecue."

Shona laughs. "Cheeky beggar." She puts the phone back in it's charger.

After arranging a warrant she grabs Nina. "Bring Mrs Green in for more questioning. Take the lads with you for safety. Use an unmarked or she'll be shouting about harassment and her good name being maligned in front of the neighbours."

"Do we get danger money for this?" asks Nina.

"Don't be such a sissy. Mind you, I think everyone should wear stab vests just in case."

"In the words of Captain Lawrence Oates, I am just going outside. I may be some time."

"Stop being so dramatic, Nina. Man up. You're a detective not a ballerina. Go get 'em."

"Yes Ma'am. Remember me bravely." They both laugh, although Nina's is a touch high pitched.

Her concern is justified, as is apparent when they get back. Jason is sporting a black eye and Roy's lip is bleeding.

"Did you two do that to each other or is Mrs Green not keen to help us with our enquiries?"

"You can add resisting arrest and assaulting a police officer to any charges you bring against her. When she's found guilty of murder I hope they bring back hanging. That poor sod in the mortuary's better off out of it," says Roy.

"It pains me to say it but I agree with everything he says," adds Jason.

"Well, well. Our Mrs Green seems to have managed the almost impossible task of bringing you pair together. Maybe I should employ her. Have you got her in an interview room?"

"Yep."

"Nina, you can do the interview with me. See if you can get a couple of uniforms to be in there as well. She's done enough damage to our team. Roy and Jason get yourselves examined by first aid and fill in incident reports. Jason, you might have to go to A&E. Your eye's swelling shut."

Gathering up their courage Nina and Shona go to interview the formidable, and possibly murderous, Mrs Green.

Mrs Green is still handcuffed.

"What do you fuc...?"

"Mrs Green. Sit down and shut up. You're in enough trouble as it is. Have you phoned a lawyer?"

"Where would eh get money for a lawyer? Eh wouldn't need one if you lot hadn't arrested me for nothing."

"You were arrested for assaulting a police officer. Now, would you like us to get you a lawyer from legal aid?"

"Aye."

Going outside Shona addresses the large crowd of officers who are peering through the interview room window. "You lot are like a committee of vultures. One of you make yourself useful and get a legal aid lawyer for Mrs Green."

"Better make it Stephen Slater, he does wrestling in his spare time," one of the coppers quips.

She returns to the interview. "Would you like us to wait until your lawyer gets here before answering our questions or are you happy for us to proceed?"

"I've nothing tae hide so carry on. I've no' done nothing."

Most of their customers have an amazing ability to delude themselves, which never ceases to amaze Shona.

"Mrs Green, I am sorry to have to inform you that your husband was found dead in the early hours of this morning."

"Deid. How can he be deid? He only went out for a pint." Shona can see the blood drain from her face. She's either a brilliant actress or she's got nothing to do with her husbands death, thinks Shona.

"How am eh meant tae pay the bills without his wage coming in?"

"I'm sure that's something social services will be able to help you with, Mrs Green." You've got more on your plate than that love, she adds to herself.

"It says in our records that your husband reported a number of times that you beat him. Is this true?"

"The stupid old sod used tae do that every time he got drunk He never went through with it when he sobered up."

"Your husband also attended A&E numerous times with broken bones, cuts and bruises."

"So he was clumsy. That doesn't mean eh beat him. What are you getting at? You'd better no' be trying to fit me up."

"Where were you between the hours of midnight and 3 am last night Mrs Green?"

Mrs Green's bulk shoots into the air. "Are you trying to frame me You fuc..?"

The slap of Shona's hand on the table reverberates around the cramped room. "I'll ask you to keep a civil tongue in your head. Sit down."

"Eh want my lawyer. Eh know my rights. I'm not saying another word."

"Interview ended at 1933 following the request by Mrs Green for her lawyer to be present."

"Sometimes I wonder why we do this job," says Nina. "We need danger money. I'd rather deal with most of the scumbags in the Dundee underworld than people like her."

"Me too. Phone in an order and get pizza for

everyone. I've had nothing since this morning's roll. I need sustenance to deal with Big Daddy in there. The usual mixture and get a vegetarian for the newbies just in case and a supreme for me."

"You're a woman after my own heart. Consider it done. Can we blue light someone to pick it up?"

"No we can't, you cheeky sod. You can just wait."

By the time they have eaten their fill, Mrs Green's lawyer has arrived. They continue the questioning.

"Where were you between the hours of Midnight and 3 am?"

"My client doesn't have to answer that. She has been charged with assault not murdering her husband."

"I am also investigating the murder of your client's husband and I am sure she will want to do anything she can to help us find the murderer. Now where were you?"

"At home asleep."

"Can anyone confirm that?"

"I rang my daughter just before midnight. She could tell you I was at home then."

The thought of this odd pair having kids is too much. It makes Shona feel weak.

"Can we have your daughter's name, address and phone number?"

Mrs Green seems a bit calmer and hands the information over without a fuss. She is escorted to a cell where she will stay overnight following the GBH charge.

Roy catches Shona as she returns to her office. "I've got a bit more info on the convent. It urgently needs a new roof and the Mother Superior arranged for the work to be done next week. She made the arrangements a week ago."

"Thanks Roy, that's great. I think we've enough

evidence for an arrest but it will wait till morning."

Going into the squad room she says, "It's time we called it a day. Anyone fancy a drink?"

Coats are grabbed as they dash for the pub. Shona sighs. It has been one hell of a day.

7

With no early morning call to disturb her sleep Shona feels more like her normal cheery self the next morning. Feeding a mewing Shakespeare, she downs a cup of scalding Brazilian blend coffee, before braving the still atrocious weather to drive to work. She needs a run but isn't going in these conditions. Besides, she has to start work soonest, in order to get a warrant to enter, search and seize at the convent. She has a feeling the Sheriff is going to take some convincing.

This is her first task on arriving at work. Phoning, she's put through immediately.

"Good morning Shona. How may I help?"

"We have a problem at St Winifred's Convent Sheriff Strothers." She explains the situation. "I need a warrant to enter, search and seize all computers."

"In a convent? That's a new one even for you. On balance I think you have grounds." She has her warrant. Hanging up the phone she punches the air. "Yes!"

When Peter arrives she calls him into her office. "You, I, Jason and Iain are off on an enter, search and seize."

"I've not had my morning roll and cup of tea yet. Can it not wait half an hour?"

"No it flaming well can't. Stop thinking about your stomach for a minute and go and fetch the boys."

Peter turns, back stiff, and leaves the room. "That's a bit rich. She eats more than the rest of us put together," he mutters. Peter plus no breakfast equals one grumpy policeman.

By the time they get in the car Peter has managed to snatch a muffin to keep body and soul together. "When I was being taught by nuns at school I never thought I'd be doing a dawn raid at the convent." He sounds cheery at the prospect.

"It's half past nine. Hardly a dawn raid."

"Aye. Well you know what I mean. Anyway we'd have tae be affy early to get this lot at dawn. Three in the morning's not my favourite part of the day."

"Not unless you're still out clubbing," comes from the back seat.

"My clubbing days are over, but I could've give you a run for your money as a youngster. I could shake a mean heel at the Palais."

"I didn't think they had nightclubs when Robert Peel was in charge."

The good natured banter keeps up as they trudge up the snow covered drive.

Ringing the bell they wait an interminable amount of time until the solid wood door creaks open. An elderly nun is dwarfed by the enormous doorframe. Which nun, Shona has no clue. They all look the same to her.

"Good morning Sister. I have a warrant here to enter and search the premises." She hands it over.

"I'll have to get the Reverend Mother."

"I'm afraid we can't wait until you do," Shona says keeping her voice soft. "Please, let us in."

The nun complies. As they enter the Reverend Mother herself appears. Peter hands her the warrant and Shona says, "This allows us to search the building for computers and take them back to the station. One of my PCs will stay with everyone in the building whilst we complete our search."

After half an hour they have searched the building and seized one PC and two laptops.

"It seems a lot for a bunch of people who don't even have a telly," says Jason.

"I agree. This is one strange convent. Not that I know a great deal about convents. This being the only one I've set foot in," says Shona.

Finding the Mother Superior she hands her the receipt for the computers. "These will be held as evidence in a murder enquiry. You will be informed when you can have them back."

The Mother Superior's face is implacable.

Returning to Bell Street they dump the computers on Roy's desk. "This will keep you occupied for a while. Did you get the passwords?

"I surely did Ma'am. He performs a sloppy salute. Not that we needed to. They're all things like 'MaryandJoseph' and 'Christmas'. I could have cracked them in about 2 minutes."

"What's with the cowboy impersonation? Stick to English." Shona smiles.

Roy laughs. He's grateful it isn't the usual telling off. He always seems to be in the doghouse with the DI.

A couple of hours later Shona is interrupted, in the act of devouring a greasy pie from the canteen, by a knock on her office door.

"I've found some interesting things on that computer Ma'am," says Roy.

"Round up the others and meet me in the incident room in five minutes. We might as well all hear it," she mumbles through a mouthful of pie. She wipes the grease dribbling down her chin. Arriving in the briefing room she finds everyone gathered eager to hear what Iain has to say.

"It didn't take me long to go through emails and find the ones which were deleted and removed. Not a tech savvy person amongst them in that convent."

"Well they are nuns. They've not had much opportunity tae build up their careers in Silicon Valley," says Peter.

To a chorus of laughter, Roy continues, "Their emails are interesting. Here I've printed a few copies."

People start reading and a few of them gasp.

"Some of these would give *50 Shades* a run for its money," says Nina.

"They're not that bad Nina. I'm more interested in the ones from the Mother Superior. It looks like the convents finances are so dire the diocese is threatening closure. Our Reverend Mother Mary Joseph has said she would do anything she could to find a way to keep it open."

"It looks like we have our motive then. Do we arrest her?" asks Abigail.

"Affirmative. Iain, have you found anything that would incriminate any of the other nuns."

"No. Most of the emails were between the nuns and their families. Nothing of interest."

"Peter. You and I are off to arrest the Reverend Mother. This has to be a first."

Shona stops to update the Chief. "I think she arranged to have the nuns killed to collect the life insurance. She also managed to get rid of someone who was bringing the order into disrepute at the same time."

"It does seem likely. Are you confident in making the arrest?"

"I am, Sir."

"Report to me when you get back and have interviewed her again. Remember to use her real name."

Good point. Shona has forgotten nuns are born with a different name. The Chief occasionally has his uses.

By the time they get to the convent, reporters from the *Evening Telegraph* are sniffing around. To say Shona is annoyed would be an understatement. How do they find out about these things, she wonders? Ignoring them, Peter Rings the bell and they are soon reading the Mother Superior her rights.

"Sarah Jean Smith, we are arresting you for incitement to commit murder. You do not have to say anything, but it may harm your defence if you do not mention when questioned something, which you later rely on in court. Anything you do say may be given in evidence," says Shona.

A camera flash goes off as they leave the building. Brilliant. She will be on the front of that nights paper, arresting a nun. That will go down well with the fine upstanding citizens of Dundee. Many Dundee citizens already think the police are a bunch of numpties. This will seal the deal as far as the public is concerned.

After allowing the Mother Superior, or Sarah Jean Smith, to phone the diocesan lawyer Shona parks her in a cell. "Can I have a bible and may I have my rosary beads back and my crucifix?"

"I'm sorry but you can't have your rosary beads or the crucifix. However, of course we can get you a bible."

"A catholic one?"

"I'll see what I can do." She hurries down to the desk sergeant. "Can you get one of your PC's to bring in a Catholic Bible. As far as I know we've only got the ones The Gideons hand out which are not Catholic."

She drops into the squad room, which has the look and smell of a late night Asian street market. "When did the grenade go off?"

Most of the team ignore her but Peter looks up, "What?"

"The only explanation for the state of this place

must be that someone threw in a grenade."

"It's no' that bad."

"Peter, it's a pig sty. You're a sergeant, step to it and get the troops to clean up."

Leaving she hears Peter say, "Right, you clarty sods, you heard the DI. She's got her knickers in a twist about the state o' the office. I agree. You're a slovenly bunch so get your marigolds out and put some welly into it."

He's got a cheek considering his desk's the worst of the lot thinks Shona.

It doesn't take long for Sarah Jean Smith's lawyers to arrive, finding Shona back in the interview room. At least the Mother Superior isn't likely to lamp her unless she calls down the wrath of God on her head she thinks.

The diocesan lawyer is quick to get in first. "This is outrageous. How can you believe that my client, a longstanding stalwart of our community, could be guilty of such a crime?"

"If we didn't have evidence to the contrary we wouldn't be sitting here. I need to ask your client a few more questions. I would suggest you keep quiet and let us get on with it." She glances at the papers in her hand. "Sarah. How long have you been the Mother Superior of the convent?"

"Thirty years." Nuns obviously believe in keeping things simple in speech as well as life. This one does anyway.

"Is it true that during this time the finances of the convent have deteriorated?"

"Yes, but that has nothing to do with me. There are fewer people going to church in the city, so collections are down."

"Just how bad is the financial situation at the convent?"

"My client doesn't have to answer that. It has no

bearing on the charges."

"I disagree, and she does have to answer. If she is innocent, then there shouldn't be a problem. Now please answer the question, Sarah."

"They are bad. In fact they are worse than bad. It looks like they are going to have to shut us down."

"And yet you ordered work to start on building a new roof?"

"Yes. We are confident of a Scottish Heritage grant coming in and I wanted the work to start immediately."

"What if the money hadn't come through?"

"The roofers were aware that we would not be able to go ahead."

Shona whispers to Jason, "Go check that out with the roofers."

Shona hands over copies of the emails to the Mother Superior and her lawyer. "What did you mean when you said you would do anything to keep the convent open?"

"Wh… What? How did you get these?"

"Anything can be retrieved from a hard drive. It's not that difficult. Now what did you mean?"

"I didn't mean anything. It's just something you say."

"We have enough here to prosecute you for conspiracy to murder. Did you arrange to have the nuns murdered? It's better to tell us. The judge may be more lenient."

"I haven't done anything. There's nothing I can tell you."

"It will be up to you and your lawyer to prove that."

The nun looks resigned. "I am sure God will help us prove that."

Shona finishes the interview. It is pointless arguing with God.

In the squad room everyone is hard at work, apart from Nina who is haranguing the others. "Haven't you managed to come up with anything yet? How are we meant to solve a crime when you useless shower can't do your job?" Most people think silence is the wisest response, other than Roy.

"Time of the month is it?"

Half way out of her chair Nina says, "Say that to me again and I'll staple your nuts to the floor."

Everyone laughs. Roy turns red and says, "I'm sorry. It was a joke. It won't happen again."

Nina takes the apology in good grace, and replies "Okay. We'll leave it there."

Peter is stunned. Maybe the little prat's learning something after all, he thinks. That's the first time he's ever heard Roy apologise. Wonders will never cease.

Peace reigns by the time Shona makes it back to the squad room.

"Hi Ma'am," says Abigail. "I've been to visit the Green's daughter. She seems a lot more placid and level headed than her mother. She's confirmed her mother's alibi. Mrs Green phoned her and spent an hour complaining about the fact Archie hadn't come home."

"We can't pin Archie's murder on her then. She's still got charges for assault though but we'd better let her go. I suppose it will save Her Majesty paying for her food and board. Book her on the assault charges and throw her out. No lifts home this time. That'll teach her."

"Yes, Ma'am." Abigail looks cheerful at the thought.

"Peter, do we know what pub Archie Green was drinking at last night?"

"Aye we do. Jockie's on the High Street."

"We need to give Jockie a visit to find out who Archie Green was drinking with or speaking to. In fact anyone who even looked at him. Peter, you're with me."

"Always happy to visit a pub Ma'am."

"Don't get too excited. You won't be drinking."

"No' even a swift half."

"Not even a sniff of the barmaid's apron."

Jockie's is a typical run down pub. There are a few regulars propping up the bar mainly pensioners and the work shy. Peter and Shona flash their badges at the middle aged woman behind the bar. "DI Shona McKenzie and DS Peter Johnston. Is Jockie around? We'd like to ask him a few questions."

"I'm Bella Young, the owner. Jockie died years ago but we kept the name. This is a respectable place. There's nothing dodgy goes on here."

"We're not accusing you of anything, Mrs Young. I believe a Mr Archie Green was in here last night. Is that correct?"

"Aye. He's in here every night at 6 o'clock. You can set your watch by him. What's he done? He's never any bother in here."

"Did you see what time he left last night?"

"No. We had a karaoke night and the place was packed."

Shona's heart sinks, at the thought of all those interviews. Also more punters usually means no one sees a thing. "Did you happen to notice anyone new here, or anyone talking to Archie?"

"Are you having a laugh? It was standing room only in here and I hardly recognised a soul. We were too busy pulling pints to worry about what the punters were doing."

"Do you know what time Mr. Green left?"

"I haven't a clue but he usually leaves between eleven thirty and twelve. Probably giving that wife of his time to get to bed."

"Is there anyone that Archie regularly sits with?"

"Yes. Him and Bert Walker are as thick as thieves, but I think Bert's tucked up in a bed in Ninewells Hospital at the moment. I heard he had a bit of a stroke."

"Thanks for your help. Could you write down the names of anyone you remember being here. I'll send someone to pick it up later?"

When they get outside Shona says, "Drop me at Bell Street and then go up to the hospital and see if Bert Walker's in a fit state to speak to you. He might know something that will help."

Peter gets back about an hour later having been able to speak to Bert. "Not much help Ma'am. According to him Archie was a pillar of the community and wouldn't do anything to hurt anyone. I'm sure he wasn't a pillar of any sort but he does sound inoffensive."

"Thanks. Send some of the team around to speak to the neighbours and see what you can come up with. Has anybody looked at CCTV footage?"

"When I popped into the squad room they were going through about a millions hours of it. Not sure how far they've got," says Peter.

"I'll come and see them in a minute. Sort out who should canvas the neighbours?" says Shona.

"Nina can take Jason and Abigail can take Roy. It'll give them a chance tae work together and might solidify relations a bit more."

"Either that or it will dissolve the team completely. Okay. I trust your judgement," says Shona.

According to Iain, the CCTV footage isn't getting them very far. "Dundee has more cameras per square foot than any other City in the UK and still they're no use when it comes to solving a crime. Half the cameras are broken and there wasn't enough light for the others. Most of the streetlights in the area are broken." Peter is his usual glum self.

"I know it's hard going slogging through footage but keep at it. Hopefully there will be something in there."

8

Talk is easy and time is cheap thinks the killer.

"How much?"

"Depends what you want and how much time."

"I've not got much time. Just the basics."

"Forty quid."

The lying little slut. That's much more than the going rate.

"Fine." The killer shoves dirty notes into fingernails tipped with chipped purple polish.

An agreement is reached before they move up the snowy hillside. Woods provide some shelter from the snow, but not much. Deep inside the majestic splendour of the snow-covered trees, the killer makes his move. They kiss. A short rope is pulled from a pocket. The killer's hands move. 'Stroking' her neck, the rope is slipped in place and pulled tight. As it grows tighter terror blazes from the woman's bulging eyes, which turn fatalistic and then dim. Her life breath is frozen, as if by the snow itself. She will ply her trade no more. The killer strips her and leaves her lying, in the pose associated with death. Hands crossed on her breast. This place has been transformed from one of beauty to one of evil. The killer gazes at this masterpiece. Surveying this snapshot of time, and storing it in his mind, the killer slips away. Still the snow falls.

9

Shona is running along the icy esplanade at Broughty Ferry, the cold burning her lungs with every steady breath. With all this snow and ice it's probably the most stupid stunt she's ever pulled. She doesn't care. She needs the exercise. Each strong, carefully placed, step moves her further past the beach, as the pure white snow dances off the brooding grey of the river Tay. The sound of Tchaikovsky's 1812 Overture drags her from this reverie. Her mobile.

"Shona McKenzie."

"I hate to be the bringer of bad news but there's another body been found. It's in Baxter Park. Looks like a suspicious death."

"At least you've left it till 8 o'clock this morning," she replies.

"Nothing to do with me Ma'am. I'm just the messenger."

"Thanks, sergeant. Tell them I'll be on my way in about half an hour. I'm out running."

Stopping only for a shower and to feed Shakespeare, she pours coffee in a thermal cup and is out of the door. The cat is vociferous in her objections to being left again. "Tough luck old girl, your views on the subject are being dismissed." Sipping the strong brew en route, she mentally thanks her mother for the Tassimo machine she gave her for Christmas. She quaffs like Henry the VIII at a banquette.

At Baxter Park most parking spaces have been taken.

Shona parks on double yellows and puts a police sign on the dash. Might as well use any little vestige of power I've got she thinks. Saying good morning to the young PC at the gate she steps over the crime scene tape. The usual cast of characters are assembled. Here we are again, happy as can be, floats through her head. "What have we got Peter?"

"A woman who's been strangled by the sounds of it. No' that I've been up there. The POLSA wanted Iain to take photos before he'd let anyone up the hill. He's doing them now. Yon' laddie shivering over there, is the one that found her."

Shona moves over to the young man. Flashing her badge as way of introduction she says, "Detective Inspector Shona McKenzie. I believe you found the body?"

The lad can't force a word out through chattering teeth. He is dressed only in a thin top, Ron Hill tracksters and expensive running shoes. A full rucksack sits beside him

"Yeh. Yeh, I did. I'm j... j... joining the Marines next week so need to keep my fitness up. I ran round and round the park and then started hill sprints. That's when I f... found her."

He looks like he's in shock. He'll not get far in battle if he's in this state over one dead body thinks Shona.

"Did you see anyone or anything else in the park?"

"No, nothing. As far as I know there was only me."

"What about in the street?"

"I ran here from home and didn't see anyone. There's only me stupid enough to be out at 7 o'clock in the morning in this weather." Shona is thankful his colour is improving.

"What's in the pack?"

"It's full of books. I needed to run with weight."

"Do you mind if I look?"

He nods his assent and Shona opens the bag. Books indeed.

"Thank you. I'm going to get someone to take you down to the station to give a statement. I'm sure they'll find you a blanket and a mug of hot coffee." Witnesses with hypothermia are not a good look for the CID.

The Police surgeon arrives, a straggler as usual. "No break in the weather then Shona. It's Baltic."

Why do Dundonians always feel the need to comment on the weather? They're obsessed with it. Shona has only seen two versions so far, rain and snow. Out of politeness she murmers, "Morning Larry. You're right."

He makes an uneventful journey up the hill but his return is spectacular. Skidding, he slides down the slope on his backside before sprawling, at her feet. She can see shoulders shaking as everyone controls the urge to laugh. He is not a man who will take kindly to anything like that. No one says a word. They can't. Pulling his wits and his dignity together, he stands up grasping Peter's outstretched hand.

"Certified dead and from the look of her I would say she's been strangled." With that he goes carefully on his way, his back ramrod stiff. It is then everyone bursts out laughing.

"It's worth coming oot at this time o' the morning just tae see that." Peter sums it up for the rest of the team.

"If you're finished having fun at the police surgeon's expense, let's go and see the body," says Shona. Trooping up the hill they keep a close eye on the ground in case they tread on any evidence. It also means that they won't repeat the police surgeon's impressive gymnastics.

The girl, who is about twenty years old, looks

small and pitiful.

"I ken her," says Peter. "Her name's Tilly Methven. She's a prossie and we've had her in the cells a few times for Trading in Prostitution."

"She looks like she's been posed. Why are her arms crossed across her chest? I'd say it smacks of some sort of religious slaying like the nuns." Shona moves closer. "There are burn marks on her neck which is indicative of strangulation with a rope. Again, it seems close to what happened to the nuns. The murder weapon's gone this time though."

"We had a spate of murders like this in the Highlands and Islands," says Abigail. "Someone was murdering pensioners and leaving them in the same pose. I don't think it's the Highland killer though, unless he's escaped from Shotts Maximum Security, where he should be doing twenty-five to life. He's a nutjob. Said he wanted to put them out of their misery and he thought they looked peaceful after he'd helped them."

"Maybe we've got a copycat ridding the world of prossies," Nina chips in.

"It's something to think about but unlikely as we've only one dead prostitute. Despite the shenanigans of one of the nuns we can't in all fairness put them in the same category. They're a decent bunch on the whole and do good works. We'll continue this at the station. Looks like the body's about to depart for the mortuary."

There is a rush to leave, the thought of heat galvanising them. Shona stops short at the gate when she sees a reporter arguing with an irate PC.

"The sharks are circling. How the hell did you lot find out about this?"

"It doesn't matter how we found out. We're entitled to be here."

"We can't stop you being in the street." She turns to the PC. "If they put one toe inside this park you have my permission to arrest them."

"The Press have freedom in this country. You can't suppress what we have to say."

"No but I can throw you in a cell for interfering with a police investigation."

Shona spends several entertaining minutes thinking of ways in which she could suppress them for good. This cheery thought sustains her until she returns to Gulag Bell Street.

Gathered over drinks, and piping hot sausage and egg rolls, the ideas continue coming. "Maybe she was murdered for her takings," says Roy.

"At £10 a trick I don't think she would have made enough to be murdered for them. The prossies around here are not exactly park lane quality." Nina worked in Vice for a while.

"Is that all they make? Imagine going out in this weather and exposing yourself to disease and worse for a measly ten quid." Jason's mouth is lolling.

"For someone who's been in the Army you've led a sheltered life, Soldier Boy," quips Iain.

"We'll leave that one to the side for a minute but we might come back to it. Thanks for bringing it up, Roy. Abigail, I'd like you to go to Shotts and speak to your boy from Skye. See if you can dig anything up. Take Roy with you."

Shona turns to Peter. "As you seem to know Tilly could you find the address of her next of kin and we'll go and break the news to them that their nearest and dearest is dead."

10

Whitfield is still quiet this Monday morning. The houses are modern and new although many have a downtrodden look. They knock on a red painted door and wait. A small woman answers. Showing the woman her card Shona introduces both herself and Peter.

"Please come in. How can I help you?" The woman is, thankfully, dressed and the house is polished to a shine Shona envies.

"Mrs Methven?" asks Shona.

"Yes. What's this all about?" She has a wary look in her eyes.

"Do you have a daughter called Tilly?"

"Yes. Yes, I do." Wariness is replaced by fear. "What has she been up to now?"

"I am sorry to have to inform you, but a girl answering the description of your daughter was found dead in the early hours of this morning."

"No. Oh please God no." The woman starts rocking back and forwards.

"Do you know where Tilly was last night?"

"No, I don't. I haven't seen or spoken to her in six months. I can imagine though."

"I take it you and your daughter were estranged?"

"That's putting it mildly. She walked out eight months ago saying I stifled her. She said she couldn't breathe with all my rules." She stops. Mascara stained rivulets run down her cheeks. Shona hands her a tissue.

"I wish I'd tried harder to get in touch with her. I never imagined this would happen."

"We need you to come and identify your daughter. Is there anyone who can come with you?"

"My husband, Tilly's stepfather. He's a nurse at a care home in town. He's on shift."

"Peter, drive up and get him. I'll wait here with Mrs Methven."

Harriet Methven's sagging posture and keening cry tells Shona everything she needs to know. The young woman lying on the table in the Mortuary is Tilly.

"I am so sorry for your loss, Mrs Methven. Have you got an address where Tilly stayed?"

"Yes, she lived with her boyfriend in a flat in Baffin Street. I worry about her but what could I do. She's 24 what could I do." As she realises her daughter will never see another birthday, deep, shuddering sobs shake her feeble frame. Her bewildered husband puts his arm around her and pulls her close.

"You've been really helpful Mrs. Methven. Thank you. We'll take you home now."

"When will we get her..." Fresh sobbing then, "her body back? We'll need to arrange her funeral."

"I'm not sure. There will have to be an autopsy. The Procurator Fiscal will be in touch when they have done everything they need to. They'll look after Tilly."

They drop the couple home on their way back to the station.

"Could I have her locket? She had it for her 18th and had a picture of me in it."

"I don't remember her having a locket when we found her. I'll check the pathologist didn't put it somewhere safe or it may have gone into evidence. Maybe she left it in her flat so it didn't get lost."

"It's more likely she pawned her locket," says Peter as they leave the couple. "When she wisnae turning tricks, we'd find her begging outside the

Wellgate."

Back at the station Shona rallies the troops.

"Any thoughts Peter, as you knew her?"

"Not that well. I've never been up close and personal with her."

Once the laughter and racy comments die down he continues.

"I don't think this couple could have had anything tae do with it. I know it's necessary to keep an open mind but they did seem genuine and helpful."

"You're right but you know better than I do, that a lot of people fake it."

"Probably a trick gone wrong," says Jason.

"I'm inclined to agree. Round up all the known prossies in Dundee and see if anybody saw anything. Widen the search if necessary. Ask them if they've had any rough clients recently."

"That's an affy lot of people," says Peter.

"I've learnt enough about Dundee to agree with you. We'll have to do it anyway. Find names and addresses and go talk to them. Split up into pairs. One lot can go and speak to anyone in the houses backing on to the park."

"Make sure there's a female officer in each pair. We don't want the boys getting accused of anything nasty," adds Peter.

Roy splutters, "I wouldn't touch that lot with a policeman's truncheon, never mind get up to anything with them."

"I know you wouldn't Roy, but when it comes to dealing with the seedy underbelly of Dundee it's better to be safe than sorry. I'll get you another woman from uniform. I'm staying here," says Shona.

Peace is reigning in Shona's office until a shout is heard

"DI McKenzie get in here."

Resigned, she rises, and goes to speak to the Chief. "You wanted me sir."

"What's this I hear about another dead body? I would like to know why I heard about it from uniform and not you?"

She'd forgotten to let the Chief know. Epic fail. "I'm sorry Sir. I should have informed you straight away."

"That's not good enough. So what's happened now?"

Shona fills him in on the latest developments.

"Are you telling me that we now have five murders on our hands and so far all we've got is one nun in our cells on conspiracy to murder? We're not even out of January yet, Shona. Get it sorted."

"Yes sir." It is pointless arguing with the boss when he is in this mood.

She returns to her office and picks up the ringing phone.

"It's Bella Young from Jockie's pub. I've got that list you asked for."

"Thanks Bella, I'll have one of my team drop round to pick it up."

Ringing Nina she asks her to drop into Jockie's on her way back. She then calls the pathologist. "Morning Mary. How are you?"

"I'm suffering from terminal exhaustion due to the number of bodies you're sending me. At least it's not as bad as last time - yet."

Shona thinks back to their previous case and shudders. "I never want to talk about that again. Have you got anything yet on my bodies?"

"I'm still on young Tilly but can update you on the others. Looks like the nuns were silenced with chloroform and tape put over their mouths. One of the nuns was allergic to either the chloroform or tape. I can confirm death by strangulation. There's one thing you will want to know," and she rattles off her findings. Shona is past being surprised but this is indeed a major piece of the puzzle.

"I knew you'd like that. Archie Green, poor sod, was beaten to death as we thought. From the pattern of the wounds I'd say with an iron bar or something like that. I'll get the results for Tilly back to you once she's thawed out enough for me to examine her properly."

Shona hangs up and is in deep thought when she hears a quiet voice say "Hello Shona." Looking up she sees three pairs of eyes peering at her.

"Rory, what a fright. What are you guys doing here?"

"Daddy's speaking to your boss. I wanted to see you. This is my friend Freya," says Alice.

"And jolly pleased I am to see you all. I'm sure there's cake in the squad room. Do you want to join the police as well, Freya?"

"No, I want to be a crime writer like my Auntie." Shame, thinks Shona. She is hoping to palm her job off onto any willing child who walks through the door.

"I liked my steam train you gave me for Christmas. It fits my track and everything."

"An elf told me it would."

"Rory let me play with it."

"That was very nice of Rory."

The kids are happily munching on a slab of post Christmas Dundee cake when their father appears.

"I see you're bribing my kids with cake again."

"Shona always gives us cake, Daddy. I like cake."

"I know you do, Alice, and it's very good of Shona. I hope you said thank you."

"Of course we did." Rory isn't letting his father away with anything.

Shona interrupts this fascinating insight into the domestic life of the average British family. "Hi, Douglas. What brings you to the Gulags?"

"With all this snow I have to agree it does resemble Siberia. I had to come in for a meeting with the Super and catch up with you on the latest murder. The kids are at work with me this morning as their gran can't have them. Freya's mum is a nurse so can't have her."

"Are they not meant to be at school?"

"Inset day."

"Already? They've only just gone back."

"Tell me about it? The vagaries of the Scottish school system never cease to amaze me."

"We're going sledging this afternoon," contributes Alice. "In the park," she adds, just in case there is any room for misunderstanding.

"That sounds like great fun."

As the kids wait outside, Shona briefs Douglas, and then goes out to say goodbye to the kids.

"Can you not come sledging with us?" asks Rory.

"Sorry. I wish I could but I'm hard at work catching the bad guys. Maybe next time."

"I don't want your job after all Shona. You don't seem to get much time for playing."

"You're right Rory. Maybe I'll get time to come and play with you all soon."

As the team return, Shona yells from her office, "Meet in the incident room in 5 minutes."

They just about make it in five minutes whilst slopping tea and dropping biscuits.

Shona asks, "Anything to report?"

"Not a thing. Every prossie we interviewed said they were at home. The weather's too bad for them," says Peter.

"Same here." Nina and Jason had no luck either.

"Have any of their tricks turned nasty recently?"

"No more than the usual slapping that seems to turn their tricks on. They all swore that they'd call the police on anything too way out," says Peter. "I'm inclined to believe them. The lassies do tend to look out for each other."

"I'm glad to hear it," says Shona. "What about the neighbours?"

"We went to every house bordering on the park. No one saw anything. Most people said, and I quote "Who'd want to look in there and see a bunch of drug doped whores touting for business?" The ones who did look out the window said they could see nothing for the snow," says Abigail.

"Have we managed to interview every prostitute?"

"Nope, we can't find half of them. Nobody seems tae know where they are."

"I suppose they are a rather flighty bunch. So we're no further forwards." Shona hands over a list. "These are the people who were in Jockie's the night Archie Green was killed. Bring them in and see if they know anything."

"A rather flighty bunch. You're no half posh Ma'am. You need to learn some Dundonian," says Peter.

"You've a cheek to take the mickey out of my choice of words, Peter." Her grin softens the words. "Abigail, have you arranged to interview your Skye killer?"

"The roads are impassable around Shotts. Their snow's worse than ours. They did let me speak to him on Skype though."

"My, the wonders of modern science. Who'd have thought we'd be speaking to prisoners over a computer," says Peter.

"It wasn't much help I'm afraid. He's complete

fruitcake material. He just ranted about peace and tranquillity and him being the agent of God. I've arranged for the prison psychiatrist to speak to him. He might be able to untangle what he's saying."

"Thanks, Abigail. Park it and chase it up in a few days if you haven't heard. On a completely different note, you'll love the latest news from the Mortuary. It turns out Sister Mary Claire was pregnant."

"This just gets better and better. I wonder if the Reverend Mother knew about that?" asks Peter.

"That's exactly what I'm about to find out. Nina, come with me and we'll interview her again."

Once more in an interview room, Shona switches on the recording equipment. She tries to keep her voice gentle but firm. "Reverend Mother, new evidence has come to light. Is there anything else you would like to tell us?"

"No. I've told you everything I know. I can only repeat I was not involved in any of this."

Despite the trouble she is in the Reverend Mother displays an inner peace, which Shona envies. Shona would sacrifice her left arm for a bit of calm in her life right now.

"Are you sure, because now would be a good time to tell us?"

"I'm sure. I cannot tell you what I don't know."

"Were you aware that Sister Mary Claire was pregnant?"

The Reverend Mother turns white and slumps in her chair. Shona leaps to her feet, afraid the nun is going to faint. "Get some water," she instructs Nina.

Recovering, the Reverend Mother whispers, "No, I did not. I didn't think this could get any worse but now a child has died too."

Nina returns with the water and the Reverend Mother grasps the glass like a lifeline. Shona would swear on all of Shakespeare's nine lives that she is telling the truth.

Instead of returning to her office she goes to break the news to the Chief that the murder count is now six, including a dead baby. His mouth tightens. He says, "One of these days you'll come to me with good news rather than sky high body counts. I'll let the Superintendent know."

"Thank you Sir. I'll keep you posted." The Mother Superior is right. Things are getting worse. Shona feels she could do with even a nano glimmer of good news.

The team has been busy and the station is full of people lounging around moaning and waiting to be interviewed. Although disgruntled they are at least staying calm. Shona hears one mutter, "Wasting valuable drinking time." She has no sympathy. It'll do your liver good to have a break you old soak. You've probably drunk the equivalent of the Tay Estuary in your lifetime.

Back in her office she realises that the Chief is on the warpath, and heading in her direction.

"We need a Press conference. The editor from the *Dundee Evening Telegraph* has phoned saying you're breaking their right to free speech. If you find any reporters sniffing round, apart from the Press conference, you have my permission to break anything else you would like. Legs, arms, heads, take your pick." The Chief is well known for his hatred of reporters. It is about the only thing they agree on.

"I'll get on it right away, sir. When's best for you?" Of course, she means for the Press conference but thinks longingly of having fun with reporters' bones.

"At 1600 hours today. Oh, another thing. Have you

done all the usual internet malarkey as well? Facetwit or whatever it's called. Waste of time if you ask me but we've been told we've to keep up with the times."

"Yes sir. It's in hand. We've put out the usual calls for help. Facebook and Twitter are awash with requests for assistance."

"That's all. Come and find me at 1550 hours."

Returning to the squad room she finds a full complement of staff. "Have you dug up any useful information?"

All of the team shake their heads, except Abigail. "One woman, Miss Edna McKay, thinks she saw two men walking up the high street about 2330. It was dark and snowing though so she couldn't give us anything else."

"What about CCTV? Is there anything from that now we've narrowed down the time?"

"Nothing," says Iain. "Most of them are broken and the snow obliterated anything from the ones which were working."

"Peter, get on to the council now and tell them to get these CCTV camera's fixed. How are we meant to solve crimes with the council doing their level best to help the criminals? They're a useless bunch of layabouts."

"Yes, Ma'am." Any other response is pointless. The DI must be in a damned bad mood if she is slagging off the council. They are usually helpful and willing to pull out all the stops for the police.

Shona sits thinking with her head propped on her hands. The boss's opinion of her is going down quicker than the demolition of the Derby Street multis and her reputation as the grim reaper is growing. Could these murders have anything in common? Nothing springs to mind. What about the strangulations? They have a strong case against the Reverend Mother for the nuns. Where does Archie fit in, and what about the young prostitute. The cogs in her head are spinning and nothing is making any sense. Something is bothering her. She needs to discuss it with someone else. Peter can always be relied on for discretion.

Peter comes at her bidding, bearing coffee and cakes. "No problem can be solved without tea and a wee bittie cake."

She smiles. "Thanks, Peter, I'm ready for a bite to eat. There's something puzzling me. How come the newspapers always seem to turn up at the crime scene? It can't be they're scanning radios because we're all using mobile phones. Do you think we've got a leak?"

Peter is silent for a minute and says, "It does seem the most likely explanation. Mind you I can't see anyone in the team leaking information. Even Roy wouldn't be that stupid."

"He's always wearing designer gear. How can he afford that on a DC's salary."

"Aye, but so is Nina. Roy still lives with his parents. I'd bet a month's fag money he's mummy's little boy and doesn't pay a penny in keep."

"Is there any way we can check up on them?"

"You'd have tae get warrants to monitor their mobiles."

"I know. I don't want to go down that route at the moment. We'll have to park it."

.

11

As the Press conference approaches she heads towards the Chief. She stops en route at the squad room to see if any progress has been made.

"Here comes the stations supermodel. The slightest hint of a camera and the DI's all dolled up. Are you hoping a reporter from Vogue will be there?" says Peter.

The entire squad room bursts out laughing.

"Don't forget us when you're famous," says Nina.

"Looking for a change of career are we?" asks Iain.

"You lot had better have some evidence for me when I get back or you'll all be looking for a change of career." She is glad to hear laughter again. It has been a bit subdued since the contretemps between Roy and Jason.

The Chief, spit shiny in his number one uniform, takes the lead.

"I am sure you are aware that there have been a number of murders in Dundee over the past couple of weeks. The victim's families have been told, so we are able to release the names. We have reason to believe these murders are not connected. The first incident took place in the early hours of Monday seventh of January. Three nuns were murdered inside St Winifred's Convent. They were Sister Mary Claire, Sister Mary Elizabeth and Sister Mary Josephine. Many Dundonians will know them from their work in both teaching and nursing. They will be sadly missed within the community. We have one suspect in custody."

"Can you tell us more about the suspect?" One of the reporters cuts in.

"No, and I would thank you to keep any comments or questions until the end." The Chief, like Queen Victoria, is not amused.

"The second incident involved the murder of a Mr Archie Green. He was last seen drinking in Jockie's pub in Lochee High Street. Witnesses say he may have been walking up the high street with another person. He was found, beaten to death in Reids Lane, Lochee in the early morning of Thursday the 10th of January." He takes a sip of water.

"The third incident involved a young woman found strangled in Baxter Park in the early hours of this morning. Her name is Tilly Methven. If anyone has any information that could help us with any of these cases then please contact the Chief Investigation Officer, Detective Inspector Shona McKenzie on 0300 572 8761."

Hands shoot up as reporters vie to ask questions.

"Mackie Stuart, *Dundee Courier*. I heard that the suspect you have in custody is the Mother Superior of the Convent. Is that correct?"

"As this is an on-going investigation we cannot comment on that at this time."

"John Laird, Dundee *Evening Telegraph* and *The Courier*. As the girl was found in Baxter Park is it likely she was a prostitute?"

"You will agree that we cannot answer questions like that as we have to maintain privacy for the relatives."

"Miranda Greg, *The Scotsman*. Do you think this could be another serial killer?"

"As I said, we do not believe these crimes are related."

John Laird is confident. "Chief Inspector, it would

seem to me that since you have been in post the murder rate in Dundee has risen significantly. Have you anything to say about that?"

The Chief, somehow keeping his cool, says "No comment. We will take no further questions." he swivels and walks off.

Once they are back in the building he says, "My office. Now."

"How dare you put me in that position. I would agree, the murder rate has risen. Since you arrived, not me. I will not take the blame for your inadequacies."

"But sir. I'm not responsible for the murders. It's no one's fault."

"Do not argue with me. Get these murders solved and do it quickly. This does not look good on anyone's record. If anyone is having an interview without coffee in the Superintendent's office, it will be you, not me." He dismisses her with a curt wave of the hand.

Her stoic nature is beginning to crumble. I've had enough of this she thinks. She is beginning to wonder why she comes in day after day and take all this crap. It's not as if she seems to be doing any good anyway. Thinking that a swift kick to the Chief's unmentionables might give her a well-needed boost, she resists, for the sake of her career, and finds the others. The team still seem to be in a good mood. At least something's going right for her. "Have you found anything? Please say you've found something."

"We have Ma'am. One of the men we interviewed this afternoon came back of his own accord. Said he had more information and felt guilty. Archie Green was in debt tae Chick Anderson, our local back street moneylender. It turns out Archie liked a flutter on the gee-gees and borrowed a hundred quid. The debt's racked up to two thousand big ones."

"Two thousand quid! That's some interest rate. I'm

in the wrong job. So it looks like Chick or his henchmen could have got a bit carried away?"

"Aye, it does, Ma'am."

"We've also got a bit more info on Tilly. We've had an anonymous tip off. Her boyfriend and pimp is Jimmy McTaggart. He's a complete bampot and been arrested by uniform multiple times," says Burns. "I've had dealings with him and he's as violent as they come. His business card says GBH R US. Done a couple of stints in Perth Prison but he's out at the moment."

"There's no' any GBH in Scotland. It's Assault to severe injury," says Peter.

"I know but it doesn't have the same ring as GBH R US."

Shona is suddenly feeling much more cheery. "Peter, you and Roy go and bring in Chick Anderson for questioning. Burns you seem to know Jimmy McTaggart. Take Iain and bring him in."

"With all due respect, Ma'am, he's nuts. It might take more than two of us."

"Take Jason as well. I'm sure he learned a few tricks in the Army that will help you. Abigail and Nina, come with me."

Everyone disperses leaving the women to file off to the police canteen.

"I need sustenance. I would say Chick and Jimmy are a main and pudding job. You can't face the dregs of Dundee society on an empty stomach."

The canteen is dead. "I'll have your best steak and kidney pie with all the trimmings Annie. Make it a large portion." Annie, having a soft spot for Shona, she leaves the counter with a plate piled high. Her lunch is a heart attack on a plate.

"I don't know where you put it," says Abigail. "You're rake thin."

"You've a cheek to speak. You're not exactly fat

yourself and that plate's as full as mine."

"Touché." Silence descends as they devour steaming platefuls of stodge whilst awaiting the arrival of Chick and Jimmy.

12

The pair are dragged through the door, handcuffed and bellowing like walruses in heat. Interspersed with a colourful array of obscenities is their accusation, "This is police brutality." It never ceases to amaze Shona that most of Dundee's criminals, not having a grey cell to share between them, still know those words. She believes they came with their mother's milk. A sharp yelp from Jason means a kicking foot has met its mark. Poor Jason isn't doing well during these arrests. Not that Shona is bothered. It would toughen him up. Despite vociferous objections the pair are, literally, thrown into separate interview rooms still roaring like the demons of hell.

"Peter, which one do you want? I'll take the other."

"I'd better take Jimmy. He doesn't think much o' women and we might not get much out of him if there's a woman involved."

"Much as I'd love to bring him down to size you're probably right. Take one of the boys with you, preferably one that won't antagonise him. I'll take Burns in with me and interview Chick. Best of luck."

"If I'm no out by supper time send reinforcements."

"All you ever worry about is where your next meal's coming from. Man up and go interview. It can't be that bad."

Entering the interview room, Shona is confronted by a very irate moneylender indeed. Chick is all flash suit, dazzling white teeth and righteous anger.

"What's going on? I'd like tae know why you've dragged me away from my business."

"Mr. Anderson, as part of an on-going investigation we need to ask you if you know a Mr. Archie Green?"

"Yes I do. He's always in and out of my pawnshop."

"Pawnshop? Is that what you call it?"

"Aye, it's a respectable business."

Gritting her teeth, she just about manages to stop laughing. "When did you last see Archie Green?"

"I think it was about a month ago. How the hell would I know without my records? Why do you want to know about him anyway?"

"I'm sure you've heard on the Lochee grapevine that someone murdered him a few nights ago."

"I'd heard rumours but wisnnae sure." Chick's accent is getting stronger.

"I have reason to believe that you lent him a hundred pounds recently and he hasn't repaid the debt."

"He pawned a watch. I gave him a hundred quid for it."

"Are you trying to tell me that Archie Green had a watch a pawnbroker would give him a hundred pounds for? I find that incredible. Stop playing games. We both know what you do on the QT." Shona looks down at the papers in front of her. Roy has done her proud. "Do you recognise the names, Stephan and Gregor Alexeyev?"

"Yes. They work for me in my business."

"Why would you need a couple of Russian thugs to work in a two-bit pawnshop? I believe they go out and collect your money. I want an answer and don't even think about lying."

"No, whoever is saying that is lying."

"I think you got them to teach Archie a lesson and they got carried away."

"That's not true. You cannae prove anything. I'm not saying another word until I get a lawyer."

"Guilty are you, Chick, and want your lawyer to step in? It would look better if you cooperated."

"Get me a lawyer. I'm not having you lot fitting me up for anything."

"So Jimmy. What have ye been up to now?" asks Peter.

"What the **** you talking about?"

"Now now, Jimmy there's nae need for language like that."

"Awa an bile yer heid. I'll speak however I want. Since when has it ever bothered you before."

"We've a new boss and she doesn't hold with such language. Now play nicely."

"I've nae time for champing my gums wi' you. What do you want?"

"I know you're missing one of your girls."

"I dinnae know what you mean."

"Come on Jimmy. Don't play the innocent with me. We've known each other too long. I'm no' interested in your business, just Tilly Methven."

"What's up with her now?"

"You know fine well she's dead. Now do you know what happened to her?"

"I didn't even know she was dead. It's nothing tae do with me."

"Are you sure about that?"

"Of course I'm sure. Now I'm leaving. You've nothing on me."

"You're not going anywhere. You'd better tell me everything you know or I'm sending a bunch of bobbies, with warrants and guns, around to your gaff. I'm sure they'll find it interesting."

"You're hurting my feelings throwing accusations around."

"We've a wee lassie that's been murdered. We're not that worried about your feelings. Answer the questions."

"Tilly went out last night and she never came home. I was waiting for her and when I went tae find her, the place was crawling with polis. That's it. I swear."

"Are you sure she wasn't a liability and you killed her?"

"I'm positive. I've four other women would swear to that on their mothers lives. The only one who went out was Tilly. She was desperate for money."

"You wait here nice and comfy and I'll send one of my boys round your house tae check your story."

"Nice and comfy! It's a fu..."

"I've told you. Mind your language. I want you speaking like a choirboy when I get back."

As Peter slams the door a barrage of obscenities can be heard. He grins. I love this job. The DI has added a certain little enjoyable something to the role he thinks.

Seeing Peter over at the kettle Shona joins him. "Good grief Peter you could tar the road with that tea."

"I like it nice and strong. Who are you to speak anyway, drinking the crud that comes out of that coffee pot. Are you even sure it's coffee?"

Shona squints at the pseudo mud in her cup. "Sometimes I'm not sure. How did you get on with Jimmy?"

"He's declaring his innocence as usual. He's about as innocent as Burke and Hare. I've sent Jason round to check his alibi. He's borrowed a female officer from uniform. Jimmy's girls are as mad as him and might try something on."

"Chick's clammed up and wants a lawyer. All this

hurry up and wait is driving me nuts."

They stand cogitating for a few minutes focussing on their respective, noxious brews.

"I'm sure you've heard of Stephan and Gregor Alexeyev. What's the skinny on them?"

"The Russian Twins! If you think Jimmy's a bampot you need to meet that pair. They make oor Jimmy look like Tinkerbelle. Their idea of a good night out is shoving broken glass in the eyes of the unsuspecting public."

"How come they're roaming the streets and not serving twenty five to life in Carstairs?"

"Everybody, including most of Dundee's underworld, is terrified of them. None of them will testify. Why are they featuring in your enquiries?"

"It appears they're currently 'gainfully employed' by Chick Anderson. Roy tripped over the info while doing his stuff on the web."

"God help us if Chick and the Russians are in cahoots. I'm off to fill out the papers to emigrate."

"Right Mr. Anderson, now that you're all suited up with your own freshly squeezed lawyer, maybe we can get going." The lawyer looks to be about sixteen.

"You can't speak to my client like that."

"Like what? I haven't said anything yet. If you interrupt every time I open my mouth we'll be here all night."

The lawyer splutters a bit and mutters, "Outrageous," but takes the hint and shuts up. Self-righteous prig thinks Shona.

"Mr. Anderson. How do you know Stephan and Gregor Alexeyev?"

"I've already told you. They work for me."

"In what capacity?"

"Just odds and ends."

"Could you be more specific?"

"They go out and bring things in that are a bit heavier. They'll look and make a decision."

"It seems a bit like overload to pay them just for that. Is there anything else you're not telling me?"

"They go out and collect money sometimes."

"Ah. Now we're getting to the nitty gritty. Does this involve extorting money with menace?"

"I run a respectable business."

"So you keep saying. Could you tell me how a hundred pound loan on a watch turned into a two thousand pound payback?"

"That's a load of rubbish."

"Is it now?" Shona places some papers in front of him. "What do you have to say about this?"

"Where Did You Get That?"

"Keep your tone civil and your voice down. It doesn't matter where I got it. It seems to prove that Archie owed you the equivalent of the GDP of a small nation and wasn't very good at paying it back. Did you send Tweedledee and Tweedledum after him?"

"I asked them to talk to him. I never said anything about touching him. I don't believe in violence."

"Oh I'm sure you're a positive angel, Chick. It still doesn't excuse the fact that I have a dead body and it looks like your so-called 'business' is involved somehow."

"You can't blame my client or his business for the murder."

Showing the lawyer all the respect he deserves, Shona ignores him. "Where can I find Stephan and Gregor Alexeyev?"

"They'll probably be at Cat's Eyes Club later tonight."

"Thanks for your very helpful cooperation. Now in the matter of money lending. I am arresting you on suspicion of..."

As Chick throws himself at Shona, Burns catches him, using a rather spectacular dive. She is impressed.

"Finish reading him his rights and chuck him in a cell. I believe cell 14 is free as Jock has just left us." Burns and Shona grin. Revenge is sweet.

Back in the squad room she finds the others knee deep in paperwork. Silence reigns. "Meet in the briefing room. We need a catch up." Chatter breaks out and everyone moves en masse. Nothing like a spot of paperwork to make a briefing seem exciting.

"Peter, are you any further forward with Jimmy?"

"According to his girls he's lily white. Their stories tie up with his. Tilly went out late last night. Jimmy was home with them all night blah, blah, blah. His alibi is as tight as a ducks backside, so I've had to send him on his way."

"That's a shame. I am in the mood for charging him with murder." She updates them on the interview with Chick. "Roy, delve deeper into Chick Anderson's life. I want to know everything about him right down to the colour of PJs he wears."

She pauses then, "I need a couple of volunteers to go to the Cat's Eyes Club and pick up the Russian twins." She lights the touch paper and stands back.

"I'll go. You'll need someone strong to bring them in."

"I'm stronger than him. I'd be better."

All the men are vying for the privilege. Nina stops laughing long enough to say, "You do realise Cat's Eyes is a lap dancing club."

"I had heard. It's a nightclub as well though. So we're all off clubbing. Boys don't get the idea this is a jolly. There will be a DI and two sergeants along as chaperones. Now go get yourselves fed and watered and get your clubbing gear on. Sexy for the ladies and sharp for the men. Meet back here at 2100 hours for a briefing before we hit the town."

"Shona, you dinnae mean me surely? My clubbing days are long over." His use of her Christian name highlights the full measure of his anxiety.

"Relax Peter. You're off the hook. You're free to go and have cocoa in front of the fire with the wife."

"Thanks." Picking up his coat he flies from the room before she can change her mind.

As the others leave she hears Jason saying, "Clubbing at the force's expense. I didn't see that coming." As he and Roy high five, she is cheered by the thought that the cost of this operation can be justified on the increased camaraderie of that pair alone. They may not have caught their murderers but things are looking up.

"Are you telling me that you want to spend my already over stretched budget on a night out for your team?"

Her gut feeling about the Chief's reaction is spot on.

"I know it sounds absurd sir, but there's no other way we can pick up the Russians without bloodshed."

"You don't even know this pair were involved."

"It's looking highly likely, sir."

After pausing to calm down, the Chief agrees. "No alcohol. Any consumed is paid for with their own shilling."

"Of course, sir. Wouldn't have it any other way." She leaves before he can change his mind.

Nine pm sees a veritable peacock of colours and attire congregating in the squad room.

"My, my, you lot scrub up well even if it does smell like the inside of a whore's bedroom in here.

Abigail you've got that sexy look off to a fine art. Nina you're not far behind her."

"She certainly does. Ma'am." Jason and Roy are transfixed.

"Boys, lift your eyes up from Sergeant Lai's cleavage and concentrate on the matter in hand. We need to set a few ground rules."

"Rules? It's a night out."

"What on earth gave you that idea, Burns? We're about to pick up a couple of Russian gangsters, with violence written into their DNA, not go partying. We need our wits about us. Follow me. We're going to be packing guns."

"Guns? Blimey, what do you think is going to go down in that club?" asks Iain.

"Nothing I hope and the guns should help us do that. So the first rule is no alcohol."

Everyone groans.

"The second is keep your eye on the ball not the lap dancers. The third is lose those guns and you're going to be directing traffic for the rest of your natural. Come on."

As the taxi pulls up opposite the club, Jason says, "That's one of Stephan and Gregor's henchmen standing guard at the entrance."

"How can a couple of Russian thugs have henchmen?" asks Nina.

"They've got their fingers in a lot of very large pies."

"Jason. Burns. Would they know either of you from uniform?"

"They might know me," Jason replies, "but not out of uniform."

"I've never had anything to do with any of them," adds Burns.

"Hang on Jason you still look like a cop with that haircut." Shona delves deep in her bag, pulls out a jar of hair gel, and rearranges his short back and sides. "That's more like it."

"I've always had a secret desire for a DI to ruffle her hands through my hair."

"Shut it you cocky git. Next time it might be a hairy male sergeant." She views her handiwork and turns to Abigail.

"Go put that outfit to good use and distract the doormen. In your interview you said you did acting in your spare time. Show us what you've got."

Abigail shimmies over, putting her sexy five foot four inches to good use. She might be small but every single inch is packing a punch tonight. Cleavage thrust out, and tight skirt showing wiggling buttocks to perfection, she makes short work of charming the duo of paid muscle. This leaves the rest of them to enter the club unobserved. Go Abigail thinks Shona. Despite the no alcohol rule she has already made everyone take one mouthful of whisky and asked them to swallow it. They will stand out like sore thumbs if they seem too sober.

Inside darkness is broken only by gyrating orange, yellow and green neon lights. Fumbling for purses and wallets they speak nonsense whilst buying their tickets. The club is packed. A wall of sound in the form of pulsating music and shouted conversation hits them like an Eddie Stobart truck. This is matched in ferocity by the solid smell of sweat mixed with the cloying scent of perfume and what smells like pot.

"How are we meant to find our marks in here? I can't see a thing," mutters Iain.

"You'll soon get used to it. Go up to the bar with Nina and get drinks. Here's thirty quid. You'd better get alcohol. It'll be more realistic. I don't want to draw too much attention to what we're doing. Move about. If you need help then text. Everyone else is doing it anyway."

Roy pulls out his phone, gathers everyone around and takes a selfie. "That had better be gone tomorrow and if it surfaces anywhere I'll throw you in a cell with Auld Jock and keep you there." Shona speaks in his ear.

"No worries Ma'am it's for our eyes only." He grins and shows her the photo. A group of friends relaxing and having fun.

Shona grabs Iain by the hand and pulls him off. The darkness hides his blush. They wander 'aimlessly' around the club, moving to the throbbing beat of the music.

"I'm surprised how many women are in here considering it's a lap dancing club," says Iain.

"You're right. I must be very naïve as I expected mostly men."

Shona watches the dancers. Their sensuous, writhing bodies are perfectly formed. Not an ounce of muscle or fat to be seen. The women know how to move. Men fight to thrust money into areas Shona doesn't want to think about too deeply. This is not her idea of a good night out.

"Jason's texted me. The Russians have been spotted." Iain interrupts her reverie. "They're in a semi private cubicle further back."

They go to find the others. Abigail has joined them and Shona sends her to do her stuff with another muscle mountain minder. As the others fool around causing a distraction, Shona and Jason stumble 'drunkenly' past the Russians, who find that they are no longer watching a private lap dancer. They are now gazing into the barrels of two police revolvers, and a hand holding a warrant card. Blue eyes turn to steely grey, reminiscent of a Siberian sky during the worst excesses of winter.

"Time to go, boys. As you can see we're carrying

so don't try any funny business and no one will get hurt. Oh, by the way, I'm DI McKenzie and I'd like to invite you to join me at the station for a little chat."

As Stephan, or is it Gregor, lurches to his feet screaming obscenities, Shona shoves the muzzle of her gun in his mouth. This is repeated with Jason and the brother. Twins right enough. Before they can say arrest they have handcuffs on and are being marched from the club. Okay, it is more struggling and dragging than marching, and there is a lot of noise involved, but they are soon slung into a waiting police car.

"Charge them with interfering with a police officer in the course of her duty and throw them in separate cells overnight. I'll come and talk to them in the morning."

The officer leans out of the window and almost whispers. "You do know this pair are nuts. They make Attila the Hun's rampage through Europe look like a peaceful demonstration. The duty officers will struggle to contain them."

"And I should worry about that, why? Tell the duty officers to grow some and get on with it."

"You'll need to put sedatives in their porridge if you want to interview them."

"Thanks for the advice. I'll bear it in mind."

Turning, she dismisses the team. Roy says, "We're taking Abigail to Ali's Kebab House. She's educationally lacking. Never had a kebab."

"Ali's? What has Abigail ever done to you?"

"Ali's is great. It's an authentic Middle East cafe."

"Yeh, right. With authentic Montezuma's revenge thrown in for good measure."

Roy's grin says it all.

"You're evil, Roy."

She leaves them to it and heads for home, a shower and a nightcap. Her priority, get this gunge out of her hair and this makeup off. Going out dressed as a vamp isn't all it is cut out to be. How can women be bothered, week in week out? Her thoughts are of PJs and bed.

13

Despite the relentless snow the killer is off on a recce visit. The next murder needs to be perfectly choreographed if it is to be pulled off undetected. Everything he wears is flawless. Prepared for maximum disguise. Jeans with holes. Doc martins. A Guns n Roses T-shirt and a hoody. The perfect picture of a poor student, or another unemployment statistic, heading to the pub. With a nod to the snow he pulls on a fleece and drives to a road, several streets away from his destination. Slouching, as he walks his eyes scan every direction. He knows every street, every closed or empty shop, every house and every window intimately, like the body of his lover.

If he had one. No one is good enough for him. He is the master of his own life and his own destiny. No one, of course, knows this. Only him. His mother had known when she was alive. From the first minute he can remember, she had told him he was different. He would be someone. He was better than everyone else. The killer believes this to his very core. He will be someone. People will talk about him in wonder. She would have been proud of his accomplishments.

He knows everything. What time occupants come home, what time they switch on their lights and close the curtains. Each paving stone is memorised down to cracks and uneven slabs. This practiced familiarity of the normal is necessary to give him a heightened perception of the abnormal. Entering the seedy bar he nods to the barman.

"Evening Murray. The usual?"

"Thanks."

The barman places a half pint of Tennent's in front of the killer and he takes it to a table by the window. Seemingly immersed in his Stephen King novel, he is watching, memorising every inch of the room. He nurses his drink until closing time and then leaves. A sad reflection of a society in which no one pays him any notice. He exists only as a familiar part of the background. Leaving the pub he takes another meandering route back to his car. He has covered every street within a mile radius of the pub in the past few months. He has memorised everything down to the last little detail including what time the milkman comes. His meticulous planning is about to come to fruition. It is time.

14

The alarm wakes Shona from a dream where a masked killer is suffocating her. She peels one eye open and stares straight into the green eyes of Shakespeare, her cat, who is lounging, jauntily on her chest. Shakespeare's thunderous purr vibrates though her lungs.

"Get off, Shakespeare." Shakespeare is a girl but Shona had only found out after the cat presented her with a full litter of kittens a few months back. Shakespeare objected to a name change so the name remains. Shakespeare knows her own mind. Hitting the off button Shona forces herself up.

Switching on the Tassimo coffee machine she hurries to get dressed. She pulls on Chino's and a jumper, drags a brush through her thick hair and tugs it up in a ponytail. The fact she can relax over coffee, toast and *The Times* newspaper makes a change from recent events.

The Kingsway is snarled up so she arrives at work a whisker shy of her starting time. Most of the others are noticeably absent, Abigail being the only occupant of the squad room.

"Are the others having a wee lie in after their night out?"

"Peter and Roy rang and said they were caught up in traffic. There have been a few accidents. Peter is stuck half way across the bridge because the town's at a standstill."

"For pity's sake. These road and rebuilding works

are going on for about another ten years. You'd think the council could sort something out. How are we meant to interview the Alexeyevs with most of the team missing? We'll have to get started. Go and get some muscle from uniform. A night in a cell probably has the two of them ready to strangle someone."

Little does she know how right she is. Three officers drag in a furious Gregor.

"Why did you bring us here. We have done nothing. I want my lawyer. We will not speak to a woman." Shona is pleased that he speaks excellent English even if his accent is strong and he spits out the words. She isn't so pleased that he spits in her direction and a glob lands on the papers in front of her.

"Get a box of tissues." One of the officers scurries to do her bidding.

"You're not doing yourself any favours here mate."

"I am not your friend. I do not need any favours. I have done nothing. You will regret this." Shona could swear she is staring into the eyes of Satan himself.

Putting her face close to his, quite bravely given the recent spitting incident, she says, "No, *you* will regret it. I am the senior officer here, so you will deal with me and lump it." Shona suppresses her fear. Showing fear to this puffed up, misogynistic thug is not an option.

"I want my lawyer."

"Interview terminated at 0937 hours. Take him to phone his shyster lawyer."

The others still being missing in action, the arrival of the lawyer finds Abigail and Shona back on interview duty. The lawyer is Angus Runcie. He is, allegedly, a bigger crook than the low lives he represents. By this time Shona's mood is such that she would take no prisoners, or any crap off this pompous windbag.

Before they return to the interview room, the lawyer asks, "What right have you to arrest my clients? What evidence have you got that they have committed a crime?"

"Mr. Runcie, we only wanted to ask your clients a few questions. They wouldn't play nicely so we arrested them for interfering with the police in the course of their duty."

"You arrested them at gunpoint, in front of half the city. What about their reputation?"

"Their reputation!" Shona can't seem to form the next word, then, "With their reputation you're lucky I didn't pull the trigger."

"That's preposterous."

"Much as I'd love to stand and chat with you all day about the finer points of arrest procedure we need to go and speak to your clients." Shona turns and leaves him scurrying to catch up.

The interview room is a bit cramped with three bobbies, two detectives and the suspect and his lawyer. Shona can see one of the bobbies loosening the collar of his uniform. Starting the recording she says, "Can I confirm that you are Gregor Alexeyev?" She thinks she'd better clarify, as the twins are cut from the same sperm. Mind you he might lie through his teeth.

"Yes."

She decides to run with that for now. "Do you know a man named Chick Anderson?"

"Yes. He is a business colleague."

Yeah, right.

"What sort of business?"

"We help him to keep his books in order. We collect payments for him."

"Does your money collecting involve the use of physical violence?"

"That is a lie. Who told you this? You cannot prove it."

Shona picks up the papers she has brought. "It says here several complaints have been brought against you for assault leading to severe injury."

Runcie pipes up, "Those were never proven. All the complainants retracted their statements. These people were trying to sully my clients' reputations."

"Here we go with the reputation again. Mr Alexeyev, have you heard of a man called Archie Green?"

"No, I have never heard of him." His eyes dare Shona to contradict him.

"That's funny because Chick swears you went to collect money from him."

"He is mistaken. This did not happen." Shona doesn't think much of Chick's chances. If he has any sense he'll be on a rocket to Mars by now.

"I beg to differ. I think you went to collect money and got a bit carried away with the persuasion."

"That is a lie. You have no evidence."

The bad part is he's right. They are clutching at the snow here. Disappears the minute you grasp it.

"You have been very helpful Mr. Alexeyev. I would like you to stay until we've interviewed your brother."

Interviewing Stephan gives Shona a strong feeling of déjà vu. It's unsettling. She and Abigail leave the interview room none the wiser.

"How eerie," says Abigail.

"You're telling me."

The squad room has a full house by the time they enter. "Good of you to join us. I know it was a late night but a couple of us managed to crawl out of bed and get here."

"Abigail lives in Bell Street. She only has a 200

yard walk to get here," says Nina.

"That's immaterial. I came from the Ferry."

"The town's a car park. Our colleagues from traffic are involved but seem to be making things worse. Mind you I dinnae envy them that job."

"While you lot have been sitting listening to Radio Tay in your cars, Abigail and I have interviewed the Alexeyev Twins."

"Did you get anything useful?"

"Not a thing and we're probably at the top of the Russian mob's hit list. I need a strong coffee. A whisky in it would seal the deal."

"Do ye no' think it's a bit early tae be toping."

"After a couple of hours of Russian mobsters and Angus Runcie you'd be begging for a drink too."

"I didnae know Angus Runcie was involved. I'll pour you that drink myself and join you out of sympathy."

"Joking apart, grab Abigail and Nina and come into my office. We need to pool our brain cells."

"Before I do, have you seen this morning's *Courier?*"

"Nope, What 's it saying now?"

He chucks the paper over and Shona glances at the headlines.

"Highly Regarded Mother Superior, in Police Custody."

Underneath is a picture of the Reverend Mother handcuffed and flanked by Shona and Peter. Every detail can be seen in its full, multi-coloured glory. *The Courier*'s photographer is at the top of his game.

The article goes on to describe what a fine, upstanding citizen she is and how she can't be involved in murder.

"Someone should shut that rag down."

"It's not a rag, Ma'am. It's a historical stalwart of

Dundee society. So they might get it a bit wrong every now and then, but they're reporting the news."

"Whatever. How come it's taken so long to get to the front page?"

"Ex Lord Provost George Brown has been caught en flagrante with a prossie. That's much bigger news than something as trivial as the arrest of the Mother Superior for the murder of three of her flock."

"Dundee's a hotbed of sin and debauchery. Oxford, even with 22,000 students on its books, is positively provincial compared to this."

"Aye, we seem to know how to do crime well. Not as well as we do weather mind you."

"What is it with you lot? Can't you have a conversation without mentioning the weather?"

"Why would we want to?"

There is no arguing with that.

Ten minutes later, coffee, cakes and three accompanying sergeants arrive in her office. Office is a bit of a misnomer. It's more of a cubicle. But they manage to squeeze in by dint of Abigail sharing space with the printer.

"It's a good job I'm not that big." Abigail takes her inferior perch with her usual good grace.

"Thanks, Abigail. I'd hate to trust the vagaries of my office furniture to Peter. He'd probably break it. Any more of that cake and he'll break the chair." They all laugh, including Peter.

"Moving on to more important matters. Here we are, yet again, with a positive plethora of murders on our hands. Being the most experienced of the troops I thought you might have some ideas."

Silence descends and they all look blank. Abigail fills the gap. "Do you think they're connected?"

Nina asks, "What could possibly connect the

murder of three nuns, a prostitute and an old drunk?"

"I agree it does sound like something out of an episode of *Midsummer Murders*. Let's take the nuns out of the equation. What could link Archie and Tilly?"

"Could he have been using Tilly for a bit of 'light' relief?"

"That joke is awful even for you Nina. I can't see Archie mustering up the energy tae stagger over to Baxter Park. Seems tae me he's only interested in drinking and never steps over the boundaries of Lochee."

"You're probably right Peter, but we ought to look into it anyway. I'm ready to clutch at any straw, as the saying goes."

They sip their coffee, each of them deep in thought.

"One thing they do have in common is that they all seem to have an item of jewellery missing." Abigail speaks into the silence.

"We're not 100% sure that Tilly's is missing. I think she might have pawned or sold it. It could well be in her flat and she wasn't wearing it. Abigail, when we're finished here take Burns and go and find out."

"It doesn't seem much of a haul, three crosses, a locket and a wedding ring."

"I agree Nina, but if it is a serial killer then it will make some sort of twisted sense to him, or her, I suppose."

They sip their drinks in silence then Shona says, "Changing the subject, I'm still suspicious about the fact that the Press are all over us like botulism. Does anyone else suspect a leak?"

"Nobody on the team's acting any differently to usual. Doesn't seem like there's backhander's flying around."

"What about Roy and his designer clothes." The idea is stuck in Shona's mind.

"Shona, I'm dressed from my hat to my shoes in Diane Von Furstenberg. How do you think I can afford that on my salary? It's all cheap, knock off copies from India. He's probably the same. You can buy them off Dodgy Dougie at the market in Main Street."

"There goes another great idea. Wait a minute. I hope you pair aren't up to anything dubious. If my knowledge of consumer law holds firm isn't it illegal to buy or sell copy designer goods?"

"I'm not doing anything suspect. Mine are all presents from my huge, and loving, extended family from visits to the homeland. I wouldn't worry about the market. Uniform seem to be turning a blind eye for the minute."

"I'm lost for words. Going back to what we were talking about I still think we have a leak though."

"Who could it be?" asks Abigail. "You obviously don't think it's one of us. That leaves the four DCs. Is that likely?"

"I'm not sure. Keep a close eye on them and see if they do anything unusual. In the meantime Roy can trawl through HOLMES. It might come up with something that links our victims."

Before she reaches the squad room the Chief intercepts her. "DI McKenzie, my office now." Exchanging surprised glances with the others, she follows him.

"I've just had Angus Runcie on the phone saying you threatened to shoot his clients. Is this true?"

She gives him a run down of what had transpired and adds, "He's lucky I didn't shoot them."

"DI McKenzie, I realise that Runcie and his clients are the cess pit of the city but keep things civil. No matter how provoked, you cannot, I repeat, cannot, go around threatening to shoot people. I've managed to calm him down for now but you will act professionally in future. Do I make myself clear."

"Yes Sir." Shona leaves muttering, "I'd like to shoot you next time as well. Sod the lot of you." Unsolved murders tend to make her rather belligerent. She feels the need for another large cream cake to salvage her wounded pride. Having set Roy to on scouring HOLMES, she returns to her office. Despite five murders, the office furniture catalogues are calling her. Time, tide and new office furniture wait for no woman. The Chief will regret telling her off when she orders from the dirty bit at the back of the book. The super deluxe, everything top of the range, section. A smile flits over her face.

After a pleasant hour poring over catalogues she has chosen a new workstation with every bell and whistle, topped off by a huge leather chair. She's also ordered fancy furnishings for the team. CID will have the best-dressed offices in the station. Feeling a bit like God, she looks and sees that it is good. Satisfied, she finds Roy who is, for once, hard at work. Thankful for small mercies, she says, "What's HOLMES thrown up?"

"Not a thing Ma'am. I've done every permutation I can think of but nothing. Would you like me to try internationally?"

"Sure. We've knack all to go on anyway so it can't hurt."

She turns her hands waving. "Oi, you lot. Why is Roy the only one working in here?" She can see Roy's smile out of the corner of her eye. You enjoy it while you can son. It makes a pleasant change for you to be the good guy.

"We're at an impasse, Ma'am. We can't seem to get a handle on anything to do with our cases," says Abigail.

"Surely there must be a cold case or two you can

gnaw on while you're waiting. Get some flaming work done or I'll send you to walk the streets."

The flurry of activity in the office is stronger than the fiercest flurry of arctic snow. Shona can't cast off a feeling of impending doom. Her finely tuned detective radar, or is it female intuition, is telling her something else is going to happen.

15

The cellar provides a fairly comfortable hiding place. Sitting in a dark corner the killer thinks about his next move. he can feel the thrumming of the base from the pulsating music in the bar above. It is somehow all too distant here. He is a world away from the one overhead. Silence tells him that closing time has arrived. He listens for the sound of footsteps pounding on the stairs.

The publican has feet the size of Angus, no light step for him. He stops, listens. "Hello, is anyone there?" The only reply is his own voice echoing round the stone walled cavern. He speaks words of comfort to himself. "You're jumping at shadows Stan. Get on with it." His solid footsteps continue.

Then, his size cannot protect him as he faces a long bladed knife.

"On your knees."

"What the ...?"

"Shut up. On your knees."

"If you want the takings you can have them," he says, still going for bravado, but does as he is commanded.

Taping his mouth the killer guarantees silence. "Turn round and put your hands behind your back."

He tries to punch the killer. A blood-drawing jab from the knife soon has him in a more compliant mood. Once his hands are tied a strong kick has him face down on the floor. His feet are tied. Using the sharpened knife the killer cuts Stan's trousers and

Mickey Mouse boxers and removes them. Propping him up in a corner, the killer watches, detached, as a lone spider scurries up the publican's leg and across his genitals. He strains against his bonds. The smell of terror oozes from every pore with his sweat and is joined by the stink of other bodily fluids. The killer gazes for a moment then his blade is used for much more lethal purposes. He knows exactly where he will cut and how. There are books full of notes to ensure all goes to plan. He stands back and surveys his handiwork. It is good. It is always good.

16

The next morning Shona and Shakespeare are sitting, in a rare moment of peace, in the kitchen. Shakespeare is munching on a plate of salmon Whiskas, and Shona on a bowl of muesli. Yes, she's usually a full cooked breakfast kind of gal, but sometimes even she needs to make an effort. As she lifts the freshly brewed coffee to take the first restorative sip, her mobile rings. "It never fails Shakespeare."

Shakespeare's insouciant look says, I don't know what you're complaining about, it doesn't affect me, and she turns back to her fishy breakfast.

"Thanks for your support." She answers the phone. "DI McKenzie."

"It's the duty sergeant Ma'am. How do you fancy a wee jaunt to Blairgowrie?"

"Blairgowrie? What's happened there?"

"The publican of the Glenshee Arms pub in Blairgowrie has been found dead under suspicious circumstances."

"Blairgowrie's not my beat, it's Angus CID's. Let them sort out their own dead bodies."

"They've requested you take it on as a Major Incident Team. None of them can get to it for the snow. The gritters have been up the A923 so it's just about passable. You should be able to get there."

"I knew this Police Scotland reorganisation would be a right dog's breakfast. I haven't got time to act as a MIT team so the Angus guys can stay tucked up all cosy in their beds."

"Would you like me to tell them you can't do it?"

"No. We'd better cooperate now that we're all meant to be working together. Let the rest of my team know."

Although resigned, Shona is still belligerent so finishes her coffee and pours another mug. A trip to the barren wastes of Blairgowrie is a two-mug job if she ever saw one.

The town in question is a warren of hills and old houses. Despite her state of the art, sat nav system, she gets lost. Eventually, finding somewhere to park, she steps out into a white maelstrom. Sliding down the icy pavement, melting snow dripping down her neck, she finds the pub. She is the last to arrive. Everyone else is standing outside the yellow crime scene tape looking miserable. The POLSA is on guard at the door with a determined glint in his eye.

"I can't believe we've had to trail all the way out here in weather like this. What's the point of having an Angus force if they can't cope with a spot of snow? And then the Sergeant Major there won't even let us in the pub to shelter." Even Nina, the most cheerful copper in the nick, is fed up.

"A spot of snow? It's a full-scale blizzard. We're all one big happy family in Scotland now, Nina, so it is our job. We'll all just have to put our big girl pants on and get on with it."

Shona might be moaning about taking on extra duties but there is no way she's letting the rest of them get away with it.

"Morning Sergeant Muir. How are you this fine morning? I see you've done a sterling job. Not that I expected anything less."

"Morning, Ma'am. I don't think your team's very happy."

"You're as observant as ever Sergeant. Is it okay if we go in now?"

"Of course, Ma'am. I've kept the scene clean for you."

"You're a scholar and a gentleman. Right, let's see what we've got."

She turns towards Nina, "You're with me. Come on." She thought she'd better throw the poor girl a crumb.

Before Shona gets through the door Nina is behind her.

The doorframe is splintered and the door lock hangs askew.

"Was this like this when you arrived, Sergeant Muir?"

"Yes. Uniform did it when his wife reported that he'd not come home. She came looking for him and when she found the door locked and just one light on she panicked. The beat bobbies thought it was suspicious to so called it in and broke the door down."

"Does our corpse have a name?"

"Stan Adam Zack. He's Polish."

"Doesn't sound very Polish to me."

"Stan A-d-a-m-c-z-a-c. Stan's short for Stanislaus."

Shona calls to Peter and Roy. "Go and speak to uniform and find out precisely what happened and who's been in here."

"Can we do it inside?"

"No you flaming well can't. Get on with it."

The scene is not a pretty one. The smell of beer mixed with blood and faeces is knockout strong. Despite sub-zero temperatures outside the room is warm. Most of the lights are off. The body of a corpulent man aged about fifty, or thereabouts, is propped up in the corner. The knife protruding from his neck probably accounts for the vast amounts of blood spattered on the wall, the nearby beer barrels and the floor. It soaks his jumper. There is also evidence of a beating. He is wearing nothing on his bottom half, exposing his genitals to the world. Through blood, Shona can see a deep laceration all the way round the man's genitals, which are almost hanging off. They can see this because a spotlight, so bright it would rival the sun at its core, is focussed on him.

It is difficult to get too close to the corpse without standing in blood. Shona studies the area as though she can conjure something out of the mess.

"Do you think it's a sex encounter gone wrong? It looks like a sex crime to me," says Nina.

"Difficult to say, but it's one theory. The cut around his genitals would suggest that. Could be a hate crime as well seeing as he's Polish." Switching on the remaining lights Shona looks around the basement.

"Can you see his trousers anywhere?"

They search the basement but find nothing resembling the missing garments. Donning rubber gloves, she pokes at a pile of old rags but they are only discarded cloths for polishing glasses.

"Get Iain in here. We need photographs. Fingerprinting this place will be all his worst nightmares rolled into one. On the other hand, knowing Iain's love of his job, he'll probably view it as all his birthdays and Christmases rolled into one."

"I wouldn't fancy his job for all the sweets in Keiller's factory."

"What are you talking about? What's Keiller's factory?"

"They used to make jam and sweets. It's the jam bit from Jam, Jute and Journalism. It's what we're famous for."

"For goodness sake I don't need a history lesson, I

need Iain. Step to it."

"Yes, Ma'am."

She reappears a couple of minutes later with Iain in tow and he sets to work.

Waiting upstairs for the Police Surgeon to arrive Shona asks Nina, "Did you notice anything unusual down there?"

"Apart from the fact his meat and two veg were swinging in the wind you mean?"

"Of course that's what I mean. I know a half naked corpse is unusual even in Blairgowrie."

"Nothing springs to mind." She starts giggling.

"Get a grip. I'm not even going to ask what it is you find so funny. You're meant to be a professional. Act like one. There is nothing funny about this poor man's murder."

She gasps out, "Springs to mind."

"Go outside and look for the Police Surgeon. A blast of cold air might rein you in."

"Rein... me... in." She bursts out laughing again and leaves Shona shaking her head. The nuances of that have completely passed her by. What on earth does Nina find funny in any of this?

After about fifteen minutes of thinking time Larry Baird, arrives. "Here we are again Shona. I knew it wouldn't be long until we met. At least you kept this one to a decent time. Where is the unfortunate gentleman?"

Shona points to the cellar door. "Down there. Iain will help if you need anything. Watch the stairs, they're a bit steep. I wouldn't want you to repeat your unfortunate slide down the hill at Baxter Park."

She might as well have Jack the Ripper tattooed on her forehead the way everyone feels about her she thinks. As if it's her fault that there are several dead bodies lying around the highways and byways. This is wearing thin. At least he hasn't mentioned the weather.

She doesn't have to wait long until he reappears. "It won't be a surprise to you that I've pronounced him dead. I'd say the knife sticking out his neck is a giveaway as to the probable cause, but Mary will tell you for sure. Have a great day Shona, and try to keep the body count down. I'm off to face the blizzard."

She knew the weather would make an appearance.

Perhaps Larry Baird's body could join the rising count in her imaginary murder spree. She is beginning to understand how people can be tempted to kill.

Shona joins Iain in the basement. She is trying to work out what it is her brain is trying to tell her.

"I'm almost done, Ma'am. I'll be about another ten minutes with the photos. After that I'll start fingerprinting."

"That's going to be fun in a pub. Mind you there shouldn't be that many down here."

She falls quiet and lets her eyes wander around the cellar. What is wrong? She mentally ticks off everything in the cellar, bottles of spirit, wine bottles, beer barrels, hoses... Then it clicks. One of the hoses is not attached to the barrel. It looks like something is missing.

"Do you know anything about beer barrels?"

"Not a thing, Ma'am. I've never worked in a pub. I think Roy did though, while he was at Uni."

Shona dashes up the stairs and hollers Roy. Dragging him downstairs, she points. "What's wrong with that barrel?"

"The tap or coupler's missing."

"Can you tell if there's a problem with the barrel?"

"Not at first glance." He moves over to the barrel in question and tips it a bit. "I'd say it's about half full so the tap should be in place."

"When we speak to the other barmen, or maids, we need to find out if they know anything about it."

"Duly noted, Ma'am."

"Iain, you're on your own. Would you like any help?"

"Can you spare Burns? He's shown an interest in what I do and he has a real aptitude."

"I'll send him in."

Going outside Shona assigns Burns his duties. With an excited gleam in his eye he bolts towards the cellar.

"Someone's happy in their work."

"I'm glad someone is, Peter. It's time to canvas the area. Nina take Roy, Abigail you're with Jason. Nina you're in charge. Stay until the body's picked up."

"Okay. I'll keep their noses to the grindstone." She winks.

"Peter, we need to speak with Mrs Adamczac."

"You made a decent job of that, Ma'am. I'm not even going tae make an attempt at pronouncing it."

"The publican lives a couple of streets away. Or should I say his widow does as he's now dead." Shona ponders the nuances of the English language as they negotiate snowdrifts. No wonder Angus CID couldn't get here. She is having trouble slogging through two streets. She wonders how the Chief would feel about adding snowshoes to the equipment inventory for Tayside CID.

17

Mrs Adamczac isn't as large as her husband but would have given him a run for his money. "DI Shona McKenzie and DS Peter Johnston." They flash their IDs. "We are sorry for your loss Mrs Adamczac. Can we come in and have a word with you?"

"Of..." She stops and then tries again "Of cccourse"

Shona isn't sure if the woman's teeth are chattering with the shock or the cold, but either way they need to get her inside.

"Would you like my Sergeant to get you a drink, Mrs Adamczac?"

"Call me Rrrr...osie. The other one's too much of a tongue twister. Tea please. You'll have one too?"

As Peter tends to his buttling duties, Shona says, "Rosie. Your husband had a Polish name. When did he come from Poland?"

"He was born in the Dundee Royal Infirmary so born and bred Dundee. His parents came over from Poland after the war. They wanted him to have a good Polish name."

"Did you ever have any problems because of his name? Any racist comments or attacks?"

"No never. Everyone liked Stan. He had a broad Dundonian accent, supported Celtic and got on with every single person he met. To be honest he wasn't that Polish. Neither were his parents. They wanted to settle into Scottish life."

Shona supposes there's not a big problem with racism in Blairgowrie full stop. She's sure the nearest they get to people of another race or cultures are the ones who own the Chinese or Indian Restaurants. Most of them were probably born in Blairgowrie. Worth digging about just in case though.

"How is the pub doing? Has the recession hit you?"

"Not at all. Our punters are loyal and they always seem to find money for beer and fags."

That would be about right. Peter reappears with a tray bearing three Winnie the Pooh mugs. Who would know that a woman this big would be into cuddly teddies? There's no accounting for taste. "Thanks, Peter," as he hands her a mug of coffee.

After they all drink deeply from the mugs she says, "What was your husband wearing last night?"

"Blue trousers, white shirt and dark blue jumper."

"What about his underwear?"

"What do you need to know about his underwear for?"

"It's important Rosie, or I wouldn't be asking," Shona says, tone gentle

"Simmet, mickey mouse boxers and mickey mouse socks. I gave him the boxers and socks for his Christmas."

Geeze, this pair are Disney mad. She can't believe she's going to have to hunt for a pair of Mickey Mouse boxers. "I'm sorry but what's a simmet?"

Rosie looks at Shona as though she were simple. "A string vest."

"You'll need tae excuse the DI, Rosie, she's no' been living around here for very long."

Good grief. Shona moves on from her inadequacies with Scottish Vernacular. "Did your husband have any close friends?"

"Only the ones from the Celtic Club. He knocked about with Barry McLeish and Glen Morris but he mainly saw them in the pub. He worked all the time."

"Are you employed in the pub?"

"Only occasionally, for cover. I was never as keen on it as him but it was his dream. He bought it with his redundancy money from the National Cash Register factory."

"You've been very helpful Rosie. Have you got contact details for his friends?"

She writes them down and they depart. Glancing at the paper Shona says, "One of them lives in Glenshee. There's no way we're going up the Glens in this. Let's visit Barry and see what he has to say."

Barry lives in a tidy bungalow on the edge of the town.

They explain why they are there. Looking shocked Barry says, "Come in. Quick come in out of the snow," and leads them to an immaculate living room.

"I can't believe it. What happened?"

"I am sure you will appreciate that we can't tell you that."

"Of course. Sorry."

"Were you in the pub last night?"

"Yes. I'm in there every night since my wife left me."

Shona wonders where she went. "Did you notice anything out of the ordinary?"

"No. The place was busy but they were all regulars as far as I know."

"Did Stan have an argument with anyone or take offence with anyone."

"No. Everything was quiet. I was the last person out."

Shona is sure he doesn't realise he has just put himself in the frame for murder. Or maybe he is boxing clever.

"How did you and Stan know each other?"

"We started primary school on the same day and

have been friends ever since."

"Have you been as friendly with him since your wife left."

"Even more so. He's been a great help tae me." It's funny how a Scottish twang creeps in when people are stressed thinks Shona.

"Did Stan seem the same as usual last night?"

"Yes. He was always cheerful and full of chat and good humour. Nothing different last night." He stops and gazes into the distance.

"Thank you Mr McLeish. That will be all for now, but we may ask you to come into the station for more questions later."

"No bother. I'll do anything I can to help."

After treading snowy cobbles on the return journey, they find the POLSA still has the area taped off and secured, with a couple of bobbies guarding it. "Have they picked up the body yet?" asks Shona.

"I wish. They're saying they can't get through." The look on the bobbies' faces highlights the mood that accompanies the words.

"Can I get you a take away coffee? I know you're not meant to but this weather calls for desperate measures."

"You're an angel, Ma'am, says the older of the pair. Strong, with milk and three sugars. If there's anything you ever need help with you can count on me."

Thinking that it is always helpful to have a willing slave in uniform, Shona purchases the restorative beverages. She can't believe she is doing this in the middle of a murder enquiry. Anybody would think she has nothing better to do.

Drinks in waiting, appreciative hands, she turns around and bangs into a reporter and cameraman from

The Dundee Evening Telegraph.

"For goodness sake what are you pair doing here? Surely the Dundee Press have better things to do with their time than tip up at a crime scene in Blairgowrie in the worst snowstorm the country's ever seen."

"This is news and the people of Dundee and Angus deserve to hear the news."

"So you pair of vultures are here to provide them with it. How noble of you."

"PC ..." Shona peers at their badges, "James and PC Eldridge you have my permission to shoot this pair if they put one toe near the crime tape."

They look confused. "The Scottish Police aren't usually armed, Ma'am."

"Shame. We could have had fun with this pair."

Leaving the PCs to it she looks for the rest of the team. Iain and Burns are still hard at work, photographing and fingerprinting, paying proper attention to every detail like they were Sherlock's acolytes. The others are busy knocking on doors. No one has come up with anything yet.

"As well as knocking doors you need to search the bins. I'd say for a mile radius. Some of the coppers will jump at the chance to help. You're looking for the missing trousers which are blue in colour and his boxer shorts and socks both of which have Mickey Mouse on them."

"Nina, don't even think about laughing," Shona says, as she sees the corners of Nina's mouth twitch up.

There being nothing much for her to do she leaves them to it. "See you back at the station. I'll put the kettle on."

She starts to thaw out on the way back and completes the process with scalding hot coffee at the station. For once it doesn't taste too bad. Probably because she's brought in a nice Brazilian dark roast, and made it fresh. She's sure if someone tested the usual muck they'd find it contained the sort of poison that Agatha Christie would allude to in the pages of her books. Gulping the steaming beverage down she is soon warm enough to face the Chief Inspector.

"You again. Can't I have a day without your coming to pester me? What is it now?"

"Another murder I'm afraid Sir. A Blairgowrie licensee found dead in the cellar of his pub."

"There's no need to look so cheerful about it." He pauses then, "Why are *we* dealing with the man's demise if he lives and works in Angus?"

Flash to bang in three hours. "They asked us in as a Major Incident Team. Most of their guys are snowed in."

"Useless bunch of layabouts. Don't make a habit of doing every other Forces work for them. I haven't got enough officers for you to be chasing around the country."

"Sir, now that we're..."

It is pointless continuing. His silence and bent head are dismissive. Sometimes she wonders why she bothers to report to him. He's about as useful as a bottle of beer in a distillery. She thinks she must stop fantasising about drowning the boss in scalding coffee, even though it does cheer her up.

Back in the office she casts her mind over every tiny detail of the case. The scene looks staged to her. As though the murderer is making a point. She can't quite place what that point might be. Why remove his trousers? Nina is probably right and it is a sex crime. A bizarre sexual fantasy gone wrong. As her Naval brother is prone to say, stranger things have happened at sea. It might be a cliché but it is true. She still wants a few questions answered like why kill him, and why now? Surely some mysterious lover wouldn't want to take him out. Maybe he was having an affair and the wife has done it. They need to get her in here and a warrant to search the house.

The team arrive back in the office with frozen extremities, chattering teeth and red faces.

"I need a large cuppie and one of Doreen's finest rolls." Pulling twenty quid from his pocket Peter continues, "Jason, you're on roll duty. Hop to it and remember the broon sauce." Jason obliges and grabs Roy to help him. Things must be bad if Peter is doling out cash thinks Shona. He could have given name to the myth of the miserly Scot.

"They seem to be getting on a bit better," says Shona.

"It's amazing what a joint love of football and Dundee United can do for male bonding," replies Peter.

"Well, I never thought I would hear myself say this, but praise the Lord for football."

Once they are thawed out, and replete, they congregate in the incident room. "Abigail, did you come up with anything in the house to house?" asks Shona.

"Not much. A Mrs..." She looks at her notes "Banarjee said she looked out of her window at about 0300 to see what the snow was doing. She saw someone walk up the hill past her house."

"Did she manage to get a good look at him? Could she identify him?"

"No such luck. She's about 90 and doesn't see very well. She thinks he was tall and he had on one of those puffer jackets with the hood up. It was a dark colour. She could see that because there's a street light just opposite her house."

"It's not much to go on. Roy, put out an appeal for this bloke on Facebook and Twitter. See if he comes in and can give us any information. Better do it now."

"On it," and he bounds off. It's astonishing what mention of a computer can do to transform Roy from his impression of a sulky teenager into a skilled investigator.

"Peter, give Glen Morris a ring and see if the snow ploughs have made Glenshee passable. If they have, get one of the Angus lot to bring him to the station in a four by four. They should have plenty available seeing as we're doing all their work for them. Ask Angus if one of their CID can bring him as their local knowledge could be useful."

Back in her office she picks up the phone and dials Douglas's number.

"Hi Shona. Lovely to hear from you. How are you? I hope this is a social call."

"I'm afraid not. Has anyone told you about the latest dead body?"

"No, which I'm surprised about. Uniform always call me the minute they think it's a suspicious death."

"This was a 50 year old man found dead in the cellar of his pub in Blairgowrie."

"Ah. That explains why. Blairgowrie has its own Procurator Fiscal, Sara Blenhem. Angus bobbies would contact her."

"Thanks Douglas. I'll give her a ring. How are the kids?"

"As lively as ever and they want to see you."

"As soon as I get a free minute we'll get together. Speak soon."

Hanging up she phones the correct Procurator Fiscal and explains who she is.

"Ah. The infamous Shona McKenzie. I've heard all about your propensity for collecting dead bodies."

"That's me." She decides it's easier to give in to the inevitable rather than argue the toss. If she is going to be seen as second cousin to Burke and Hare, she might as well accept it. "Did anyone let you know about the body found in the cellar of the Glenshee Arms?"

"They did, but I've five kids and couldn't leave them. My husband's stranded in London with all the snow. School's closed so they're in the office with me now."

Shona brings her up to speed and assures her she will let her know about any developments. Hanging up she thinks how on earth can she work with five kids in her office. Shona can barely cope with the cat.

Two mugs of coffee later her equivalent from Blairgowrie arrives at her door.

"Thanks for picking up that murder, Shona. None of us could get in despite the best efforts of the council gritters. I appreciate it."

"Don't worry about it, Neil. We're always glad to help. You would have done the same for us." The relative warmth of the office and strong coffee has made her magnanimous. "I'm glad you've come as your local insight could help us. Did you know Stan?"

"I did. Everyone knew him. He and his pub were popular in town. In fact it was one of the few pubs that was doing well despite the smoking ban."

"Is there any reason why someone would have wanted to murder him?"

"Not that I can think of. Everyone spoke highly of him and his wife. There were a few rumours but as far as I know they were only rumours. The usual gossip that goes nowhere."

"Can you tell me what they were?"

"Some people said that Stan, Barry and Glen were

a bit too close, if you know what I mean. I never saw any evidence of it, and even if they were it's got nothing to do with us. They're free to do what they want."

"I know, but it's worth bearing in mind. Could your team do a bit of digging around town and see what you can come up with. When we interview Glen I'll ask a few probing questions."

"Right you are. Are you happy to keep the murder on your books?"

"Might as well as we've done the ground work. We can work together."

"Anything you need just ask. My team's at your disposal if you need more warm bodies. The snow seems to be keeping the crazies at bay on the whole so we're fairly quiet."

"I wish I could say the same."

"I heard you were thigh deep in murders here. I'll leave you to it and get back to you with anything I hear."

"Thanks, Neil."

Shona and Nina interview Glen. He is sitting in room two with a mug of NATO standard tea - thick, white and with copious amounts of sugar. Someone must be feeling generous. More likely they think he would be chattier once he melted a bit.

"Interview with Mr. Glen Morris. Started 1314 hours. DI Shona McKenzie and DS Nina Chakrabarti in attendance. Thank you for coming in Mr Morris."

"No problem. I'm not sure what you want though."

"Did you know a Mr. Stanislaus Adamczac?"

"Stan? He's one of my best pals. Everyone knows Stan." Then as the past tense sinks in he adds, "What do you mean *did* I know him? What are you saying?"

Shona hates to kill the hopeful look in his eyes. She

can't believe no one has told him about the death. You'd think Barry would have rung. Maybe he's just playing it cool.

"Mr. Morris, I am sorry to say that Stan is dead."

With chalky white cheeks he gulps his tea. No actor is this good so Shona would bet her granny on his not knowing. After a few seconds his colour is restored although he still doesn't look in the pink of health. Shona is hoping he doesn't have a heart attack leaving her with another dead body.

"What… what… what happened?"

"When did you last see Stan?"

"Last night. I left the pub about 8 o'clock, as the missus wanted me home. He was okay then. He didnae look sick or anything."

"Did he seem any different to you?"

"No. He was the same as ever. Joking with everyone. Did he have a heart attack? He was overweight so he might have had a heart attack."

"No, he didn't have a heart attack. What was the nature of your relationship with Mr. Morris?"

"Me, him and Barry were best pals. We did everything together."

"How close were you to him?"

"Why…" Then the penny drops. His face pales again. "What are you getting at? How dare you. I came in here of my own free will to have a chat and now you're trying to libel me. I won't have it." The chair clatters back. He bends over the desk. Nina grabs him.

"Sit down, Mr. Morris. I think you'll find it's slander not libel and no one is trying to do any such thing. I am running a murder enquiry here and if I'm to solve it then I need to ask difficult questions."

The chair screeches like a castrated cat as he sits down. "Murder, I didn't murder anyone." His voice, suddenly falsetto, is as squeaky as the chair.

"No one's saying you did. Now how close were you to Stan? You must have heard the rumours."

His right eye twitches. "People are always talking about someone. If it isn't me it's some other poor sod. There was nothing dodgy going on between Stan and me. Or any of us for that matter."

Shona leans across the table. "No one cares what you get up to behind closed doors. However, if there is anything you want to tell us it would be better to do it now. If we find out you've been lying then we may think you're lying about everything else."

"I want my…"

"Lawyer. Of course you do." Shona finishes for him.

"Interview suspended at 1348 hours at the request of Mr. Morris." She switches off the recording. "My sergeant will take you to ring your lawyer and then you can wait in here until he arrives."

"Can I have another cup of tea while I wait?"

"We're not running a café, but I'll see what I can do."

"What do you think?" she asks Nina who has returned from phoning Glen's lawyer.

"I think he's hiding something."

"I agree. His facial expressions gave him away."

"The daft part is, if they are all having a sexual encounter, nobody cares. We're only interested in whether it all went wrong and led to murder. Do you think Glen and Barry might have done it together?"

"Who knows? We're going to have to wield our largest vocal shovel and dig deep. I might leave Glen and his lawyer to stew for a couple of hours to see if Neil Stanner comes up with anything. He's asking around in the highways and byways."

"It might take his lawyer longer than a couple of

hours to get here," says Nina.

"True. I'm interested in why an old boy from Blairgowrie has a lawyer on speed dial. It's not exactly the criminal capital of the world. We need to ask him what he does."

"Maybe he runs the Blairgowrie Mafia?"

"He wouldn't be a millionaire on it that's for sure. There can't be more than a few hundred residents."

"It's about eight thousand, Ma'am it's bigger than you think."

"Still it's not mafia numbers. Now stop talking complete drivel and get some work done."

"Aye Aye Cap'ain."

Shona follows Nina down the narrow corridor and grabs Roy at his desk.

"Anything back from social media yet?"

"Not yet but it's a slack time for Facebook, Twitter et al."

"I need you to do something else for me. Do a search on Stan Adamczac, Glen Morris and Barry McLeish. See if you turn anything up."

Nina is right. It does take Glen Morris's lawyer a couple of hours to get there. Maria Cabarelli is one of the more sensible lawyers around these parts.

"Maria, nice to see you."

"You too Shona, although we'd better not look to chummy or my client will be shouting collaboration from the steps of every courthouse in Dundee and Angus."

"Sure. I'll speak to you later. I'll take you to Interview room two where your client is patiently waiting."

"Hmff. If I know Glen Morris the word patient won't come into it. I'll need time to talk to him first."

"You've got it. Take your time. Never let it be said

the Dundee force are not cooperative. Would you like a drink?"

"Black coffee would be great. Extra strong."

Shona hands in a brew strong enough to be classed as a nuclear deterrent and then finds Roy. "Have you come up with anything on our merry band of brothers yet aka Stan, Glen and Barry?"

"I've got a lot on them but nothing that could help us. It looks like they were bosom buddies but nothing unsavoury. I'll keep digging down in the nether reaches and see if any mud is thrown up."

"Let me know as soon as you find anything."

Just as she is picking up the phone to ring Neil, the man himself rings her.

"Hi Shona. Sorry it's taken so long to get back to you. I've sent my guys round to speak to their friends. As I say, there are rumours that they were a bit too close and possibly gay. Nothing more than that."

"Thanks Neil. It doesn't look like a sex game gone wrong then. That's helpful."

"I'll keep asking round and see if I can dig anything else up. Bye, Shona."

"Glen Morris and his lawyer are ready for another interview. Nina, escort them through please."

When they are all settled, Shona does the usual round of preliminaries for the benefit of the recording. Then Maria speaks. "My client does have information. However, he insists that this information has nothing to do with the murder of Mr Stan Adamczac."

"I am sure that you will appreciate , Miss Cabarelli, that I will make the final decision on that."

"My client expects a fair hearing, without prejudice."

"And that is what he will get. Now what do you have to say Mr Morris?"

Glen sits with his head down, not speaking.

"Mr Morris, I don't have all day. What have you got to say?"

He slowly lifts his head. He looks anguished. " I'm gay. I always have been. I was arrested when I was young for…"

His head drops and he can't speak.

"What were you arrested for, Glen?" asks Shona, her voice soft.

"For soliciting sex with a man. No one knows. My wife doesn't know. If this comes out, it will break her. She's got cancer."

"We're not going to tell her, Glen. I need to ask, was Stan gay as well?"

"Not as such, but he did have the odd encounter with men. I think it was more an experiment for him."

"What about Barry?"

"He's bisexual. None of us actually do anything. The reason we're such close pals is because we were able to talk to each other."

"Do you have any reason to believe that Stan was meeting anyone that night?"

"No. No, he didn't say anything about it if he was."

"Where were you the night of the murder?"

"I was at home in bed with the missus. She'll tell you. Please don't say anything about what I've told you." His eyes are pleading.

"We won't, Glen. It stays in this room. That will be all for now. Thanks for your cooperation." She lets the poor man go. He looks devastated. Not surprising as he's heard of his best friends murder and been outed, all in the space of one afternoon.

Maria escorts her client out of the station and Shona returns to the office with Nina. "Peter, we need to speak to Barry McLeish again. Get Angus to bring him in? Then, everyone to the briefing room so I can bring you all up to date."

With a feeling of déjà vu, Shona is once more sitting in interview room two. This time the cast includes Peter rather than Nina.

"Thank you for coming in to see us, Mr McLeish. We just have a few more questions to ask."

"Of course. If it will help you find the sadistic bastard who killed Stan, I don't mind."

"I appreciate your sentiments but please mind your language, Mr McLeish. I just need to clarify your relationship with Stan?"

"We were friends. Good friends. End of."

"Was there anything more to it than that?"

"What are you getting at?"

"I am giving you chance to tell us if your relationship with Stan was merely one of friendship."

Shona can almost hear his thoughts. How much do they know? What should he say?

"You've heard the rumours?" he asks.

"What would they be?"

"If you're asking me what my relationship with Stan was, then you must know."

He is still trying for bravado. Silly old fool. Fessing up is much less damaging than making the police guess. "I'd like you to tell me, Mr McLeish, and do it quickly. I've a murder to solve and I haven't got time to spare waiting whilst you concoct a story."

"The rumours that me and the others are gay."

"And is there any truth to this rumour?"

He thinks for a minute and then says, "Yes. Yes, the three of us were gay. We didn't do anything with each other. It was a relief to be able to talk with people who understood."

"Where were you the night that Stan died?"

"I went and got a fish supper from the chippie and

went home. I ate my tea and then went to bed."

"Can anyone verify this?"

"I don't have an alibi but I didn't do it. Do I need a lawyer?"

"No, Mr McLeish, you are free to go. I may have to call you back for more questions later so please don't leave the area." He is up and out the door before Shona gets the last words out. Rather nervous, she thinks. Another one whose past they need to scrutinize.

Roy is still working on ferreting out information on their victim and his friends. "I might have something but I'd like to look a bit more closely before I give you the info if that's okay, Ma'am?"

Surprised that he's even bothered asking, Shona tells him it is more than okay. "Come and find me when you've got something tangible."

"Will do," but he is back at the computer screen and not paying attention to her. He'd make a good Chief Inspector with the qualities he displays. He's got the Chief's annoying mannerisms off to a tee.

Talking of the Chief, Shona once again finds herself tapping the boards in front of his desk.

"What's this I hear about you threatening to shoot the Press?"

Shona feigns innocence. "How on earth could we shoot the Press? None of us are armed."

"You can wipe that look off your face. I know you're as guilty as sin." Then a grin splits his face. "Nice one. I'd love to have target practice with a few reporters. Just don't make a habit of it." The stern look is back but accompanied by a twinkle in the eye. "Consider yourself reprimanded, Shona. That's all."

"Yes sir. Thank you Sir." She'd got off lightly. Maybe she ought to curb her enthusiasm for pissing off the Press and anyone who disagrees with her she thinks. For a few days anyway. No use courting trouble.

Shona is in her office going over all the cases again when Roy knocks.

"I've turned up a few interesting facts about Glen and Barry. Seems the pair of them are heavily into gay S&M sites. They spend a lot of money exploring, what we would call, the dark side of the web."

"What about Stan?"

"Everything on him seems gen up. He's on Facebook and twitter posting about his pub and his family. Newspaper articles about opening the pub. Normal stuff. Not a hint of anything sexual and I've looked in all the usual places and most of the more hidden ones."

"How do you manage to do that? No, on second thoughts don't tell me. I don't want to know."

"One thing you might want to know is that the sites our guys were entering don't come cheap. They were spending obscene amounts of money. Looks like their savings are pretty much gone. Glen isn't quite as bad as our boy, Barry."

"Interesting. Glen probably keeps himself in check so his wife doesn't find out. Thanks, Roy. You've done a great job. Do you think you'll be able to uncover anything else?"

"There're some places I haven't tried so I could carry on if you would like me to. What I'm doing might not be a hundred percent legal though."

"Do whatever you need to. If we need a warrant, I'll get one."

"Thanks, Ma'am," and he almost leaps through the door doing an outstanding impression of a dog with its tail wagging.

Shona decides it's time for another chat with the ever-obliging Neil. He should be obliging seeing as Shona's team are doing all his work.

"Neil, it's Shona."

"What's up?"

"Could you go round and have a word with Glen's wife? We need to check out his alibi. He says he was tucked up with her all night."

"Sure. I'll do it now and ring you right back."

True to his word he calls within the hour. "Sorry, Shona, the roads are still horrendous or I'd have got back quicker. Rhona Morris confirms that her husband was in bed all night. Rhona has chronic insomnia so was awake most of the night. She would have known if he'd left."

"Thanks, Neil. Any chance you could get someone to bring Barry McLeish back in?"

"Sure, why not? My petrol bill's going to rival that of Tesco, Asda and Sainsbury's deliveries put together, but that's for the Chief to worry about."

"Great. We'll let the Chiefs slug out the cost of fuel between them. Hopefully I'll see you soon if the roads are passable."

"I should be there within the hour if Barry's around. The council are keeping the main roads clear. There are gritters and snowploughs everywhere."

"Hooray for the council."

By 1900 Shona is sitting in an interview room with Nina, Barry and his lawyer, who also turns out to be Maria Cabarelli. She must specialise in this sort of crime thinks Shona. Either that or Barry has asked Glen for the name of his lawyer. She isn't sure why he feels he needs a lawyer. He must have a guilty conscience.

"Interview blah, blah, blah." She gets the preliminaries over with. It's time to turn up the heat.

"Thank you for coming back in to speak to us, Mr McLeish. I just have a few more questions to ask."

"I don't know why you keep bringing me back in here. I'm too busy to be trailing back and forwards from Blairgowrie to Dundee half a dozen times a day."

"I am sure you are busy, Mr McLeish, but we're even more busy. I'm trying to solve a murder and that takes priority over whatever you feel you should be doing. What is it exactly you are too busy doing?"

Maria breaks in. "What my client does in his spare time has no bearing on your case. I am sure you will appreciate that his private life is just that, private."

"I'm sure *you* will appreciate Miss Cabarelli that it is my job to ascertain if his private life has any bearing on my case."

Shona gives the solicitor a chance to respond but she remains quiet. Her gaze is placid. Shona is sure Maria's brain is busy trying to work out where this is going.

"Mr McLeish, I have reason to believe that you spend a lot of time on gay porn sites on the Internet. Is this true?"

Despite his face going the colour of Peter's newly washed, Persil bright, white shirt, Barry continues to brave it out.

"That's nae true. Where did you hear that?"

"Mr McLeish, I've not got time for this. Take a look at these." Shona throws the computer printouts in front of him.

"What...? Where...?"

Maria looks at them and says, "I would like to talk to my client alone."

"Of course. Please feel free, especially if it helps us to get to the bottom of this more quickly." Would you like a cup of tea and a sticky bun as well, thinks Shona. For goodness sake make it quick so we can get on with solving this murder.

"I'm assuming you do want us to solve your friend's murder Mr McLeish."

Maria turns to look at her and says, "We will be as long as it takes. However, I am sure my client appreciates the importance of speed in this matter."

It doesn't take as long as Shona thinks because half a cup of coffee later she is back in the interview room going through her opening speech.

"Well, Mr McLeish what have you got to say for yourself."

"I'm sorry I shouldn't have lied. I was scared. I did access those sites and have been doing for years."

"Your candour in light of the evidence is less than impressive. Why were you lying to me in the first place?"

"I'm ashamed about doing it. I don't want anyone to know. I've never acted on the things I saw in real life though."

"Forgive me if I have difficulty believing you. It looks suspiciously like you were acting this out with Stan Adamczac and it all went wrong."

"No. That's not true. I never did anything with Stan."

"I don't believe you."

"My client is telling you the truth."

"Your client hasn't said one thing that's true since he walked in here. Why should I listen to the lying dirtbag now?"

"This is preposterous. My client is trying to help you."

"Is he now? So, Mr McLeish, in what way are you trying to help me? Do you know anything about Stan's murder?"

"No. I swear on my mother's grave I don't know anything. I don't know what happened to him. If I knew anything, anything at all, I would tell you."

He is pleading and Shona, for the first time that day, believes him. That doesn't excuse the fact that he doesn't have an alibi. Brows puckered, she nibbles her lip. A bomb explodes in her brain. She grabs the computer printouts and looks at the dates and times of access to the sites.

"Mr McLeish, you're off the hook. It turns out your sordid little hobby has given you an alibi. It looks like you were cruising the sites during the time of the murder. Why didn't you tell us this before?"

"I told you. I'm ashamed."

"If you'd been upfront with us from the beginning you could have saved us all a lot of time. I've a good mind to charge you with wasting police time."

"I wasn't trying to waste your time. Honestly. I'm sorry."

Shona doesn't have the heart to charge the poor man. He seems terrified.

"I'll leave it this time. You're free to go." He bolts without a bye-your-leave. Maria turns to talk to Shona. "You're scary when you get going. I'm glad I'm not on the wrong side of you."

"You believe it. I've umpteen murders on my hands and so far I've only got one nun in the stocks for them."

"A nun? I saw that in the papers. Why on earth would you want to arrest a nun? Surely she wouldn't murder anyone."

"If you think that's bad it's actually the Mother Superior. She's in the frame for incitement to commit murder. Hang on, you're not involved in that case are you?"

"No. I don't know a lot about the convent but I'm sure they must have their own lawyers. All fine upstanding Catholics to a man."

"Nice chatting but I'd better get on. I hope I don't see you again too soon."

"Roy, I'm usually au fait with online matters but I have a question. Would someone be able to fake the fact they were online at a certain time? How would they do it?" Roy hesitates. "It would be difficult to fake they were online unless someone else did it for them. I'd need to start by tracking what computer they were using and its location. If it's a laptop we could look at where they accessed WiFi. With regards to time that would be pretty difficult to fake."

"Could you take a look at where Barry McLeish accessed the internet that night?"

"I'll do it now. Shouldn't take too long as the right paths will be in place."

"Whatever! Just see what you can find."

Despite the fact that Roy is hard at work everyone else seems to be busy devouring four extra large Pizzas. Shona joins them and grabs a couple of pieces, which look like they are the Full Monty, calorie laden and satisfying. They are just what she needs. Never mind the fact she can't run it off at the moment. She'll just have to sign up to a gym.

"Besides eating pizza what have you lot been up to. It's been remarkably quiet whilst Nina and I were slaving away."

Peter answers, "I've had them hard at it, dinnae you worry. We got a list of all the punters in the pub that night and we've been ringing round them all. We've managed to get hold of about 70% o' them. The others seem to be missing in action. We might need to try later tonight."

Abigail takes over. "According to the ones I spoke to, all was quiet. The punters were mostly regulars but with a couple of businessmen. The last ones out swear the pub was empty when they left. They heard Stan lock the door behind them. That was between quarter to and quarter past midnight depending on who you listen to. They'd all had a skin full so weren't sure of the exact time."

"What about the rest of you. Anything different?"

"Pretty much the same all round," says Jason.

"Where are Iain and Burns?"

"In the deepest darkest reaches of Iain's lab. We couldnae split them up. I'm led to believe they're doing extraordinary things with fingerprints."

Shona goes to find them. Peter is right. They are messing around with chemicals, photos and fingerprints. "How's it going, boys? Have you found anything useful?"

"We've got eight separate sets of fingerprints. We were just about to head out to Blairgowrie to fingerprint the bar staff and Mrs Adam Zack."

"I applaud your enthusiasm but it might be better to leave it until the morning. It's still snowing and the roads will be lethal. Go as soon as the bar opens tomorrow. You're off the hook for the night so off you go home to the bosoms of your loving families.

Heading home Shona has visions of lamb korma and Rioja, dancing in her head. Her troubles start when she, and the korma, reaches her flat. A figure rises from her sitting position on the floor of the landing. Her little sister, Blair.

"Hi Shona."

"Never mind 'Hi Shona', what are you doing here?"

"I've come to stay for a while."

Opening the door and yanking her inside, Shona says, "You're meant to be at Cambridge. Hasn't Uni started again?"

"I've quit."

Shona isn't in the mood for this. She shoves a twenty quid note in Blair's hand and points her in the direction of the Gullistan Indian Restaurant. "Go and get more food."

The minute she takes off her coat she pours a large glass of her long awaited Rioja and slugs it down. She doesn't need her wild sister tipping up. What is she going to do with a runaway twenty year old? Blair can be difficult to deal with at the best of times, but right now the situation is unpalatable. She pours another glass of wine but forces herself to wait until the food arrives before she drinks it. It is going to be a long night.

"What do you mean you've quit uni? You're in the second year of a law degree. This is no time to bunk off."

"I hate law. I only did it because I thought it would be fun."

"What on earth gave you the idea law would be fun? How the frick did you get into Cambridge to do a degree you're not even interested in?"

"You know my IQ's off the planet. It wasn't hard."

"With a genius level IQ you should be able to do this course standing on your head and still have heaps of time to have fun."

"But Anthony's always studying. He's never around to have fun."

"Who's Anthony?"

"My boyfriend. He's studying law as well."

Ah now they are getting to the crux of things. Shona doesn't have the energy for a genius young adult who still seems to have the emotional IQ of a 15 year old. "Have you told Mum and Dad?"

"No. I thought you could."

"Not in this lifetime lady." Shona picks up the phone and hands it to her sister.

Blair goes into the spare room and returns ten minutes later, mascara running down her cheeks.

"They didn't take it well?"

"Dad's never spoken to me like that before. He's furious."

"I'm sure he is, considering the amount of money he's paying for you to study there."

"What am I going to do?" Blair runs her hands through her wild blonde hair. Shona's heart melts. She's still her baby sister.

"Nothing tonight, but tomorrow you are going to have to think long and hard about that very question.".

18

Shona wakes late the next morning and with a headache. She swallows a couple of paracetamol washed down with a strong cup of coffee. Blair is still asleep. Shona leaves her money and a note saying to go and get groceries and that she will ring later. She's never been so glad to go to work in all her life. It is only delaying the inevitable, however. She will have to deal with her sister later.

"Blair will look after you," Shona says to Shakespeare. The cat throws her a look, which seems to say, "Are you having a laugh? Your sister can't even look after herself."

Shona is the last one at the office; even the Chief has beaten her to it.

"You looked knackered. What were you up to last night?" asks Nina.

"Blair was camped out on my doorstep when I got home."

"Blair? Your sister Blair?"

"The very one. She's up and left Cambridge."

"You're joking. Did she actually quit and tell them she wasn't coming back?"

"Who knows? She's only got a small case so I assume she still has a room in college. This gives me hope that she hasn't entirely burned her bridges."

"Let's hope not. Where are we going with the cases?"

"I'm hoping Iain and Burns have gone straight to

Blairgowrie. This is so confusing. Why did my parents have to call my kid sister after a town near Dundee?"

"I dinnae suppose it was much of a problem when you were all in Oxford."

"True. I'm hopeful I can convince her to shimmy off back to Cambridge and we can all go back to normal. Peter, can you split everyone up and get them working on all the different cases? See if we can come up with a new angle. I'm off to the mortuary to speak to Mary. She might be able to shed some light on things."

Mary is busy autopsying their latest victim. He smells just as bad today as he did the day before.

"Morning, Shona. I'm just about to start. Would you like to watch?"

"Sure, I'll gown up." Mary waits patiently until Shona returns. Then all four foot eight inches of Mary moves over to the autopsy table and stands on a stool.

Her lilting Scottish accent is clear.

"Adult male, approximately 50-55 years of age. Height 182cm. Overweight at…" she looks at the scale on the autopsy table, "120 kg which makes him obese, bordering on very obese. Well hydrated, well cared for. Buttocks and thighs covered in dried faeces. Face neck and chest covered in dried blood. A deep laceration encircles the testicles and penis. These are partially severed. The deceased has a long handled knife sticking from his neck. Photographs have been taken for legal use. We will now wash the body."

The pathology technician brings out a hose and washes down Stan's body. Shona has to remind herself that this is a real person. His chalky white skin looks more waxwork than real. Once the technician is finished Mary continues in the same vein. She makes the first cut. Every organ is examined, weighed and measured. Despite the grisly reason for this it is almost a pleasure to watch Mary work. Every inch of her diminutive frame is put to good use, making her a true professional, expert in what she does.

Once finished, Mary strips off her gown and gloves. "Let's have a coffee. I'll give you the edited highlights before you go back."

"Thanks, Mary, I need to know about the others as well. The reports haven't reached me yet."

Mary has made her office surprisingly comfy. Shona throws herself into an armchair, covered with a bright fleecy throw, and sighs. Bliss. She supposes Mary needs somewhere to think after dealing with dead bodies all day. Mary sits in the matching chair and brings Shona up to speed with the various reports.

"Your man today, Stan, died from a stab wound to the neck as you well know. However, he was a ticking time bomb anyway as he had an aortic aneurism. It could have burst any time. I'm surprised that the attack didn't kill him before the knife. Otherwise he seemed in good health for someone of his size.

"Can you tell if he had sex before he died?"

"It didn't look like it to me. I paid particular attention given the circumstances."

"It's not looking like a sex crime then?"

"I wouldn't say so but you never know. It could be that he was killed before they got going. I've seen that happen before."

"I won't strike it off the books just yet then. Are you able to give a time of death?"

"Between Larry's and my findings I'd say anywhere between midnight and 0400. Difficult to put an exact time otherwise."

"Thanks. What about Tilly?"

"It will come as no surprise that young Tilly did have sex before she died, or that the cause of death is strangulation. With a rope I would say. I have fibres from the rope to put into evidence. She was also a user. Track marks up the ying yang, all over her body."

"Did you manage to get DNA on the semen?" Shona is hopeful.

Her bubble is soon burst. "No such luck I'm afraid. They used a condom. That's not surprising. The word in the bazaars is that everyone uses a condom when they go with a prossie these days."

"I'm not surprised either. Doesn't help me much though. Thanks, Mary, you've been a great help. Would you like me to take the fibre samples with me?"

"We'd better play it by the book. If everything's hunky dory then there's less chance the murderer will wriggle out of it when he's caught. Or she I suppose."

"Good point. I'll leave you to your dead bodies and I'll go and try to find the sadistic pigs who produce them for you."

"The next one on the agenda died of natural causes at age 96, but as she'd only been in the hospital an hour she comes to my attention."

"Okay, I hope I don't see you again too soon."

Iain and Burns are still out in the wilds of Blairgowrie when she returns to Bell Street. She doubles back from the lab to the office. "We need a briefing to pull everything together but I'd rather wait until Iain and Burns are here. In the meantime is there anyone spare to trawl the pawnshops for Tilly's locket?"

Nina, Abigail, and Jason agree to go. "What does the locket look like?" asks Jason.

"There should be a photo in the briefing room. Her mother gave us one of her wearing it."

Abigail says, "I'll get it copied and we can take one each and split up. It'll be quicker. Have we any idea what's inside it?"

"It should be a picture of her on one side and her mother on the other. Goodness only knows what's inside it now. It could be drugs for all we know."

"I hope it's an unusual locket and not a chain store special. We haven't a snowball's chance in hell of finding it if it is."

"I think her mother said it belonged to her great grandmother. She gave it to Tilly on her eighteenth birthday."

"Let's go on a treasure hunt," Nina takes charge.

Peace descends and for once the Chief inspector doesn't want to hang her backside out to dry. In fact he is very quiet. Shona wonders if he's gone home or out for lunch. She doesn't have to wait long as the phone rings and he asks her to come into his office. Quite pleasantly, she thinks. The reason becomes clear the minute she walks through the door. The Chief Constable, Sir Malcolm Rennie, stands up as she enters.

"Sir, this is DI Shona McKenzie."

The Chief Constable extends his hand and Shona shakes it in a daze. What's he doing here?

"Shona, it's a pleasure to meet you. I've been hearing great things about you from Thomas."

To say she is speechless would have been stretching credibility. She remembers through a sudden fug that the Chief Inspector's first name is Thomas.

She manages to stutter, "Nice to meet you, Sir."

"Shona, I would like you to brief the Chief Constable on what's been happening with your cases."

Somehow she manages to form the words and comply. After about 10 minutes she halts.

"Thank you, Shona. I can see you have everything under control. If there is anything I can do to help you to move things forward then let me know." The Chief Constable is a real gentleman, and very good looking to boot thinks Shona.

"Thank you Sir. I appreciate that."

"I will be along to meet your team later."

"Most of them are out at the moment, Sir, but I will let you know the minute they return."

"That will be all, Shona. Thank you."

For once she leaves the Chief's office without planning ways to bump him off. She feels like Alice in the rabbit hole.

Peter and Roy are hard at it on computers when she arrives in their office. "Stop everything and get this pig sty tidied up. The Chief Constable wants to meet you all the minute everyone's back."

"It's no' April Fools Day Ma'am."

"I'm being serious. He's in the Chief's office as we speak."

The urgency in her voice convinces them and they leap into action. Shona helps and they soon have the place looking spick and span. It's never going to be a showroom for Police Offices R Us but it would pass muster.

"Grab yourselves drinks but that's all until he's been for his wee chat. Let me know the minute the others are back."

What a day. In the space of 24 hours she's had unexpected visits from her halfwit sister and the Chief Constable. She doesn't know which is worse. She must have been horrific in a past life to put up with what's thrown at her in this one she thinks.

Once they are a full complement they gather in the briefing room. Shona fetches the Chief Constable and the Chief follows. She's sure he's never been in the briefing room. It is a hive of activity with the team updating various media.

"Good morning, everyone. It looks like you've got your hands full. How many murders is this so far?" asks the Chief Constable.

Shona lets Peter answer. "Six sir. Three nuns, one prostitute, one drunk and one publican."

"Thank you Sergeant...?"

"Johnston, Sir."

"Sergeant Johnston. There isn't much to connect them. I suppose the prostitute, the drunk and the publican might be connected, but I'm puzzled as to why anyone would want to kill a nun?"

Him and the rest of Scotland.

Nina answers, "You probably already know we have the Mother Superior of the convent in custody for collusion, sir? The others we are treating as individual cases."

"You seem to have it under control. I believe you have three new members in your team. I hope it's going well. Sgt Lau, how are you settling into the Dundee force?"

"Quickly Sir. It's certainly been an eye opener."

Shona is impressed with his knowledge of her team and what is happening.

"I will leave you to it as I am sure you want to get on with solving your cases. It is a pleasure to meet you all."

As they turn to leave, the Chief adds, "Good work, everyone. Keep it up."

Two compliments from the Chief in one day is just about more than Shona can take. She's not sure how she's managed to stay upright.

After they leave Abigail says, "I don't know how I stopped myself laughing when you gave the litany of cases. I wanted to put it to the tune of the 12 days of Christmas."

Everyone burst out laughing saying, "Me too."

"Okay, light relief over. What have we got? Roy you start."

"Barry McLeish is definitely into gay S&M. I've gone as far as I can go looking at what he gets up to in the deepest, darkest reaches of the 'Interweb'. It looks pretty much like he was logged into, and using, the websites, in the time frame we're looking at for Stan's murder. Unless he got someone else to log into the site for him of course, in which case his alibi dies."

"Thanks, Roy. Did anyone else pick up anything about him in the pub or with the neighbours?"

"As far as his neighbours are concerned, he's a bit of a loner. Looks like his only friends were Glen and Stan. No one has seen him with anyone else. Blairgowrie's a small town so most people know everything about everyone."

"We'd better put that to one side then. Did anything else come up that we should know about?"

"Two of the regulars a Mr Sam Leasman and a Mr Brian Green did short stints in prison for assault when they were younger. Nothing since, or they haven't been caught since. Maybe Roy could slip into the nether regions of the net and see if he can pull up anything incriminating?" says Abigail.

"Leap to it, Roy. Might as well get on it straight away."

There is nothing else of interest. If Roy came up with anything they would bring in Leaman and Green. Sounds like a pair of dodgy solicitors thinks Shona. They are more likely to be a couple of Blairgowrie wide boys. Still she will leave no stone unturned as the saying goes.

"What about Tilly's locket?"

"No joy," says Nina. "We've been to every pawnbrokers in Dundee. I didn't realise how many there were. How can we have twenty eight pawnbrokers in a city with a population of only 150,000."

"Times are hard, Nina. Hadn't you heard?"

"I know, but still it's obscene the way these people prey on the unfortunate. Anyway, none of them had Tilly's locket."

"Do you think Chick Anderson might have given her something for it?" asks Jason.

"I don't think even Chick would be stupid enough to touch Tilly with a bargepole. By the sounds of it she was on her last legs due to her prolific drug habit. Might be worth checking out though. Peter can you take Jason and go and have a gentle word."

"Aye, I'll go after the briefing."

"Iain, what's the deal with the fingerprints? Do they all pan out with legitimate users of the cellar?"

"Most of the prints belong to Stan, his wife or the barmen and barmaids. One of the others belongs to our man Barry. There are several others but they could belong to anyone who handled the barrels in the brewery."

"Seems like we're no further forward. Thanks, though. Keep them on file. They might come in useful if we do arrest anyone. Right everyone, back to the salt mines."

Shona grabs a coffee and on the way back bumps into Peter. He is swinging an old fashioned truncheon like he was born to it.

"Where did you get that and where are you going with it?" Her tone is sharp.

"I've always had it. It belonged to my granddad and he gave it tae me when I joined the police."

"What exactly are you planning to do with it?"

"I'm going tae use it tae scare the bejesus out of Chick."

"You can't go beating up witnesses with a police truncheon even if they deserve it."

"I'm no gonnae use it. I'll just gi' him a fright."

"For goodness sake speak English. Give it here. You're not going to be wandering around Dundee wielding it like a scene from Ripper Street."

He hands it over. "I'll get more from Chick if I use it as a prop."

"You're not an actor. You don't need props. Use good policing and intuition like you always do. If you're scared Chick will set the Russians on you, then Jason will protect you. He was in the Army so he's a big strong lad."

Peter says, "Hmpf," pulls himself up to his full 6' 2", back ramrod stiff, and stomps off. Indignation is heard in every heavy footstep. Good grief what is the CID coming to. She has to admit to a sneaky feeling that his is the best route. Damn this management stuff it means she has to spoil people's fun.

The office is a hive of activity when she enters to find Roy. "Have you managed to get anything on Leasman or Green?"

"Not yet Ma'am. It looks like they learnt their lesson in prison and have kept their noses clean since. I'll keep looking."

"Thanks I'll speak to Neil in Blairgowrie, and see if he knows anything about them."

Five minutes later she hangs up the phone. Another dead end, as it would seem that the pair have cleaned up their act. They are now model citizens and involved in charity work raising money for Guide Dogs for the Blind in Forfar.

Peter isn't one to hold a grudge and by the time he returns he is smiling and daintily carrying three boxes of cream cakes. Jason is carrying another three.

"Thought these would make sure the troops were in

fine fettle. I couldn't resist a wee trip to Fisher and Donaldson's in Lochee on the way back to the sweat shop."

Shona bags a huge cream horn and puts it aside. "Thanks. It will put me in fine fettle. How did it go with Chick?"

"One look at Jason's muscles and Chick cooperated. Not that it got us anywhere. I quote, "I wouldn't have anything to do with that foxtrot druggie whore. She was no use to me." He didn't exactly say foxtrot but you get the gist."

"I'm sure I can substitute the correct word. Did you believe him?"

"Aye, I have to say I did. I know Chick of old and can usually tell if he's lying. He lies most of the time but I think he is genuine this time."

"Afternoon Ma'am."

Shona turns and comes face to face with Brian Gevers from Uniform.

"Oh hello Brian. How's that scooter of yours? Don't tell me you're riding it in all this snow?"

"It's great, Ma'am. I've had no trouble getting in and out. Angus council have been troopers at getting the roads open."

"Good grief. You be careful the roads might be clear but they're icy."

"You sound just like my mother, Ma'am." He smiles taking the sting out of his words.

"I suppose I do. What brings you to the wilds of CID?"

"My sergeant said you were busy up here and might need an extra pair of hands."

"I'm not going to turn down a free PC. How are your computer skills?"

"They're excellent. I'm a whizz on computers."

"That's what I like to hear. Have you done

anything with HOLMES yet, during your training?"

"We had a bit on it. I'm sure I could work it out."

"Great stuff. Peter, give the lad a cream cake and a mug of whatever beverage he fancies and show him to a spare desk. Brian, the team will provide you with their notes and you can bring HOLMES up to speed." Hallelujah. There is a God and he loves me thinks Shona.

By the end of the day they seem to be no further forward. Looking on the bright side they have eliminated some lines of enquiry, and know who they can
strike off their list. That in itself is an achievement. It means they can focus their energies elsewhere.

"Guys it's time to knock off. Go home to your nearest and dearest and remind them that you're alive. The hours we work they've probably all forgotten who you are." Then she remembers that one of her nearest and dearest is waiting at home. At least she hopes she is waiting at home. You can never tell where Blair is concerned. She could be anywhere doing anything.

The delicious smell of lamb and rosemary assaults Shona as she walks through the door into a warm flat. The feeling is almost sensuous. She has forgotten that Blair is a fabulous cook. Maybe if she gives up law she can become a chef. On second thoughts, strike that, she'd be thrown out of any serious kitchen after about an hour for arguing with the head chef. Going into the sitting room she trips over Shakespeare who is winding round her feet and meowing furiously. Translated, she is saying why did you leave me here all day with her? She's manic.

"You're absolutely right, Shakespeare. How remiss of me."

"Why are you talking to the cat? I didn't think you'd be home yet so I was going to plate yours up so you could microwave it later. Come on it's almost ready."

"I'll open a bottle of wine to have with the meal. I'll be there in a few seconds." In a lot of ways it is nice to have company rather than come home to an empty flat.

19

The bitch has to die. He's known that for a long time. In fact it is past time for her to die. The time has come. Tonight it will happen. His preparations are controlled. Well thought out. She will never suspect a thing. He has brought in a take away. Indian. Her favourite. She will enjoy her last night on earth. Not that she will know this. Meat Samosa, Cauliflower Pakora, Lamb Bhuna, Chicken Korma, Pilau rice and Peshwari naan. A feast fit for a condemned woman. A 2000 vintage merlot is breathing on the table. He pours a glass as she sidles into the room, dressed in a provocative outfit, moving like the whore she is.

"Darling, have you done all this just for little old me." Her eyelids flutter. He responds with a smile. He kisses her and hands over a glass of wine. She gulps it down, as he knows she will.

As they sit at the table she says, "Pour me another glass. You are so sweet to me. Of course you know I'll repay you later. We'll have fun, you and I." Her lips brush his cheek. Her tongue traces his lips in a sensuous caress. They eat the curry and he watches her relax. More than she knows.

He says, "Let's come back to this later," and pulls her through to the bedroom. She begins to stagger. "The wine... wine, stronger than I thought"

With clumsy hands she shrugs off her skimpy robe exposing underwear that comes only in a plain brown envelope from a catalogue. He lays her on the bed and kisses her but she is too drowsy to respond. Too involved in her own world, she hadn't noticed that he wasn't drinking. Within minutes she is insensible. It is easy to place a pillow over her face and smother her. It doesn't take long. "Goodbye my love."

Taking his leave, he moves along dark streets. Much of this place is still awaiting streetlights. As he walks down a country road he pulls off his gloves. The ones he always wears because of his 'psoriasis'. She said she found the leather sexual. That it added something to the game. He puts the gloves in his pocket and looked at his clear and healthy hands. It is finished. It is time to move on.

20

The shrill ringing of the phone wakes Shona at 5 a.m. after only a couple of hours sleep. She and Blair were in heated discussion until 2 a.m. at which point she agreed to go back to Cambridge. It turns out she hasn't really quit but is 'considering her options'. She can just as easily consider her options in Cambridge as Dundee. Shona thinks the unrelenting snow is a major factor. Apparently they don't have any in Cambridge.

"DI McKenzie. This had better be good."

"It's the Duty Sergeant Ma'am. Suspicious death in Balumbie."

Even Shona knows Balumbie is a suburb on the outskirts of Dundee. Shame. She could do with palming it off on to someone else. If it is a murder why couldn't the killer have gone a few hundred yards up the road and it would belong to Angus? "What's the address?" she says, sitting up and grabbing a pen and paper. She buries herself back under the duvet. Shakespeare buries further. "Tell them I'm on my way. Shouldn't be too long." In the kitchen she shovels food into Shakespeare's dish and heads to the shower. Then she scribbles a quick note to Blair, stuffs £50 in the envelope with it, and finally wakens her up enough to say she is off.

Blair prizes open one eye and mumbles, "Thanks. Love you lots," and goes back to sleep again

Shona smooths Blair's tangled hair. "Love you more."

She puts the note in front of the Tassimo machine,

where Blair will find it. Costa Coffee opens at 5 am so she nips in and orders a grande double shot Americano. That should keep her awake long enough to carry out a decent investigation. The snow is off and the main roads are fairly clear. Things get a bit trickier in Balumbie itself but she manages to get the car there in one piece. She has always admired the houses in Balumbie, a new private housing estate. She regards the white stone buildings as she drives. Each house seems bigger than the last. The one she is looking for is the grandest of the lot and has a front lawn bigger than Camperdown Park. Well she assumes it's a lawn. She can't really tell for snow.

Apart from the POLSA and his crew she is the first one at the scene. That's because she lives nearer Balumbie than anyone else. The others live on the other side of town.

"Morning, Ma'am. I can't believe we're seeing each other again so soon."

"Me neither, Sgt Muir. I'd say it a pleasure to see you but we both know it wouldn't be true. Not on either of our parts."

"Don't take this the wrong way, Ma'am but I agree."

"What have you got?"

"The neighbour called it in. She was worried as the light was on all night, which is unusual. The front door was ajar but the neighbour was scared to go in. When the local bobbies turned up they went in and found the body. She's upstairs in the bedroom."

"Have we a name for the deceased?"

"Sienna Laing. Her husband's Fergus Laing the importer and exporter."

"That's if the corpse is Sienna. It could be someone using the house for a bit of hanky panky. Do we know where her husband is?"

"Abroad on business. The neighbour didn't know where he is, or when he would be back."

"She could be with him. We need to contact him. Can I go in or do you want me to wait for Iain to do the photos?"

"You might as well go in. Goodness knows when Iain will arrive."

She walks through an imposing front door, which is painted green. The house is well maintained. Inside is a tiled hallway. The light is on. The lights in every other room seem to be on as well. She isn't keen to step inside in case she disturbs any footprints. It doesn't look like there are any footprints, however, she thinks it's better to be safe than sorry. She returns to speak to Sgt Muir. "Which neighbour found her? I think I'll go and see her first."

"A Mrs Janet Kilfoyle. She's in the house opposite. Number 139."

Mrs Kilfoyle's house seems to be a mirror image of the one opposite but with a red front door as a nod to individuality. Shona knocks on the door and a smartly dressed woman opens it. It stops hard against a chain.

"Yes."

Shona shows her warrant card. "Mrs. Kilfoyle I'm Detective Inspector Shona McKenzie. May I come in and talk to you."

She studies the card and then undoes the chain.

"You can't be too sure with all that's going on but you seem genuine. Please. Come in."

It is the first time Shona's been taken for a criminal but she supposes there's a first time for everything. Maybe she should stop thinking about murdering the boss. It might be showing on her face.

"Thank you, Mrs Kilfoyle. Can we sit down?"

"Come into the kitchen and I'll make you a drink." Her kitchen is about as big as Shona's whole flat. Gleaming utensils sit on granite worktops and Shona is willing to bet next month's pay packet that the cupboards are real wood. How the other half live.

"Can I get you a tea or a coffee?"

"Coffee please." She pulls out dark roast beans and grinds them before putting them in a filter coffee machine. This beat the usual Nescafé instant that appears in the houses she frequents in the line of duty. She takes a sip of the divine brew and takes a moment to savour it. Ambrosia. Mrs Gilfoyle's stare brings her back to reality.

"I believe it was you who reported the situation at the house across the road?"

"Yes."

This is going to be harder than she thinks. Usually in these situations the witness is so nervous they tell her everything in one long adrenaline burst.

"Can you tell me what happened?"

"I don't sleep well. I have to get up to go to the toilet several times. Last night, each time I got up, I realised that the lights were blazing in the house opposite. That's unusual. It's normally only the bedroom light that's on, if you know what I mean."

"Can you clarify for me?"

"She seems to entertain a lot of men when her husband is away on business. I'm surprised she doesn't put a red light in the window."

"Do you know if she was entertaining anyone last night?"

"I don't, I'm afraid. My daughter took me to the Caird Hall for a concert and didn't get back until late."

"What time would that be?"

"About 1030 pm. I came in and went straight to bed."

"I believe the door was ajar and that's what prompted you to ring the police?"

"Yes. Even she doesn't leave her door swinging in the wind."

"Did you see anyone go in or out?"

"I didn't see anyone. This weather has everyone behind closed doors. The place was deserted. Not that you see many people around here anyway. It's very private."

I'm sure it is, apart from you peering through your nets. Shona supposes she should be grateful for nosy neighbours. They make her job so much easier.

"Thank you Mrs Gilfoyle. You've been very helpful."

Shona takes her leave and crosses the road. The POLSA tells her that Iain has arrived and is inside the house taking photos. Nina and Abigail have arrived but there is no sign of anyone else.

"Many of the roads are blocked so it might take the others longer to get here," says Nina. The snowploughs and gritters are doing their best but it's wild over the other side. I picked Abby up on the way. Bell Street's like an ice rink."

"Much as I'd love to stand and chat about the state of the roads in Dundee City the deceased Mrs. Laing awaits our attention."

The hallway is large with a sweeping wooden staircase at the end. Shona walks through one of the doors into an enormous sitting room. There is obviously no expense spared with the luxurious cream and dark brown furnishings. The dining room is tastefully furnished, as is the small sitting room beyond. Only the study is different, panelled and full of bookcases and filing cabinets, with an imposing desk and a stuffed armchair. This is a man's room. The kitchen is fitted with all mod cons and every gadget you could ever imagine. However, Shona gets the impression these are never used. This feeling is supported by the array of takeaway dishes and plates, filled with congealing food, which sit on a huge pine table. This would account for the strong smell of Indian spices which permeates the downstairs rooms.

"This is some house," Abigail comments. "I thought our house in Skye was impressive but it stands in the shadow of this one."

"I know. If there wasn't a dead body decorating one of the rooms I might even be jealous." It is the first time Shona has seen Nina in awe of anything. Her parents aren't short of a bob or two and live in a ginormous house in the Perth Road. Many of the houses in the Perth Road used to belong to Mill owners who spared no expense on their homes.

Climbing the stairs they note six bedrooms, four of which have en suite bathrooms. The body is in the largest room, lying on the bed, dressed in red and black underwear that leaves nothing to the imagination. If it weren't for the swollen, purple tongue, protruding from her mouth she would look fairly peaceful. This is no normal slumber.

"Keep well back, ladies, until the police surgeon arrives."

"Look at those jewels." Nina sounds almost envious. "That's some rock she's got on her finger and those earrings are flawless diamonds, if I'm not mistaken."

Shona's sure she is right. Nina is an expert when it comes to all things expensive. They turn when they hear someone coming up the stairs. It's the procurator fiscal. Shona walks across the spacious room to meet him.

"Shona." There is that smile which lights up his face and dances on her emotions. His eyes crinkle in just the right way.

"Hi, Douglas. I'm beginning to get to the stage where I'm longing for a dead body just so I can see you."

"Now, now, Shona, that's grizzly even for you. Mind you it's odd that most of our dates seem to have an escort in the shape of a corpse. What's happened this time?"

"The neighbour found the lights on and the door swinging in the wind so she called the cops. According to said neighbour our dead woman was always having secret assignations. Allegedly, of course. I'd say she was smothered with the pillow next to her, but I didn't want to get up close and personal until Larry arrived and declared her dead."

"Good call. At least it gives us a chance to chat."

"How are the kids, in fact, where are the kids?"

"Rory's on a sleepover with his best friend and Alice is on a sleepover with her gran. That left me with a blessedly kid free night, until this came up, of course. It's a shame your sister is here we could have gone out for a meal."

"I know. Talking of Blair, she's gone back from whence she came. At least she will be when she wakens up. I've convinced her that continuing with her course is the best option. I think it had more to do with her boyfriend than the course to be honest. She either needs to put up or ship out in the boyfriend stakes."

They've been whispering sweet nothings for about 5 minutes when Larry lopes through the door. "Good morning to both of you."

He moves over to the body and beckons them both over. Lifting up the eyelids he says, "Perfect example of smothering - ?e around the nose and mouth, bloodshot eyes, petechiae." He tries to move limbs. "I'd say she died between 2300 and 0300 but it will need to be confirmed with Mary. I don't want to do anal temperature in case she had anal sex before she died. It could interfere with evidence. It's not likely as she still has her underwear on but I can't rule it out. Mary will be able to do a more detailed examination and give you a definitive answer. Anything else I can help you with?"

"You're fine Larry. That's great. Gives us something to work on."

Douglas and Shona move closer to the body. "With underwear like that it looks like she's running a one woman brothel. Not the sort of lingerie you expect to see around palatial estates."

"You'd be shocked at the things you see everywhere in Dundee. In my time as Procurator Fiscal I've learnt to keep an open mind. I've seen some sights. Even in the posher parts of the city."

"I'm sure you have. From the indentations on the pillow next to her I'd say she was smothered with that. Nina, get it into evidence."

"Could be natural, her having slept in the bed," says Abigail.

"The bed linen looks fresh. No creases other than where the body is. That would seem to rule out sex as well. Mind you they could have done the deed elsewhere first and then moved to the bedroom for the finale."

Roy joins them. "Grief, Ma'am. I sometimes wonder about the way your mind works."

"The way my mind works? That's rich coming from you," says Shona

"I'll give you that. She must have been stunning."

"I agree, and all of 26 years old. If it's the Fergus Laing I'm thinking of he must be 60, 65, something like that."

"No wonder she was playing a home match whilst he was playing away."

"That's enough Roy. Get your mind out of the gutter. Plus, what have I told you about football references. I hate football."

"Sorry, Ma'am. How can you hate football? It's impossible." He doesn't look sorry. In fact he looks decidedly cheery. Shona has to smile. The lad is growing on her. He's a bit like a spaniel, energetic, uncontrollable but somehow loveable.

She examines the area around the body but can see nothing amiss. She does look peaceful for someone who had been smothered.

"She doesn't look like she put up a fight."

Shona picks up the woman's hands and looks under the fingernails. No sign of a fight, at least with the naked eye.

"Iain, take scrapings from under her fingernails."

This could be another sex game gone wrong. Some sort of erotic stimulation. There is a good chance she may also have been drugged.

"Nina, Abigail. Go downstairs and bag all the food and the bottle of wine. Seal the wine bottle. Iain, go with them and get samples of the wine and the food. Get everything on the table into evidence."

Peter, Burns and Jason stroll through the door. "Nice of you to join us fellas. Just as the work's all done. Burns, help Iain with taking samples. Jason you're with Abigail and the others. Go through the place like a dose of salts and bag anything you think could be helpful. Peter, I need to speak to you."

"Aye Ma'am. Whit can I dae tae help?"

"You can speak English for a start."

"Whit would I dae that for? I'm Scottish no' English."

"So I can understand what the heck you're talking about. How am I meant to run an investigation if I'm trying to translate half the conversation?"

"Okay Ma'am. How can I help?"

"What do you know about this area? Is there anything that could be classed as out of the ordinary?"

"It's a nice area, quiet and, no, nothing out of the ordinary. The odd burglary is about it. There have been a couple of domestics but they didn't come to anything."

"What about Sienna and Fergus? They seem an unlikely match."

"They are. Fergus is well known in Dundee and everyone was surprised when he took up with Sienna. She was a hostess in Cat's Eyes before he met her."

"A lap dancer?"

"No she just served the drinks. There was a right hoo-ha at the time. He's well liked and respected. He left his wife for the new woman."

"Any kids from his first marriage?"

"Yes. Three. All in their twenties."

"Do you think they would have been mad enough to murder her?"

"I'm not sure but it's worth looking into. The thought of losing a sizeable inheritance does funny things to people."

"We need to get them in, and the ex wife. Also, if she was at Cat's Eyes then the Alexeyevs might have known her."

The team turn up for the body. Peter and Shona leave them to it and go and find the other team members.

"Go house to house and see if anyone saw or

knows anything. They might be reluctant to give up scandal so probe. Abigail you're in charge. I'll see you back at the station," says Shona.

The station is quiet considering it's ten o'clock. Is she missing anything? Strange. Shona knows they live in their own little world in CID but there is usually more of a buzz about the place. Puzzled she looks for the Chief. He's nowhere to be found. There is a note on her desk from the Chief's secretary about a meeting in the main conference room and CID is to attend. She hurries down to the relevant room and slips in the back. The Chief Constable is addressing the troops. Much as he likes the man, she isn't pleased that she has to listen to him two days in a row when she has a veritable banquet of murders to solve. Still hers is not to reason why, hers is but to do and work out why they die, to misquote Tennyson in his poem Charge of the Light Brigade. She listens with half an ear, as the Chief Constable waxes lyrical about Police Scotland. She thinks about the latest murder.

After spending a rather pleasant hour sitting in a nice warm conference room drinking coffee and thinking about her murders, Shona then rings Mary. "Has my latest corpse got to you yet," she asks the minute Mary answers.

"Hello, Shona, nice to speak to you too."

"Sorry, Mary, I'm ringing to ask if you can prioritise this one? I'd like to know if she was drugged and/or if she'd had sex before she died."

"You're lucky I'm low on bodies to examine. The hospital wards and nursing homes have managed to keep the population of Dundee alive despite the weather. More than I can say for you Attila. I've a couple coming in from a car smash but I'll start yours now as she's here."

"Thanks, Mary. You're a doll, despite your calling me names."

She laughs, "It's years since I've been called that. I'll ring as soon as I've got news. It will be a few hours at least and that's if I can hurry the lab up."

She goes via the squad room to find out if the others are back. Peter, Nina and Abigail have returned but the rest are missing. "Where is everyone?"

Peter says, "Iain and Burns are still up at the house doing dastardly things with noxious chemicals and taking photos. Jason and Roy had an altercation wi' a lamp post. Jason think's he's broken his arm so Roy's taken him up to A&E."

"For goodness sake. The big jessie. It's probably only a sprain. How am I meant to run an investigation with the boys taking jaunts to Ninewells?"

"That's health and safety for you, Ma'am. Jason has to get it checked out and fill in about a trillion forms in triplicate. I'm sure he's fine."

"I hope so. We haven't got the time to be one man down. Still we are bloodied but unbowed. We will live to fight another day."

"Are you thinking about joining the MPs or something, Ma'am?" asks Abigail. "You've gone all military."

"I've gone all light headed with the lack of progress on these cases. How did you get on with the neighbours? Please tell me it's good news."

"I wish I could. No one saw anything. All tucked up in their jammies with a mug of cocoa, behind closed doors and pulled curtains."

"What I wouldn't give for a real nosy parker neighbour. How come nobody sees or hears anything anymore? This is Dundee. Didn't the original nosy parker come from here?"

"Aye, you're right Ma'am. He did. Well he sort of did. He was in the *Sparky* and the *Beezer* comics. We've moved on since then."

"Shame. We'll have to wait and see what the boys have come up with. Let's pass the time in the canteen over a full cooked breakfast and a mug of builders tea." She doesn't have to ask twice. There is a stampede for the door.

Breakfast is finished, but Annie is on duty, and she is always happy to oblige Shona. The blessed saint Annie gets busy with a frying pan whilst they wrap their hands round huge mugs of strong tea. Life doesn't get any better than this. Even if they can't crack a case they are at least well fed and happy in their jobs.

21

Shona is sitting at her desk waiting for the remainder of the team to reappear when she is summonsed to the Chief's office. She feels she needs to break this habit.

"I've had ex Lord Provost George Brown on the phone. If I say he is not very happy, I would be understating the case."

"Why is Pa Broon in the middle of my investigation again? I can't seem to move without tripping over him. Does he want to join the police or something?" As part of her last major case she had been investigating the murder of his daughter. He was an obnoxious bully then and she's sure he hasn't changed much in the intervening period.

The Chief's mouth twitches. "Don't be so insolent about our esteemed ex Lord Provost, Shona. He says you're harassing his staff."

"Esteemed? He was in the Press last week caught in flagrante with one of Dundee's ladies of the night. Anyway, I don't know any of his staff so how am I meant to be harassing them?"

"Stephan and Gregor Alexeyev work for him."

"Are you telling me the Brothers Karamazov are on Pa..." The Chief's eyes narrow. "George Brown's payroll?"

"Yes. Now, I don't want you to stop investigating them, but watch your step. We both know George Brown is every noxious poison you can think of rolled into one. We don't want to get on his wrong side."

"Yes, Sir." She can't wait to tell the rest of the

team this little nugget.

There is a full complement in the office although Jason is sporting a sling.

"How's your arm? Is it broken?"

"No, Ma'am. Just bruised. I've to keep this on for 24 hours then I'm good to go."

"Glad to hear it."

As for the other matter, the team is, as she suspected, incredulous. Even Roy doesn't have a smart retort.

Peter chokes on his tea and Burns rushes over to bang his back. Recovering somewhat Peter splutters out, "I know George Broon's a bullying, Dundee wideboy, but I didn't think even he is stupid enough to get tied up with the Russian Mafia."

"I agree Peter. It came as a shock to me as well. However, the net result of this little liaison, is that we've to tread carefully when investigating the Alexeyevs."

"That shouldn't be difficult given that we've nothing on them so far," says Nina.

"What a pain in the a... ascending colon." Roy catches himself just in time, to a roar of laughter.

"Well saved, Roy, but whatever we call the orifice, I'm inclined to agree you're right. Hop to it and get down in the deepest, darkest, bowels of the net." Everyone groans. Shona continues, "See what you can find on our delightful Russian immigrants. I need them in a jail for a few days so we can interview them without their disappearing."

The flash of Roy's Gucci clad back heralds his rush from the room.

"Abigail, what's the update on your prisoner in Shotts? Has the psychiatrist been able to see him yet? I know we have Sarah Jean Smith in the frame for this, but as she's a well respected Mother Superior we need to prove we've followed every little street never mind avenue."

"He has, but no joy at all. His professional opinion is that Willie McPherson is stark raving mad. Not that he used those words but I can't remember the medical terms off the top of my head. Ordinarily he would be in Carstairs but opinion seems to be that, as long as he doesn't have an endless supply of old women to put out of their misery, he's harmless."

"Looking on the bright side, we're one step forward having eliminated one suspect. We need to keep moving on this. Abigail, pin down the whereabouts of Fergus Laing's ex wife and kids. Roy will help if you need to use his magic touch with all things Internet related. Iain, you get cracking with analysing the food. Do you want Burns' help?"

"That'd be dope. Let's go Burns."

"What's he on about?"

"Get with the programme Peter. He said it would be awesome."

"How can they no' speak English?"

This has to be the most jaw dropping statement Shona has ever heard from someone who talks like Peter. In the interests of Anglo-Scottish relations she feels it is better not to respond.

Shona is reading mind-numbing reports. "What a load of old cobblers. The only numbers you can rely on around here are the page numbers," she announces to the empty office. She crumples up the offending report and lobs it at the bin. Picking up a strawberry tart, she takes a soothing bite. There's nothing like a million sugar laden calories to take the edge off number crunching. Feeling slightly more cheerful, she picks up the next report – 'Impact Statement on the

Reorganisation of Scottish Police Forces into Police Scotland'. Taking another large bite of her cake she contemplates having another one.

A couple of hours later, Iain saves her from death by boredom, and an expanding waistline.

"I've got the results back on the food analysis. The wine was stuffed full of Valium. Enough to tranquilise an elephant never mind one skinny woman."

"Great. Not that we're any further forwards. Valium's pretty common around these parts. The GP's seem to give it out like Highland Toffee."

"Burns and I could look into who's selling it illegally if you want. I've a couple of snitches in my back pocket."

"Go for it."

Following Iain from the room she finds the team with their heads down and hard at it.

"Abigail, have you managed to pin down Fergus Laing and his nearest and dearest? Or ex nearest and dearest, I suppose."

"Fergus Laing's office says he is in Hong Kong. I've used my best Cantonese to speak to the local police who are going to break the news of his wife's demise. They said they'd interview him as well and put him on a plane to Edinburgh. He should be back tomorrow and we can speak to him then."

"Good job. Follow up with the locals once he's on the plane. What about the rest of the relatives."

"His sons live in England. Manchester and Bristol police are going to grab them and do the interviews. His ex wife and daughter live in Dundee and Arbroath respectively. I haven't contacted them yet."

"Don't bother. We'll go and visit them. Do they work?"

"The daughter does. She's a teacher at the High

School in Arbroath."

"Okay. Peter and Nina can go and interview her. You and I can interview the ex-wife. Roy, and the rest of the boys are gainfully employed so we should be safe from World War Three whilst we're out."

"Ever the optimist, Ma'am."

22

Shona and Abigail park outside a small, yet luxurious house in City Quay.

"It might be nice but it's no match for the one in Balumbie," says Abigail.

"My thoughts exactly. How the mighty have fallen. I'd say we have reasonable suspicion right here."

Ringing the bell they can hear dull chimes echo through the door.

They wait and then ring the doorbell again. There are sounds from the house and an elderly woman using a zimmer frame opens the door. "I don't require anything, thank you." She looks to be in her seventies, immaculately dressed, her voice cultured.

Shona shows her badge. "DI Shona McKenzie and my colleague, DS Abigail Lau. Are you Mrs Laing?"

"Yes I am. Although I'm divorced. What has Fergus done now?"

Interesting that she should jump to the conclusion her husband is up to no good. "Nothing as far as we know. May we come in and talk to you."

"About what? It's not one of my children is it?"

"No Mrs Laing. They are all safe. We just need to talk to you?"

She opens the door further and they follow her down the short hall into a beautifully decorated and sophisticated sitting room.

"Please sit down. May I get you a drink?"

"We're fine thank you Mrs Laing." They all sit down. Shona balances on the edge of the chair. She isn't sure what damage she might do to her antique perch.

"We would like to ask you some questions about your ex husband. How long have you been divorced?"

"About eighteen months. He moved in with his whore about a year before that."

No love lost there then. "Do you keep in contact with Mr Laing?"

"No I do not. I've had nothing to do with him since the day he told me he was moving his mistress into our house. We only saw each other through the courts. He does pay alimony but that's all done without any contact."

"How often do your children see their father?"

"Not that often. Their stepmother is many years younger than them. They cut themselves off from everything to do with their father. Why are you asking me all these questions? What's happened?"

"Mrs Sienna Laing was found dead this morning. Probably murdered."

"What? What?" Her eyes widen. "I didn't like the woman but I wouldn't wish that on her, but I can't say I'm sad. She was only out for what she could get. How is Fergus taking it?"

"We don't know Mrs. Laing. It would seem he is abroad."

"So why are you asking me all these questions?" She pauses and then, "You surely don't think I had anything to do with this?"

"You'll appreciate we have to ask difficult questions, Mrs Laing. Where were you between the hours of 11 pm and midnight last night?"

"In bed. Asleep. I take Tepazepam at night so I'm asleep by 10 pm. I didn't wake up until 8 am this morning."

"Can anyone vouch for that, Mrs Laing?"

"Of course not. Do I look like the type of person who would have people in my house at night? Whilst I'm at it, do I look like I'm capable of murdering anyone? I've had a stroke, for goodness sake." Indignation drips from every word.

Shona has to agree it does seem unlikely. She doesn't look like she has the strength to mash tatties never mind smother someone. Feisty though. She looks at Abigail who arches one perfectly manicured eyebrow. Shona interprets and echoes the sentiment. They are wasting their time.

"That will be all Mrs Laing. We will be in touch if we need anything else."

"Every time I go near a high school it makes me come over all cold. I always feel like I'm in bother with the headmaster."

"I can't believe you were ever in trouble, Peter?" says Nina. "You're a stalwart of the community."

"For the son of a bobby, I had my moments."

"Well, I never, you are a dark horse."

"Dinnae you be telling anyone mind."

"Don't worry, your secret's safe with me." Nina's grin indicates he'd better not put any bets on that.

A pleasant young woman is guarding the window of the office. They show their badges and ask if they can speak to Harriet Foster, as Fergus Laing's daughter is now called. They are informed she is teaching. She would be finished in 15 minutes and would they like a cup of tea or coffee whilst they waited. They sit in a small room, holding their drinks. Peter peers at the contents of his chipped mug.

"It doesn't look like tea to me."

"All you ever do is moan, Peter. Mind you, this coffee looks like it should be in quarantine. I didn't think anything could be worse than the station muck, but I'm wrong."

The arrival of the scowling teacher rescues them from having to drink their noxious brews.

Peter shows his warrant card. "We would like to ask you a few questions."

"What do you want? I've enough on my plate without the police tipping up to hassle me."

"We don't intend to hassle you. When did you last see your stepmother?"

"Why would you want to know about that?"

"I ask the questions? When did you last see her?"

"Not since the first time my father introduced us to her. I never intend seeing her again She's a gold digging slut."

"Where were you last night between the hours of 10 pm and 3 am?"

"Why do you need to ask me all these questions?" Abigail is getting antsy. "We wouldn't be asking them if they weren't necessary. Now where were you? Things will go a lot faster if you just answer instead of getting all defensive."

"I was in casualty down at the infirmary from 9 o'clock until midnight. My youngest was in a minor crash in the car. He managed to dislocate his shoulder."

"Thank you. Wouldn't it have been easier if you had just told us that in the first place? Where were you after that?"

"At home with my husband and kids."

"Do you know of anyone who would want to harm your stepmother?"

"Considering the line of work she was in before she weaselled her way into our lives, I'd say most of Tayside. What is this all about?"

"Sienna Laing died last night and it looks like it could be murder."

A moment of silence then, "Good riddance. It's the

best thing that could have happened to her. I wish I had done it myself, but I didn't."

"You don't sound very upset. Do you know the contents of your father's will?"

"I know nothing about his will other than, he said he would leave everything to his slag of a wife. Whether he carried through on that I don't know."

A bell rings.

"Can I go back to my class?"

"I suppose so. We'll be in touch with any more questions," says Peter.

Back in the car he says, "First stop Arbroath Infirmary to check up that alibi."

23

Returning to the station Shona rounds up the male elements of the team. "Boys I've a special little job for you and Sgt Lau. I need you to go and bring in our Russian friends. I want to find out if they had anything to do with Tilly at any point in their lives."

"Blimey, Ma'am. Don't you think I've had enough injuries recently?"

"For an ex soldier you're not half timid, Jason. You're an officer of the law. If I tell you to go and fetch Daniel from the lion's den, you'll do it. Understand."

"Okay Ma'am. No worries. I'll be big and strong."

"Sergeant Lau, you're in charge of the team. Use stab vests and you can sign out guns."

"I love being part of this team," says Roy. "We're the only bobbies in Scotland that seem to get to run around with guns in our hands."

"For goodness sakes Roy, this isn't the gunfight at the O.K. Corral. The guns are for your protection and if you need them. Make it clear to the twins they are only helping us with our enquiries."

"They're more likely to help us into a coma."

"Grief. You lads are wet. Now, off you go and arrest, I mean accompany, the Alexeyevs to the station. I'm very keen to have another wee chat with them."

A few hours later Abigail, and the boys return.

"So where are the Alexeyevs? You seem to have returned empty handed. Unless you took them straight to jail without passing go?" says Shona.

"We couldn't find them. They've disappeared,"

says Roy.

"What do you mean you couldn't find them? How can you lose a couple of six foot Russian thugs?"

"Where did you look? Did you go to Cat's Eyes?" asks Peter.

"Yep. It's locked up tight as a duck's ass. Not a soul in sight," says Abigail.

"Get yourselves round to Johnny Greig's house. He owns Cat's Eyes. You can bet your next pint on the fact that he knows their current whereabouts. Don't come back without our favourite Russians in tow. Arrest them if you have to."

"What for," asks Roy. "They haven't done anything as far as we know."

"For heavens sake." Shona continues, "Peter, take the lads and show them how it's done. I'm sure our twins will resist arrest. I don't care how you do it. Just get them here. Take Brian Gevers as well. I'm sure he'll be up for anything just to get away from updating HOLMES."

As they turn away Shona adds, "Jason, listen here soldier boy. I don't want you coming back via A&E. That's becoming a habit."

Shona, Abigail and Nina watch them disappear out the door, clutching their guns like a comfort blanket.

"They look like they're off for their last meal," says Nina.

"They might have already eaten their last meal if the Russian twins don't play nicely," adds Shona . With that cheery thought they go to find a cup of explosive level caffeine. It is the only thing that will get them through updating the incident room files.

A while later Shona thinks she had better tell the Chief that her team is gainfully employed arresting the Alexeyevs. She takes him a cup of Earl Grey to soften the blow. The Chief must be the only cop in the history of policing to drink the perfumed beverage. Seems a bit poncy to Shona but who is she to argue with the boss.

"I told you to back off the Alexeyevs. What part of that didn't you understand?"

"I realise that sir, but we just need to ask a few questions. If they come in nice and quiet then there won't be a problem."

"They don't do quiet and neither does George Brown. This will come back to savage you never mind bite you. Trust me Shona I will have no hesitation in throwing you to the lions."

Shona is dismissed in the usual cursory fashion. Sometimes she feels like feeding the Chief to the bears up at Camperdown Wildlife Park - piece by tiny piece. Not a jury in the land would convict her after listening to Thomas for five minutes.

The team doesn't return for a couple of hours. This time they do the job and arrive dragging a brace of handcuffed Russians who are thrown into separate cells. Shona can tell they are not happy about this, from several corridors away.

"We've arrested them for assault to severe injury Ma'am," says Peter.

"Assault? What in heaven's name did they do? The Chief will have a fit."

"They were at Chick's pawn shop. Chick wasn't looking good. In fact he's in an ambulance on his way to Ninewells as we speak. I've sent Roy with him to get a statement."

"Get their solicitor and let me know when they're ready to be interviewed."

"Not Angus Runcie again. That's all we need," says Peter.

"We do seem to be seeing rather a lot of him."

"Why are you persecuting my clients? They are Scottish citizens and have done nothing wrong."

"They won't be Scottish citizens for very long if I have my way."

"You can't say that."

"I just did. Now shut up and let me get on with it. I need to ask them a few questions."

She turns to Gregor.

"Why were you found standing over the badly beaten Chick Anderson?"

You can almost hear the digital clock on Shona's mobile tick in the ensuing silence.

"I would like an answer to that Gregor."

"I am Stephan."

"Whatever your name is, answer the blasted question."

"My brother and I found him like that."

"You had blood on your hands and I'm betting the bruises on your knuckles might fit with the ones all over Chick's body."

"We were helping him. The bruises happened as we went about our business."

"I'm sure they did."

"There's no need to take that tone, Inspector. My client is cooperating fully with your enquiries."

Shona gives him the respect he deserves and totally ignores him. She finds it's the best policy with Angus Runcie.

"You'd better hope Chick recovers and corroborates your story or you'll not be slipping away from a jail term this time."

Blue eyes, as cold as the River Tay itself focus on Shona. She has a feeling Stephan is memorising every line on her face. She thinks it might be worth being escorted home for a few weeks.

"I have done nothing."

"You seem to say that a lot. Forgive me if I don't believe you."

He opens his mouth but Shona continues, "I've no time to argue the matter with you. Do you know Tilly Methven?"

"No."

"Are you sure?"

"Yes. Why do you keep asking me this?"

"We've a dead prostitute on our hands as well. You both seem to have your huge Russian fingers in an awful lot of Scotch pies. Is running a prostitute ring one of them? I think you killed Tilly."

Stephan lurches from his chair, "I did not kill her, but I will kill you." Touching her throat Shona steps away from his outstretched arms. He is rugby tackled by a couple of PCs who look like they are in the Police Boxing Team. She tells them to phone for extra help and turns back to whatever half of Tweedledum and Tweedledee she is interviewing.

"Let's add assault and hindering the police to the list of charges. Now where were you in the early hours of January 14th?"

"You will regret this."

"So you keep saying. If you stopped issuing threats and got on with answering my questions we could all be home by teatime. You'll be eating your bowl of borscht, or caviar and champagne, or whatever it is you're having for your tea. Now where were you on the early hours of January 14th."

"I do not need to answer this."

"Of course you blo..." She pauses, to regain her composure. "You almost had me swearing there and that's some feat. Answer the damn question."

"Stop harassing my client."

"I'll harass you if you don't instruct your client to

answer my questions."

"He's taking the 5th."

"We're in Scotland. Even a tinpot lawyer like you must know there's no such blo..." She stops and draws breath again.

"You pair are getting on every nerve I possess and maybe even some I don't possess. Are either of you going to say something sensible?"

Roy and Jason enter having responded to the plea for help. Jason, minus his sling seems to have recovered from his arm injury. It is beginning to resemble Tannadice Park at a home game, there are so many people in the room.

Shona gives their names for the recording and continues. "Where was I? Oh yes. I remember. I was asking you to talk sense about your whereabouts when Tilly Methven was murdered."

"I was at the Cat's Eyes Club."

"Now that wasn't so difficult was it? Can anyone vouch for that?"

"Tatiana can vouch for me. I am sure she will remember me stroking her beautiful breast."

"What about your brother?"

"Her other breast would remember him."

"Where are you going with this? My client says he has nothing to do with the young woman's death. He has witnesses who say he was elsewhere. Either arrest him or we're leaving now."

"If you insist. Stephan Alexeyev we are arresting you for committing the offence of Assault to Severe Injury against Chick Anderson. You do not have to say anything..."

Stephan roars and thrusts from his seat knocking his chair over in the process. He swings a punch at Shona just as Roy pushes him to one side. His punch misses by a mile and lands squarely on Angus Runcie's eye. Roy and Jason wrestle Stephan to the ground and through Runcie's screams Shona continues, "Add to the arrest sheet assault to injury on your lawyer Angus Runcie. You do not have to say anything, but it may harm your defence if you do not mention when questioned something, which you later rely on in court. Anything you do say may be given in evidence." She glares at the struggling prisoner. "DC MacGregor and DC Roberts take him to a cell and lock him up." It's not easy but they manage to drag him off. Shona turns to the afflicted lawyer.

"Your eye's not looking good. Maybe you should take yourself off to A&E. Before you go can you fill in the relevant accident forms?"

"You did this. You antagonised my client. I am going to sue your a..."

"Now now, Angus. Stay professional please or I might have to arrest you as well."

"You haven't heard the last of this."

"I'm sure I haven't. I look forward to getting your communication. I'll just go and get those forms now."

Shona is smiling as she as she enters the squad room.

"What's got you with a grin all over your face?" asks Peter.

"I've got the Alexeyevs locked up and Angus Runcie has managed to get himself a black eye during the interview. It's the most fun I've had since this case started."

"Damn, and I missed it. Sorry Ma'am I didn't mean to swear."

"You can say damn as much as you like, I think this situation calls for it. In fact I think we're entitled to a bottle of champagne for the injury to Angus Runcie alone."

"I couldn't agree more. I gather there was a bit of a

rumpus. Jason didn't manage to get hurt did he?" asks Nina.

"Not as far as I know, although there's time yet as he is currently employed taking whichever twin we interviewed down to the cells to join his brother. Where are the other two sergeants?"

"Haven't a clue. They'll be doing something sensible wherever they are."

"I'm sure you're right. Grab your coat we're off up to Ninewells to interview our boy Chick. Hopefully he'll spill the dirt on our latter day Ronnie and Reggie." She feels she needs to get out of the station.

To pass the time, whilst driving at a crawl through a blizzard, she updates Peter on the full interview with their Slavic friend.

"The information about what they were up to in the club is a bit too much. I've pictures of the Russians and the fair Tatiana's mammary glands swimming round in my head."

"Och, Ma'am. Did you have to share that? A man o' my advanced years doesn't need to hear things like that."

"Peter, I'm sure you've seen and heard much more than that during your time in the force."

He lets out a bellow which shakes the car.

"Less of the hilarity, Peter. You'll have us in a ditch. Isn't Tatiana a Russian name?" she asks. "Cat's Eyes seems to be crawling with Russians. Do you think the Alexeyevs own it?"

"They do seem to spend an affy lot of time there. It might be worth looking into."

They manage to get to Ninewells unharmed despite the weather's best attempt to stop them. Shona takes full advantage of their exalted status by parking right at the entrance and bunging an official police business sign on the dash. A taxi driver flips her the bird and she has a sudden urge to arrest him. In truth, she's too cold to care. Jock McTaxi has a narrow escape, but she writes down his number plate for future reference.

They are directed to the acute surgical ward by the reception staff who look chilled to the bone and fed up. Shona supposes sitting next to an open automatic door in a blizzard can have that effect on you. It takes them about 10 minutes to get to the ward through miles of corridors. Ninewells is a 'mahoosive' place. It's also easy to get lost in it so she is surprised they don't end up in the mortuary.

Chick does not look happy to see them. In fact he looks dreadful. He is sporting a myriad of cuts and bruises, and a huge tube, is sprouting, from his chest. He must be in enough pain that would even knock an elephant sideways.

"My they've done some number on you Chick. Did Stephan and Gregor do this to you?"

His injuries are such that he finds it difficult to speak. He musters up the energy to force out a word that sounds suspiciously like no. Not what she wants to hear.

"Could you repeat that, Chick? I thought for a minute there you said no."

"Did." He pauses and manages another word. "Not... Them."

"Are you telling me the Alexeyevs are innocent? Surely even you are not that stupid, Chick. I could put them away for a long time for this?"

"Didn't do it."

"So why were they standing over your battered body with bruises on their ape shaped knuckles?"

"Found me."

"By all that's Holy will no one tell the truth where

our Ruskies are concerned? Chick, you know fine well they're bampots. This is your chance to get rid of them," says Peter.

"If it wasn't them then who did take their fists to you?" Shona is fed up with interviews where everyone feels the need to lie like a cheap Chinese watch.

"Don't...know."

"Chick if you are lying to me then I'll arrest you for obstruction."

"Not lying."

"Before we go I'm just going to take a few swabs from your wounds. See if there's any DNA that matches the Alexeyevs knuckles."

"No. Been cleaned."

"For..." She breathes in deeply. "Come on, Peter, we haven't time for this. You're not off the hook yet, Chick. We'll be back."

Outside his private room Shona swivels towards the nurses station.

"Where are you going? The exit's the other way."

"I'm not giving up that easily." Arriving at the nurses' station she spots a nurse who looks to be about ten years old, "Can I speak to the person in charge."

"I'm Senior Charge Nurse Smith. I'm the senior nurse in charge of the ward."

Blimey, she doesn't look old enough to have finished her training. Shona is beginning to feel old.

"Detective Inspector Shona McKenzie and Detective Sergeant Peter Johnston. Did you take swabs from Mr. Anderson's wounds?"

"I am afraid that is a matter of patient confidentiality. I can't tell you that."

"Whilst I appreciate that, this could help to pin down the person, or persons, who gave him his injuries."

"And whilst I appreciate what you are saying I still

cannot give you the information without the patient's consent."

"Could you make sure the swabs are not disposed of? I will get a warrant and be back."

"I will do my best. That's all I can say."

"Thank you." Peter and Shona hurry back down the miles of bleak corridors.

It isn't to be. The Sherriff's office won't agree to a warrant as the victim is refusing to cooperate. Blast and damn. There is no way she can keep the Alexeyevs under lock and key. They'd slip though her fingers again. She is beginning to think longingly of iron bars and beatings when the Chief summons her.

"DI McKenzie. Why is it that you can't seem to carry out your job without annoying half the City of Dundee? I've had Angus Runcie on the phone complaining that you riled his client to such an extent that the lawyer ended up injured. What happened this time?"

She gives a succinct explanation.

"It sounds to me like it was an accident. However, I am warning you. One more complaint and I'll be looking for a new DI. I'm fed up defending you. I know Angus Runcie is a lower form of pond life than anyone, including his clients. That doesn't give you an excuse to wind him up. Calm down, Shona. I mean it. That will be all."

"Yes, Sir. Sorry, Sir." Not that he has any chance of her complying with the mood she is in. I'd like to put him, Runcie and both Russians in a room and let them fight it out with the aforementioned iron bars. He wouldn't be so smug then. God spare her from Russians and any Chief Inspector who ever walked the earth.

Shona finds Roy and Jason and tells them to release the slippery Russians. Jason is looking a tad green.

"What's up with you?"

"Stephan kicked me in the privates while we were taking him back to the cells."

"For heavens sake, Jason. Can I not send you to do anything without you taking a hit? Were you as bad as this in the Army?"

"No, Ma'am."

Roy puts in his tuppence worth. "His todg..."

"Roy, I want to hear nothing more about anything below the level of Jason's chest, or any other man's chest for that matter. Get a car and take him to A&E. I'm beginning to think you fancy one of the nurses up there, Jason."

"I wish I did. It would make all my war wounds worthwhile."

"You might as well go home once you're finished."

Looking on the bright side she now has an excuse to keep Stephan in for another night. Gregor wouldn't go anywhere without him so they had their twins tucked up nice and cosy in a cell for 24 hours at least. She tells the rest of the team they are free from their shackles until the morning. Grabbing her coat she makes a call to Douglas. It turns out that he and the kids are free for a visit to Pizza Hut

24

The team is pleased to see that there is leftover pizza for breakfast the next morning.

"Top job, Ma'am" says Burns, between mouthfuls. "Best breakfast I've had in ages."

"If this is the best you've eaten then I dread to think what you feed yourself on in the morning. The minute you've finished your feast meet me in the briefing room. No loitering. I want to crack on."

"First things first. Peter you get moving on charging Stephan under section 41 assaulting a constable in the execution of his duty. I'm going to speak to the Sheriff about refusing bail. He's likely to disappear or put a hit out on Jason if we throw him out."

"We'll need to let Gregor go."

"Yep. Tell him to sling his hook. He won't be best pleased but we need to split them up." Peter leaves with a gleam in his eye, a man happy at his work.

"Nina and Abigail you're both off to Edinburgh Airport. Meet Fergus Laing off his flight and bring him back here for interview. He's on BA 7622 from London arriving Edinburgh 1324."

"On it." They are up and out the door. Anyone thinking they are a bit premature for an hour journey, has never faced the road works leading to the Forth Road Bridge. It will only take about twenty years to build the new bridge so the road works will probably be ongoing for another twenty three years.

"Roy bring up all the information you can about

the Cat's Eyes Club. I want any bit of scandal, news and the name of any creep who has a stake in it."

Another man happy at his work, he flies from the room. Shona has no doubt that Roy will come up with the goods.

"Jason and Burns, get yourselves down to Cat's Eyes. Arrange to meet Johnny Greig there. Look at every piece of paperwork he possesses regarding that club. Photocopy it and bring it back here."

As the team scurry to do her bidding, Iain returns to his lab, Shona to her office. For once it is blessedly quiet. She sits down and promptly falls to the floor as her chair collapses. Picking herself up she searches for any breakages other than the chair. Fortunately only her pride has taken a hit. Dumping the broken wood in the corridor she bumps into Peter as she rifles the squad room for another chair.

"Seems like you need to go on a diet Shona. DIs shouldnae be going around breaking chairs."

"You've a cheek, the size of you. It's a good job the new furniture will be here soon. How did you get on with the Kalashnikov brothers?"

"That would be about the right thing to call them. They're about as dangerous as the weapons themselves. Alexeyev 1 is tucked up nice and tight. Alexeyev 2 has been slung out into the snow like you said. Literally. He wasn't keen to leave the 5 star pleasure that is Bell Street nick. He says he's off to see Runcie."

"Good luck to him. I don't think even Runcie's going to be keen to be on his side. I'm sure he'll give him short shrift."

She marches purposefully up to Roy's desk. He is hard at it and she can almost see flames flying from his keyboard. Roy and a computer are an even more deadly force than the twins. "What have you got for me?"

Without looking up, "Not much yet, Ma'am, but

I'm following several trails."

"Go for it Davy Crocket. I'll be back later to see where they're leading."

She, and the chair, return to her office.

After trying out the temporary chair for size for a while she shimmies down to Uniform and bangs into her very own tame cop.

"Ah. Brian. Just the chap I want to see."

"Do you need me in CID Ma'am?"

"Not at the moment, but you're first on my list when I need spare bodies to help. At the moment I need a couple of things. Could you give traffic this number plate and tell them to keep a close watch on the driver. If he even thinks about doing something wrong book him."

"What's he done to upset you, Ma'am?"

"Him being on the planet is enough to upset me. Also, I need you and one of your pals to go and find out the current whereabouts of Auld Jock. I'm worried about him in all this snow. He left several days ago and I want to make sure he's okay. Let me know what you find."

"You're an old softie really, aren't you Ma'am?"

"Less of the old, and don't go spreading rumours that I'm nice now Brian."

"Wouldn't dream of it. Your secret's safe with me."

She will have Brian in her team one day. He'd be an asset.

She's no sooner put her backside in the new chair than the duty sergeant calls her. "Stephan Alexeyev is insisting he speaks to you. If you could come now, Ma'am, I would appreciate it. He's been roaring fit for the devil himself and my PC's are just about ready to get a gun and shoot him."

Trailing wearily down to the cells she can hear that everything the sergeant described is true. She steps up to the cell and shouts, "Shut up. How dare you treat my officers like this."

"I have been asking for you for hours. They would not bring you."

"I'm not a dog. They don't bring me. Are you ready to confess?"

"I have done nothing to confess. The food and drink they serve in here is not fit for the swine. This tea is der'mo."

"Russian's not my first language but I take it you don't like our provisions. What are you after - Russian tea and caviar? This isn't the fricking Ritz. No one gives a stuff about your eating and drinking habits." As she walks off he starts his yelling again. She turns back. "One more word out of that mouth of yours and I will arm an officer with a pistol and tell him to shoot you the minute you open it again. None of us want to listen to your bullyboy tactics. They may work with the great unwashed out there but not in here."

His mouth snaps shut and his eyes become colder. His expression has Shona considering a career in a police force on the other side of the world. At least she can ponder it in blessed silence. Whatever she did in a past life, which has left her dealing with so much crap in this one, she is truly sorry.

She is catching up with paperwork, in a rare moment of peace, when the troops return. The noise sounds like someone has let a fox loose in a henhouse. Her team doesn't know the meaning of quiet.

"Meet me in the briefing room," she calls out, passing the squad room.

"Can we go and get some food?"

"No, you flaming well can't. All you lot ever

thinks of is your stomachs. This is a nick not a 3 star Michelin restaurant. I want feedback so make it double quick."

They all appear muttering about having missed lunch but it doesn't wash. She's fed up of all this hurry up and wait.

Peter updates the team on the current position with Alexeyev 1 and 2.

"Nina and Abigail, did you manage to get your hands on Fergus Laing and escort him back?"

"We did. He's sitting in an interview room swigging strong coffee. He looks like a man on the edge of a grave waiting for a puff of wind to blow him inside."

"Do you think he's fit to be interviewed?"

"He's drunk, Ma'am, as well as suffering from terminal jet lag. I think he was either drowning his sorrows or celebrating on the long journey back from Honkers."

"That's just great. Get him sobered up. Does he seem keen to help us with our enquiries?"

"He hasn't said otherwise and he came with us calmly."

"That's good enough for me. Let me know when he's sufficiently sober to answer questions."

"Burns, Jason, what did you drag up?"

"They have a lot of paperwork in that place and none of it in any kind of order. We've photocopied everything and need to go through it all."

"Roy, have your trails led anywhere yet?"

"Not yet. It's taking me longer than I thought. There seems to be a lot of dead ends and misdirection. I'll figure it out though. You don't need to worry."

"I never worry where you and computers are concerned, Roy. Off you go back to it. Everyone else, let's get that paperwork on the table and start getting it into some semblance of order."

They have been at it for about an hour when there is a knock at the door. It is Brian from Uniform.

"What can I do for you, Brian? If you're offering to help we're a bit stalled at the moment. I've not enough to keep my own guys hard at it."

"I wish I was, Ma'am, but my boss is champing at the bit to get me doing work for him." His smile takes the sting out of the words. "I've got news on Jock. He and Maggie are both happily ensconced at the Sally Army."

"I thought the Salvation Army was fresh out of beds."

"They are, but they've somehow squeezed a borrowed bed into a large cupboard about the size of a police cell. Jock's as happy as a warthog in mud. He's got a bit of privacy but nothing fancy. They've turned a blind eye to Maggie so all is fine in her little world as well. I think they were both wagging their tails when I left."

"Thanks for that. I didn't want them wandering the streets in this snow. Much as Jock will never willingly go indoors, he adores Maggie and would do anything to keep her safe."

"If you need anything else, Ma'am, give me a yell. I'd be happy to help."

"I bet you would, but Sergeant Muir isn't going to be best pleased if I keep purloining you. I'll keep you in mind."

"Thanks, Ma'am." He takes his affable and helpful self back to his own duties.

Shona sends Nina to find out if Fergus Laing is sober enough to talk. It turns out he is. He's probably drunk triple his body weight in whisky in his lifetime and his liver's used to it. She and Shona go to interview the bereaved husband.

When Shona first claps eyes on Fergus he looks less bereaved than knackered.

"Mr Laing. I appreciate your coming in to talk to us. I realise this must be a difficult time for you, and that you are tired after your long flight. Would you be willing to answer a few questions?"

"Of course. Anything to help find my wife's killer."

"How long had you and Sienna been married?"

"Just under a year. It would have been our anniversary next week. I arranged to be home for that."

"Where did you meet?"

"We met socially. Through friends."

"Did your wife have any enemies? Anyone who would want to harm her?"

"No, everyone loved Sienna. She was gregarious, fun loving and the most sociable person I ever met."

"I am sorry to have to bring this up at a difficult time but it may have some bearing on her murder. It has come to our attention that your wife was a cocktail waitress at Cat's Eyes when you met."

"She was, but she was just a waitress. She was always fully clothed."

Fully clothed or not she still worked at the seediest club in Tayside. Perhaps best not to say that to the recently widowed Mr Laing though.

A couple of hours later, things take an interesting turn. Roy comes into the briefing room, beaming.

"I've got news. It looks like there's a lot more money making its way through Cat's Eyes than you'd expect from a scummy Dundee sleaze bar. Most of it's ending up in bank accounts in Switzerland and the Caymans."

"Well, well, well. Money laundering. Was this

information found out through legal or underhand means, Roy?"

"It was pretty legal."

Shona will have to live with that and worry about the consequences later. A lot later. Like after they've solved the murders and the Chief and the Sheriff are both in a good mood.

"That's not all though," he continues. "All the girls working at the club are living it up in fancy apartments. They're not in the cheapest parts of town either."

"Fantastic. Get printouts of what you've got and we'll marry it up with the photocopies of the official books we have here. Everyone get in touch with your loved, or maybe not so loved ones, and tell them you'll be late home."

"My boyfriend will freak. He says I never get any time off," says Nina.

"Andros will just have to cope. I can't run my investigations to suit your boyfriend, even if he does have a fabulous motorbike and nice looking sunglasses."

"Andros is long gone. I told you that. This one's called Kyle and he's a model. Do you not listen?"

"Of course I listen. I just can't keep up. Especially when I'm in the middle of trying to solve a gaggle of murders."

"I'll go and ring him. He's head over heels so I'm sure he'll still be around tomorrow." Flashing her infectious grin she goes to break the news to Kyle. Shona can't help but laugh. Nina's love life never fails to bring a smile to her face.

Working industriously they soon manage to make sense of the whole sorry mess of paperwork. Roy's thinking is right. There are huge discrepancies between the official paperwork and what is actually happening on the dark side of the business. They're not talking the odd pound or two here either, but several million a year. That's a sizeable side business for the club.

"Let's call it a night and come back to it fresh in the morning. Johnny Greig is as thick as Hadrian's Wall so he'll not work out that we're on to all his capers. Also, I think it's the Alexeyevs who are heading this up. Stephan seems to be the major brains and Gregor the willing henchman. I think we're safe for one night. In the briefing room at 0900." Shona stops Peter before he opens his mouth. "Yes, I know the snow is extraordinary but you'll just need to leave earlier. Peter, you're the only one with a free pass, and that's only if the Tay Road Bridge is completely shut. Drive safely and I'll see you all in the morning."

A starving Shakespeare greets her at the door. She is vociferous in voicing her disapproval of Shona's schedule. "I know you haven't eaten, Puss Cat, but neither have I." Shakespeare's look says she couldn't care less when Shona had last eaten. That wasn't her problem. She has a lamb dish courtesy of Whiskas; Shona has a portion of some sort of curry from the freezer. The cat fares better than her.

25

The all terrain vehicle pays no heed to the weather, eating up the miles, like a Lotus Type 125. Although bumpy it takes the rough, snow covered terrain in its stride and the killer is soon at his remote destination. Dusk hides his movements as he pulls the animal feed sacks from the trailer. The huge burlap sacks contain far more than animal fodder as he tips their precious cargo onto the ground. Soon it is hidden by the sheep as they huddle round, eager to get to the food

He doesn't look back as he leaves the body to any wild animals which may be around. There are no wolves here in this desolate spot. They've not yet been reintroduced to Scotland. Nevertheless, if the body is not found then the buzzards will soon do their work. Whatever happens, it is of no consequence. Driving away he does not look back.

26

Awakened early by a frantic cat demanding breakfast, Shona decides to visit the gym before work. A quick five miles on the treadmill and about a gallon of coffee has her wide awake and ready to face the vagaries of a Dundee police officer's day. Thankfully the wind and the bridge are getting along fine, which means the whole team arrives before the prearranged time. She has the feeling it is going to be a great day. She's in the mood for a tussle with a few of the main characters from the Dundee underworld. Before greeting the team she resolves to have a word with the Chief. She takes him a cup of coffee and a cake as a peace offering. She needs to make amends for riling half the population of Dundee. It is also a softener for what she is about to ask.

"You'd better not be bringing me news of more murders or anyone else threatening to sue us for your wild ways Inspector."

"Not at all, Sir. I've been frightfully well behaved. I haven't threatened anyone in the last couple of days." She sends up a quick prayer for forgiveness for lying through her teeth.

"Why don't I believe that? What do you want?"

"I'd like to do a raid on Cat's Eyes tonight."

The Chief always looks miserable but this sets a new record even for him. His face turns bright red and she worries he'll have a stroke.

"Are you all right, Sir?"

"I was as right as rain until you came to my station. We never had anything like this before you arrived."

"I realise it's unusual, Sir, but its crucial to the case. We've got new information." She outlines what they've discovered about Johnny Greig and his club.

There is silence but at least his face has returned to a healthier colour. The Chief might be a pain in the neck but she doesn't want him to croak in front of her.

"I would say you've got reasonable cause. Go and get a warrant from the Sherriff."

"Can I borrow more personnel from uniform?"

"Yes. Now there's something I need to speak to you about."

He outlines his latest plan and to say she is stunned would be the biggest understatement of all time. She can't wait until the team find out. She isn't going to tell them yet. She will savour the news and pick her moment. She grins. Sometimes her job has the best perks.

Plans for that night's raid on Cat's Eyes are proceeding well. She's managed to snaffle extra officers from George in Uniform. He'd handed them over fairly amicably despite muttering, "They might as well make me redundant and give all my officers to you. You seem to think they all belong to you anyway." Shona knows George, and his sense of humour, well so doesn't take offence. She is now busy working out who would do what, where, to whom, when and how. A knock at the door interrupts her. It is the desk sergeant.

"Can I talk to you, Ma'am?"

"Of course Sergeant Bell." Yes he has heard all the jokes about Bell of Bell Street nick. "You're a welcome break from pushing officers around. In a figurative sense of course."

"You might no' be saying that in a minute, Ma'am. There's been another suspicious death. The body of a young man found on a remote track near

Auchterhouse."

"Auchterhouse is Angus, it's not... Forget that, of course it's mine. They always are. Tell them we're on our way."

Leaving the papers on her desk she picks up her coat, and then the Chief.

Shona and The Chief enter the squad room to break the news of the latest murder. As the various members of the team begin to get ready to leave the Chief says, "Not so fast. I'm joining you on the job," and with that mind-blowing statement he walks out of the door.

Roy breaks the silence. "Well, I can honestly say that my gob is well and truly smacked."

"What was that all about? Surely he didnae mean it."

"He most certainly did. Orders from on high. The brass are going to get down and dirty with the troops."

"What on earth for?" Nina has found her voice.

"To remind them what the job's all about and foster better relations with the ground troops."

"I've enough relations. I don't need the Chief to swell the ranks."

"That's enough Nina. Come on you lot, stop whining and get your coats. Unless you want to go out in a blizzard in your shirt sleeves, that is."

"Hoy, Victoria Beckham," Shona adds for Nina's benefit. "You'll need to get out of the Jimmy Choo's and in to a pair of wellies. We're off to the wilds of Angus."

"We can't go out there, with a force ten gale blowing. Do you not know the police are advising everyone to stay off the road?" says Peter.

"Don't be such a big girl's blouse. You are the police so get your driving gloves and let's go. If the Chief can do it then so can we."

"What about health and safety?" says Peter.

"You wee Jessie. We've a murder to solve and we can't leave a dead body blowing about in a hoolie. We'll get four wheeled drives from the pool."

"Oooh. Listen tae you with all the Scottish talk. How come you can tell me off in Scottish but dinnae understand anything I say?"

"That will just have to remain one of the great mysteries of life." She does her best impression of the woman with the enigmatic smile. "Stop moaning and come on. We can't keep the Chief waiting."

Sometimes it would be easier to get her cat to do tricks than get her team out of the door. Anybody would think they hated their job.

At the crime scene she is beginning to think that Peter has a point. She isn't sure how long the Chief will last out here. They are in the middle of a bleak wasteland reminiscent of the Mongolian steppe. Apart from the Cheviots that is. There can't be many Scottish sheep roaming about Mongolia. The wind is whipping the snow up into a frenzy and they can barely see an inch in front of their eyes. How on earth had anyone been murdered out here and even more importantly who in the world would be out and about to find the body?

There are a couple of young coppers standing outside the crime scene. They look frozen to the gills despite police issue greatcoats. She imagines they are rapidly reevaluating their career choice.

It is more like a comedy of errors than a crime scene, with sheep everywhere and a trio of burly coppers trying to keep them at bay. More like herding cats than sheep she decides ruefully. The POLSA and his team have put up a large and fairly substantial tent over the body. Shona can see a number of people inside. Thanking her lucky stars that her days in uniform are far behind her she steps through the entrance to the tent. "Peter, watch where you're going." He had barreled in to her as he dogged her heels.

"Sorry, Ma'am. I'm a bit concerned about frost bite."

"For goodness sake, man. You're from Dundee you must be used to a bit of snow in the winter."

"This is exceptional even for us."

"It is rather spectacular. We need to work quickly as I'm not sure this tent is going to be around for very long."

"I'd bet my pension on your being right aboot that."

The Chief is already in the tent. He appears disinterested in the body and is wedged in a corner chatting to another couple of suits. Seems like all the brass are getting their quota in at the same time. None of them are paying the workers a blind bit of notice. Getting down and dirty doesn't mean doing any actual work. The Chief catches her looking and calls, "DI McKenzie, we are now in charge of the crime scene." With this important bit of business over with, he turns back to his buddies. By 'we', he means Shona.

The deceased is a young man of around twenty-five years old, tall and muscular. He has been strangled. There is a rope tied tightly around his neck. His face is blue and his tongue protrudes gargoyle like from his mouth. His legs are lying at an unnatural angle.

"Whoever did this must hae been strong. Our dead man isn't exactly wee," says Peter

"Exactly what I'm thinking. Do we know who found him?"

"According to the bobbies standing outside, it was a local farmer. He's sitting in his tractor."

"Roy, go and get the farmer. Nina, Abigail and Jason brace yourselves. We'll have to do a search." The collective groan tells her the troops aren't happy.

"Don't even think about moaning. You're cops so you'll have to suck it up."

The farmer, who turns out to be Davie Davis of Lochart Farm, looks pale. Shona thinks that's what tripping over a corpse in the snow does to a person.

"Mr. Davis, DI Shona McKenzie." She shakes a hand hardened by years of physical work outdoors. "I know you must have a lot of work to do, but it would be very helpful if you could answer a few questions."

"Of course Detective. Whatever I can do to help." His cultured voice seems out of place. Another import from south of Hadrian's Wall.

"Could you talk me through what happened?"

"I was out looking for one of my prize cows, which had somehow managed to undo the barn door and disappear. She's a bit of an escape artist. I was driving the tractor when it got stuck on something. When I looked I could see legs under the wheel. It was obvious that whoever owned the legs would not be alive under all this snow. I drove to the farm house to ring the police and then came back to show them to the body."

"Did you look at the body?"

"No. I only saw the legs and hotfooted it back to the farmhouse."

"Is it usual to see people out this far?"

"In the summer you get ramblers, but not in winter and not in this weather."

"Have you any idea who would come out this way? Were you expecting anyone?"

"No. We had our son's friends staying for Hogmanay but they all went back to Uni a couple of weeks ago."

"I hope you don't mind me asking but is it usual for so many sheep to be out in this level of snow?"

"They somehow escaped from a well secured barn.

Once one got out the rest followed I suppose. I was looking for them, and the cow, when I drove across the body." He swallows a couple of times. "I found sheep pellets all around the area. I think they were let out deliberately."

"Do you get many problems like that out here?"

"Not at all. This is unusual. My dog's down with a case of canine influenza and I need to go and borrow a dog. Can I go now?"

"Thank you Mr. Davies. If you give your telephone number to one of my Officers then you are free to go. We will be in touch if there is anything else we need."

Larry Briar has arrived to certify the body. He doesn't look happy

"I can't believe I'm doing the Angus Police Surgeon's work for him. He needs to get winter tyres and get himself to his own dead bodies."

"I know how you feel, Larry, but we're all one big happy Scottish family now and are meant to work together."

"It's not working together that bothers me, it's the fact I'm doing all the work. You won't be surprised that your man under the snow died of strangulation. He's also got two broken legs by the looks of things. Fractured in several places I'd say." Shona tells him about the tractor, and he informs her that this would tally up, before he trudges off into the snow.

They shove sheep out of the way and do a very quick search, if only to confirm they followed procedure. As expected they find nothing.

27

Collecting the Chief, they trudge back to the vehicle and return to the station. The boss wants to speak to them so they have to delay the consumption of boiling hot coffee.

"It has been most enlightening going out with you today. Now that I've been at the coalface, and watched what you were doing, I can see several ways in which we could move things forward. Once I have written my report I will discuss this further with you. Keep up the good work, Shona."

Watched what they were doing? Blooming cheek. The bloke never set eyes on them the whole time they were there. He was too busy having a cozy wee chat with his mates. Shona makes up her mind to put the report straight in the bin when it arrives.

Throwing her coat on a chair in her office she notices a message on her desk. The new furniture has arrived and maintenance want to change everything around. She tells the team to pack up their belongings and then they are all free to spend an hour in the canteen whilst the offices are tarted up. New furniture and fish and chips has Shona thinking she has died and gone to heaven. She adds a liberal dollop of Heinz Tomato Ketchup to seal the deal.

Half way through arranging her worldly goods in her sparkling, new office the Chief walks in.

"What is the meaning of this?" She knew the Sword of Damocles would fall but hadn't expected it this quickly.

"It's the new furniture sir. All the desks and chairs in the station have been replaced."

"I know that Inspector, but why is it that the desks for your department cost more than the rest of the station put together?"

"Did they, Sir? I wasn't aware." She realises that feigning innocence isn't going to work. "I just wanted the team's furniture to last so it doesn't have to be replaced so often."

"Don't ever do this again or you will be out of the force so fast you'll be wondering why you are standing in Bell Street with a box in your hands."

"Yes, Sir. Sorry, Sir." Shove off, Sir; it's too late now.

She sits down in her new chair and sighs with ecstasy. The soft leather fits her frame perfectly.

Despite the excitement of the new fixtures and fittings she still has a dead body to deal with. She calls the team to the conference room which is also looking smart.

"We need to work on the identity of the dead man. Peter and Jason go through missing persons and see if he matches the description of anyone on the list. Roy, Internet duty for you. See if you can come up with anything on Fergus Laing. Nina and Abigail, sorry but I'm casting you out into the wilderness again. I need you to go and speak to Fergus and Sienna's friends. I know he was in Hong Kong but I'm not ruling him out. I want to know everything about their relationship."

"Any chance we could do it by phone, Ma'am?" asks Nina.

"Not a chance in hell. Get your designer thermal vest on and get going."

"It was worth a try." Nina laughs and reaches for her Armani coat. Shona doesn't think much to its chances in this weather.

Nina and Abigail have news for them. Nina sums it up. "It seems the newly formed Laing family weren't as happy as Fergus made out. Sienna is a flighty besom, as they'd say round here. She would play fast and loose with any male who took her fancy. Her friends say she was a paragon of virtue and the best wife any man could want. His friends say he was a stupid old fool as she liked his bank balance but not his age. In her case at least it was the money that was the attraction."

"Interesting. If all Fergus's friends knew about her affairs then I'm sure her loving husband must have known as much, if not more."

"His friends say he knew everything as they took every opportunity to bring it to his attention."

"Get Fergus in again then. We'll have another chat with him. Abigail, get on to the businesses he dealt with in Hong Kong. Map out what he did for every second of every day. Ring the Airlines as well to make sure he didn't sneak back into the country and fly out again. He didn't make his millions by being stupid."

Fergus does come back in for a chat but he is trailing a lawyer behind him. The sight fills her with foreboding.

"Why does his lawyer have to be Margaret McCluskey? She's like a battleship in full sail with an attitude to match. I'm not sure who's worse, her or Angus Runcie," Shona says to Peter.

"You do know her and Angus are related."

"Why does that not surprise me? In what way?"

"They're brother and sister."

"Growing up in their house must have been a laugh a minute. Their poor parents."

"Their poor parents my..." Peter catches himself. "Margaret and Angus are the nicest ones in the family. They're kittens compared to their parents, one of whom was a judge and the other a lawyer. Mrs Runcie used every underhand trick she would think of whilst still staying vaguely legal. She would've got Jack the Ripper off if he had stood in a police station confessing his crimes."

"Well I can say my horn is well and truly swoggled."

"I'm not finished yet. Their godparents are George Brown and his wife."

"Stop right there, Peter. I can't take any more of this enthralling family tree. I'm ready to slit my throat."

"It's not a happy tale is it, Ma'am?"

With that they head off to face Fergus Laing and the formidable Margaret McCluskey.

The formalities over for the benefit of the recording, Shona opens her mouth to ask a question. She doesn't manage to utter a word before Margaret McCluskey butts in. It is going to be a long day.

"My client does not appreciate being dragged in here and interviewed when he is grieving the death of his wife."

Shona ignores her. "Thank you for coming in Mr Laing. We just need to ask you a few more questions."

"Make it quick. I have a business to run."

Not exactly the grieving widower. "I appreciate that, but the murder of your wife is equally, if not more, important."

"My business going down the drain isn't going to bring my wife back."

"Are you going anywhere with this," asks Mrs. McCluskey.

"I would if your client would stop mithering on about his business and let me ask my questions?"

"You can't speak..."

Shona speaks over her. "How was your

relationship with your wife?"

"Good. In fact it was more than good. We were both head over heels in love."

"Are you sure about that, Mr Laing? Lying to the police is not a good move."

"I'm telling the truth."

"That's funny because, according to most of your friends, Sienna was putting it about a bit. It seems she'd slept with half of Dundee, with a bit of Angus and Fife thrown in for good measure. These aren't the actions of a woman hopelessly in love."

His face turns the colour of an unpeeled turnip with roughly the same texture. Shona makes a mental note to stop antagonising men over a certain age before she is deemed responsible for the demise of one of them. "How dare you." He takes a deep breath. Thankfully his face is now a better colour. "How dare you slander the name of my dead wife."

"My client would like to see proof of this." Shona can see pound signs flashing in the lawyer's eyes. She is busy working out how much she could sue them for.

"We have spoken to every one of Mr Laing's friends and they all say the same thing. Several of them had spoken to your client to warn him."

"Circumstantial evidence. They were all jealous of the fact he could attract a beautiful younger woman. It's their word against his."

Problem is the old battleaxe is right. There are days when Shona hates her job.

"You are free to go, Mr Laing, but please do not leave the area."

"My business..."

"Will suffer if you can't move about. I know. However, my murder investigation trumps your business worries so please stay in the area. I will enforce this with a warrant if I have to. With the wonders of modern technology I am sure you can run your business from your Dundee office for a couple of weeks."

"My client will comply." Both she and Fergus stand to go. They leave Shona wondering why the lawyer has acquiesced so readily. What is she planning?

After that depressing interview Shona is ready for a bit of good news. Roy, of all people. provides it. Only someone in the police would consider it good news. Most would consider it to be quite the opposite.

"There's a missing person who might fit the description of our dead man. Dylan Masters. His parents reported him missing two days ago. They said he didn't come home from work. That was unusual as he went home for his tea every night."

He hands Shona a photo of a good-looking, blonde, young man, sporting a leather jacket and a confident smile.

"It's difficult to say given the state of his face but you might be right. Get details of the next of kin and you can come with me to visit them. Good job Roy," she says to his retreating back.

He turns to her and says, "Are we okay?" His puppy dog expression is almost too much to bear.
"I don't think we're ever going to be BFF's but we're okay." She smiles. As she turns away his happy sigh signals his relief. She ought to make more of an effort with the poor boy. If he would act more like a copper and less like an overgrown schoolboy she is sure they will get along famously. He does have a few redeeming features. This is a good thing otherwise he'd be back in uniform already. Still, he's growing into a valued member of the team.

28

Midday finds Roy and Shona in Gowrie Park, a middle class estate, near Ninewells Hospital. The snow has stopped, leaving blue skies and sunshine in its place. They walk up a tidy garden path. She can tell it's tidy as the occupants have taken advantage of the weather to clear the path of snow. Ringing the doorbell produces the melodic tones of *My Darling Clemantine*. A sharp elbow in his ribs stops Roy laughing. They both arrange their faces into a suitably solemn expression as the door opens. The young woman who opens it isn't old enough to have a twenty-year-old son.

"Mrs Masters?"

"No. Mrs Masters is my mother."

Showing her ID card Shona says, "Are your mother or father in, Miss Masters?"

"I'm Anwyn Evans. Is it Dylan?" Shona looks into fear dulled eyes.

"I need to speak to your parents." A man joins them and Shona introduces herself again.

"Are you here about Dylan?" His expression mirrors that of his daughter.

"Can we come in please?"

"Of course."

They are shown to a large and beautifully appointed sitting room. A woman stands up as they enter.

"The police are here to talk to us, Gwyneth." There's that expression again. For a Force meant to protect and serve they don't half cause a lot of grief thinks Shona.

"I need to ask you a few more details about your son."

"What's happened?" Gwyneth sinks down into her chair.

"I am sorry to have to tell you that we have found a body. We can't say for sure if it's your son yet. Does Dylan have any birth marks, or anything we could use to identify him?"

"He has a small tattoo of a rainbow flag on his shoulder," his father replies.

Ah, a symbol of gay pride. "Is your son gay?"

"Yes he is. He came out when he was sixteen. Do you think him disappearing could be anything to do with that?"

"We don't know anything at the moment. Which shoulder is the flag on? Could we also have his hairbrush? We will need a sample of his DNA."

"Would it help if we came to look at the body? Maybe it's not him."

"Let's wait until we examine a few more things to see if it could be him. I don't want to cause you any unnecessary distress. We'll be in touch soon." With that they take their leave.

Shona asks the lab to take a look at the DNA from the hair on the brush she has taken into evidence. She's also taken fingerprints from the brush, so passes them to Iain.

"See if they match the ones from the body."

Then she phones Mary at the mortuary.

"What can I do for you Shona? Please don't tell me you've another dead body."

"Relax, Mary. You're safe from an onslaught. To my knowledge the citizens of Dundee are well and happy. I need you to check the last young man we sent you though. Has he got a tattoo of any description?"

"I'll go and have a butchers. I haven't managed to get around to him yet." Shona is placed on hold and listens to hard-core rock music. Who on earth thought that was a good idea? It doesn't seem fitting for a mortuary.

"Hi, Shona. He most certainly does. A small rainbow flag."

"Thanks, Mary. I'll try to keep your office, body free for a few days."

"I'd appreciate that. I'm thinking of putting in for early retirement. I haven't stopped since you arrived." She sounds cheerful so Shona isn't too worried about the pathologist's imminent departure.

"In the meantime could you pretty the body up a bit? We'll have to bring his parents in to identify him."

It didn't take long for Iain to get back to her with the results of the fingerprints. It looks like Dylan and their corpse are one and the same. She finds Nina and sends her to pick up one, or both, of Dylan Masters' parents en route to the mortuary.

Nina returns and comes barging through Shona's office door.

"Don't you ever knock?"

"Sorry. It's important. Dylan's parents were asking about his watch. He had a Rolex. I've just been down to evidence and there wasn't a watch brought in."

"A Rolex? Worn by a 20 year-old man from a Dundee suburb. What on earth did he do if he could afford kit like that?"

"A gift from his extremely rich boyfriend who works for Microsoft."

"I'm in the wrong job, or rather Roy's in the wrong job if he could be making money like that."

"You're telling me. I'm thinking of signing up for a

computer course."

"The amount of jewellery which seems to be missing makes me think we've got another spree killer on our hands. One who's taking trophies. I thought the crosses might have been filched to throw us off the scent. Tilly probably pawned her locket, or Jimmy McTaggart flogged it. Still, there are too many to be a coincidence. Get the team in the briefing room. I'll join you in five minutes."

It looks like the nun who is currently incarcerated is probably innocent. Great. She's gone from one suspect to zero, and the Reverend Mother has been kept in jail for no good reason. Happy days. This will not play well with the good people of Dundee. It turns out it doesn't play well with the Chief either.

"Get this sorted, Shona. How am I going to explain that we've held the highly esteemed Mother Superior of our local convent in a cell for several days with no good reason? Let her go."

"In all fairness, Sir, we had good reason when we arrested her. She may still be guilty."

"Stop nitpicking, Shona. Let her out and solve this blasted case. I will hear no more of the matter. Call a Press conference and let me know the details."

"Of course, Sir." As usual, all she can see is his bent head. She leaves, entertaining thoughts of incarcerating him for a few blessedly peaceful days. Maybe she will join the convent. At least it will be quiet. On second thoughts it is perhaps not the best idea she's ever had. There seems to be enough going on in that place to keep things lively and anyway she doesn't look good in black.

She pops into the squad room. "Did Fergus Laing say anything about any items of jewellery being missing?" She is met with blank stares. "I'll take that as a no. I'll ring him."

Fergus Laing assures her that all his wife's jewellery is accounted for. The only things missing are tucked up nice and tight in an evidence locker. Odd. She has the feeling they might be dealing with two different cases. Leaning back in her comfy leather chair she mulls over the newest case. Why would a young gay man from Dundee be wandering about an isolated Angus field? She doesn't think he would. So how did he get there? Picturing the crime scene it strikes her that, apart from the brass, she can't recall any hangers on. The Press are conspicuous by their absence, as is the procurator fiscal. She hopes the journalists have gone missing in the blizzard and their cold dead bodies won't be found 'til spring. She grabs her phone and dials Douglas.

"Shona, good to hear from you. I take it your ringing about the latest death."

"You'd be right. I missed our usual banter over the newly deceased victim."

"Much as I would have loved to come and exchange witty repartee with you, your corpse doesn't belong to me. It belongs to Angus. We don't have to tip up at every suspicious death so Sara probably looked at the snow and gave it a miss."

"It's all right for some. Maybe procurator fiscals should be made to do my job for a few months."

"I'm sure we can manage without the indoctrination, Shona. Any clues on this one?"

"I don't know if I should tell you considering it's not your case." They both laugh.

"Joking apart, there's nothing to tell. A young man, strangled and, as far as we can tell, dumped in the wilds of Auchterhouse."

"You get about."

"You don't have to tell me that. Every dead body in Scotland somehow seems to belong to me. They'll be extending my patch to the Southern areas of Scandinavia next."

"Nice chatting about your ever expanding workload but I must get going. I'm snowed under." She can hear the smile in his voice and it makes her nerve ends tingle.

"That's bad even for you."

29

Plans are proceeding well for the raid on Cat's Eyes. Shona has managed to pilfer a few officers from Uniform. All the young officers are high on excitement and expectation. It isn't often something as high profile as this goes down. Peter, as usual, is moaning.

"I cannae believe I'm doing a raid on a nightclub at my age. I'm too old for nightclubs, you know."

"Peter, it's a raid. I'm not asking you to relive the glory days of *Saturday Night Fever*. You and I are there to coordinate things and make sure the others don't get carried away waving guns about."

"That's what I'm worried about. All that lot high on adrenaline with firearms. You'd better make sure Soldier Boy doesn't turn up with a rifle."

In their last case Jason seemed to be having a love affair with rifles. Everywhere he went there seemed to be a rifle somewhere about his body.

"He'll have a Glock 17 like the rest of us. He, and his mate who issues firearms, have been warned. If he strays anywhere near a rifle, I will put the pair of them up against a wall and shoot them myself."

"That should keep his mind focused. I love the way you think, Ma'am."

Cat's Eyes didn't know what had hit it. Shona has everyone well prepared and ready for battle.

"Peter, you stay out here and direct the Uniforms. Anyone who sets foot outside the door, without being escorted by a copper, arrest them."

Peter's whole body lightened as he realised he didn't have to go in, fists swinging, to a nightclub. "Around the building and cover every door," he says to a group of Uniforms, who are huddled together. They disperse, slapping their arms and stamping their feet, against minus figure temperatures.

The remainder of the team storm through the front door and Shona flashes her ID at the dolly bird on the till. "No one else is to come in." She turns to a couple of men who are waiting to pay. "Your sleazy adventure's over. Sling your hook."

They stare at her, defiance etched in every line of their faces.

"Move. You've got three seconds before I arrest you."

They scurry to do her bidding.

As it's early the club hasn't got up to full throttle. The team storm through the door, and Roy soon has the music off.

"Nina, stop anyone getting out. Arrest them if they're not keen to help us with our enquiries. Roy and Iain you're with me." She heads to Johnny Greig's office, with her pair of musclemen in hot pursuit.

"What the fu'…"

Shona slams her ID card into his face. "You're coming with us. We need to ask you a few questions."

Johnny doesn't quite get the seriousness of the situation, because he takes a swing at Shona. This is the cue for Roy and Iain to get involved and Johnny Greig finds himself face down on the floor, hands behind his back and handcuffed.

The raid could be written up in the Police Training Manual as an example of the perfect operation. They now have several people in their cells including Johnny Greig and his sidekick Valeriya Stravinsky. She has a foul mouth and a Glaswegian accent you could cut with an axe so Shona is willing to bet Shakespeare on the fact that not one of her relatives has even heard of Russia. Also taking advantage of their accommodation are a number of lap dancers and four idiotic men, who waded in with fists flying.

"It's time for us to knock off. If we leave them to rot overnight they might be more cooperative tomorrow. Who's coming to the pub?"

Peter leads the stampede. Shona pauses long enough to send Douglas a text asking him to join them if he is free. The barman knows her tastes and there is a measure of The Glenlivet waiting for her by the time she reaches the bar.

"Steve, will you ditch your wife and marry me?"

As Steve grins, Shona hears a voice in her ear.

"I turn my back for a minute and you're proposing to other men."

His voice makes her muscles tremble. Life is good.

30

Snow. Relentless snow. It forms a brilliant, diamond white canopy protecting the killer from the gaze of roving eyes. No one is out in this blizzard, whipped into frenzy by the gale force winds. He thanks the weather gods, Amun and Zeus for their favour. Not that he believes in such mythical beings, but their mythological selves are surely smiling on him tonight. He spies his prey in the distance, sheltering in the lee of a recessed doorway as arranged. This meeting has been arranged and planned for several months. It is one of many. Trust gained over a long period. No chance arrangement this. No chance consequence. Only meticulous planning which is about to pay off. Her trust is misplaced. This will be their last meeting.

She smiles, despite the weather, as the killer approaches. She has been paid handsomely each time. More money than she could ever hope to earn. Her arms reach out, her face melts into a dreamlike state as he nears. He responds, caresses her neck and then tightens his grip. The dreamy expression changes to one of fear. Her struggle futile, she is soon dead. Pulling her behind the pavilion, he arranges her. A work of creation and beauty now frozen in time.

31

Shona doesn't think life is good when the phone rings in the middle of the night. Well not quite the middle of the night as the clock tells her it is 0543. Shakespeare opens one eye, curls herself into a ball, and goes back to sleep. Even she feels it is too early to be up and about. The flat is freezing, as the heating hasn't yet come on. A scalding shower, and equally hot coffee gets her through until the car heater gets going. Once again she finds herself driving up to the gates of Baxter Park. This is becoming a habit. She is the first one there but the rest of the team is not far behind her.

"Morning, Ma'am." Peter hadn't stayed as late as the rest of them so is more cheery. Everyone else looks like they've spent a week trudging through the wastelands of Siberia. Apart from Nina, who is her usual bouncy self. Nina's demeanor depresses Shona at times like this.

"We can't go up yet as the POLSA isn't finished securing the site."

"Can we no' go inside the pavilion and wait? Has anyone opened it up?"

"Not a chance. The pavilion is part of the crime scene, so we'll just have to huddle together and wait like big boys and girls."

"You can be heartless sometimes, Ma'am."

Shona grins. "I know. Good isn't it?"

Peter takes it with good humour but carries on moaning about the weather. This usually means that he is in fine fettle so she doesn't pay too much attention. It isn't long before the POLSA opens the metaphorical gates and lets them approach the pavilion.

"Iain, Peter, you're with me. The rest of you wait here until we get the pavilion open."

The snow lends an eerie silence to proceedings as they gaze at the body of what was previously a beautiful young woman. Vivid splashes of red peep though the dusting of snow, which is covering the body. Whether it is blood, or clothing, is not yet apparent. They stand and examine the scene critically before approaching, wary of disturbing evidence. A dull whump makes them all jump. Skittish, they peer through the falling snow.

"See thon hummock o' sna ower there. It just fell aff the branches."

Shona lets out a breath she didn't know she was holding. For once she doesn't have the energy to tell Peter to talk English. She gets the general drift of the content and it doesn't add anything to the investigation other than to calm them down.

Iain gets busy with taking photographs before they move too close.

"Given the amount of snow cover, even with a bit of shelter, she can't have been here very long."

"Seeing as we're back in the local hangout for women o' the night, I'd say she's another prossie. Probably been here half the night and a trick went belly up."

"Peter, you know better than to make wild guesses. Do you know her?"

"Not one I've come across so she might be new to this."

Silence falls and Shona moves towards the body. Iain gently brushes away the snow. It is obvious the body has been arranged. The young woman's arms and legs splay out as though making a snow angel. The cause of the red now starkly apparent Shona says, "I don't think she expected to be out too long. I know youngsters consider it a badge of honour to go out half naked but no one would wander round a park in this weather dressed in nothing but a cocktail frock."

The POLSA finds them and says, "We're in the pavilion now if you need us."

"Thanks, Sgt Muir. Peter, find the others and tell them they're free to take shelter. Get the heating on. No use everyone dying of hypothermia. Make sure Jason's nice and cosy as I don't fancy trailing him up to Ninewells again. That lad could make Calamity Jane look like she was normal."

Peter grins and slithers down the hill whistling *The Black Hills of Dakota*. Shona is left to her thoughts until Larry climbs up the hill taking tentative steps. He doesn't seem keen to recreate his previous spectacular exit.

"Morning, Larry."

"It's not morning, it's the middle of the night. I thought I told you to keep the dead bodies to a minimum or at least until a reasonable time."

Good grief. "Sorry, Larry, but time, tide and murders wait for no man."

He approaches the young woman and carries out all the relevant tests to pronounce her dead.

"Another strangulation I would say." With that he turns and leaves. As the team are coming up the hill he trips over an unidentified object and falls flat on his face Right at their feet.

Suppressing every desire to laugh, and contorting their faces in a most imaginative manner, everyone stays composed until he has stomped gingerly down the hill. Yes, stomping and care don't go together but he somehow seems to manage it.

"Twice in a couple of weeks. I think I'll stage

another murder here myself just to see what will happen next time," says Nina.

"Leave the poor man alone. His dignity has well and truly flown the nest by now I would say. I don't think he'll be coming back here any time soon. He must have a minion or two he can send in his place. Right you lot. Instead of standing around getting your kicks at Larry's expense, spread out and get searching."

"In this? We don't have a snowballs chance in hell," says Jason.

"Very witty. Didn't you do Antarctic escape and evasion training when you were in the Army? That should help you here."

"The nearest I got to the Antarctic was Afghanistan. It was 48 degrees in the shade the whole time. If you've a handy desert you want searched I'm your man."

"The force is all about transferable skills these days, so transfer them. Nina, you're in charge of the search."

Luckily she is wearing Hunter wellies rather than Giuseppe Zanotti. Even in winter footwear, Nina is all about designer sartorial elegance. The rest of them are kitted out in Tesco's best. Wherever their footwear came from it isn't suitable for tramping around a crime scene.

"Tread as carefully as you can, keep your eyes peeled, bag any evidence immediately and get it into POLSA's hands. No putting it in your pocket." Last year one piece of evidence had returned to the station in Peter's pocket rather than the capable hands of the POLSA. It didn't go down well.

Peter and Shona move to the relative warmth of the Pavilion. It is probably a balmy -1 degree centigrade inside instead of -10. "Peter, you go back to the station and get the coffee on. I'll stay here until the others are finished and the body's gone." She's had enough of his moaning about the cold. She knows grumbling is a coping mechanism for him, but this morning it is getting on her every frozen nerve.

About an hour later she is bolting through the gate when she sees them. Reporters. She's had enough of them as well.

"Do you lot have to appear at every single crime scene I'm at? Is it a personal vendetta or do you harass every force in Scotland?"

"The publi..."

"Oh shut up. I'm not interested. If the public has the right to know then we'll hold a Press conference later today. You'll be glad to know there's heat in the Press room." With that she strides off and leaves them standing. No more than the stupid sods deserve.

By the time she arrives at the Gulags and grabs a huge mug of coffee she has thawed out and recovered her good humour. She enters the squad room. "Bacon rolls all round. Make that two each. Bring them to the briefing room" She shoves a couple of twenties into Roy's hand and sends him and Jason to do her bidding. No one can deal with an overabundance of dead bodies on an empty stomach.

"I'd say it's looking like we have another spree killer on our hands. Most of the victims have a piece of jewellery missing, apart from Sienna Laing."

"She might have a piece of jewellery missing that her husband knows nothing about." says Burns.

"Good point. Thanks for that. We're not sure of our Jane Doe, nor Tilly, but I'd say it's more than likely our killer has taken her pendant. Each one has been arranged in a certain way, apart from Dylan Masters."

"The tractor probably rearranged him," says

Abigail.

"Not the way I would have phrased it but I'm sure you're right."

"It looks like our victims have nothing in common. Who in the he... heck is targeting them?"

"Good question, Roy, and you're going to do a search on that very question. Off you go. Explore every possible connection. Pubs, clubs, wine bars, are they related, work, social media, shared hobbies or interests, schools, churches, libraries, courses, travel, everything you can think of and then some. Even down to where they buy their underwear."

"On it."

"The rest of you trawl through missing persons and see if our Jane Doe matches one of them."

Shona briefs the Chief.

"Mckenzie, can you not solve a case without half the population of Dundee being killed in the process. For goodness sake, woman, get it solved."

"Yes, Sir,"

She walks back to the office cheerfully thinking about kicking him somewhere unmentionable. Another tip to add to her future best seller, *1000 Ways to Torture Your Boss*.

Burns interrupts her a few hours later.

"I've been sent to tell you that our Jane Doe doesn't match anyone missing in Dundee or the surrounds."

"Widen your search to include Perthshire and Fife. If that turns up nothing try Stirling and Aberdeenshire." If nothing else it will keep them busy.

This still doesn't elicit any leads so the dead woman is still a Jane Doe.

"Roy, have you turned anything up that might link our

victims?"

"Not a thing. Not one single, tiny thing."

"Okay, I get the message. Right, team, grab your coats. We're off to show photos to all the victim's families. We'll see what that throws up."

Shona buddies up with Peter. For once he doesn't have an awful lot to say. In fact he seems almost morose.

"What's up with you?"

"Nothing I'm just thinking."

That is it until a few hours later they'd completed their task and returned to the station.

"Has anyone got a lead?"

"The nuns knew Tilly. They'd had dealings with her in her professional role," says Roy.

"Nuns and prostitutes. I wouldn't have put them together in the same sentence."

"The convent does an outreach to the women. Talk to them, make sure they're safe etc."

"Makes sense. Thanks Roy. Anyone else."

The silence gives her the answer. Then Peter says a tentative, "I might know what links them."

"What? Spit it out for heavens sake. We're on the edge of our seats."

"I need tae look a few things up first. Can you give me an hour or two?"

There are mutterings, variations of, "Keep us waiting why don't you," and a collective exhalation of breath.

"If it gives us a lead then you can have as long as you like. You lot, make yourselves busy before I send you out into the snow." That shuts them up and sends them scurrying.

32

Peter is true to his word and a couple of hours later they are gathered again.

"I think we might have a copycat killer on our hands." He falls silent.

"You can't come out with that and stop. Why?"

"They all bear a passing resemblance to Dundee Murders throughout the ages."

Shona snaps off the top of a whiteboard marker, cleans a whiteboard and gets ready to make notes. "Tell all."

"First, the three nuns. They could represent the murders of Agnes Waugh, Jane Simpson and Catherine Millar in No Man's Land in 1979."

"No Man's Land? This isn't the First World War."

"Nothing tae do with the war. It was a tenement block called Gray Memorial House in Kinghorn Road. Only women were allowed to rent flats there so hence the nickname. The women didnae live together but were all found in one room beaten and with stockings tied around their necks. They were dead. Two were auld and the other one a youngster. Two elderly and one young nun would be about right for a copycat."

"Gray Memorial House. That has a flavour of 50 Shades of the same colour. Leaving that aside, nuns are a far cry from three random women?"

"It's the nearest they would get these days to a bunch of women living together."

"We'll run with it for the minute. What about the rest of them?"

"New Years Day, 1957, Sandy Borland was found beaten so badly his family couldn't recognise him to identify the remains. He was a wee man only just over 5' tall. I think Archie Green was a recreation of that murder."

"Go On." Shona's pulse quickens. Peter might have a point.

"Back in 1979 again, Carol Lannen, aged eighteen, found murdered in Templeton Woods. She was a prostitute. Tilly could be a recreation of her murder. Baxter Parks a far cry from Templeton Woods though."

"Easier just to kill and leave," says Shona. "She was found in the wooded part of the park so I'd say the nearest approximation. Next?" Eagerness and adrenaline are making her impatient.

"In 1971 James Keltie, aged fifty-two, was found gagged and grievously injured from a beating, wearing nothing but his underpants. He was discovered in the garage of the Muirton House Hotel. He was the hotelier. Stan Adamczac would be a ringer for this one."

"I'd agree. More than a coincidence. There are a couple of details not quite right though. Stan wasn't found in his undies. They're missing. Also you never said anything about James Keltie being stabbed."

"You're right. He wasn't stabbed."

"Never mind. Go on."

"June 1991. Sandy Drummond, thirty-three years old, was found strangled on a farm track near Boarhill in Fife. That fits the murder o' Dylan Masters."

"Fife's a far cry from Auchterhouse but there are similarities so we'll keep it in. Carry on."

"1980, Elizabeth McCabe, twenty years old, was found strangled in Templeton Woods. There was deep snow on the ground which meant that Forensic examination was hampered."

"I know the feeling," says Iain. "Hampered's too mild a word for it. I'd say totally Fu..."

"Iain." Shona's sharp tone stops him in his tracks.

"Sorry, Ma'am."

"I think she's a match for our Jane Doe."

"Peter, I think you've cracked it. Looks like we have a copycat killer on our hands." Against a background of high fives and, "Well done Peter," she continues "Before you get too excited, there's still a couple of things to consider. Firstly, where does Sienna Laing fit in?"

"That's the one death I can't work out. We've nothing that equates to her in any way at all. The nearest I can get is Ellen Bury and Bill the Ripper."

"I, and the rest of humanity, have heard of Jack the Ripper but who in the name of all that's holy was Bill the Ripper?"

"Ellen Bury was found dead in a packing case in 1889. Her husband William (Bill) came into the nick and said his wife had committed suicide. He confessed to stabbing her dead body several times and then stuffing her into said case. He then went about his business quite cheerfully until he came to the station. He said he hadn't been in before because he was frightened people would think he was Jack the Ripper. They'd recently moved here from London. Some people still say he was the real Jack the Ripper."

"Grief. Dundee really was a hotbed of sin and debauchery. Who would have thought it? There are a few discrepancies though. Sienna was found neat and tidy in her bed. Not stabbed and stuffed in a packing case."

"Aye. That's why I don't really think Sienna's murder is part of the same pattern."

"Balumbie Estate looks pretty new to me. What was there in 1889?"

"It was farmland then," says Roy.

"How the heck can you trot that fact out of your memory bank?" asks Shona.

"I'm a member of Balumbie Golf club. So are my parents. The history is in the Club archives."

"Roy, you never cease to amaze me. I'd never have put you down as a golfer. I'd say given the location of the murder and the less than grizzly nature she's not part of the equation. It looks like we have two separate cases."

"It doesn't give us much of a clue when it comes to finding the perpetrator though," says Nina.

There is a lot of nodding.

"That brings me to the second thing we have to consider. What sort of nutjob is recreating ancient Dundee murders?"

Silence and gloom descend in equal measure.

"Well I'm from the Islands so I know very little about Dundee and the particular nutjobs who live here. I'll hand it over to my distinguished colleagues," says Abigail.

"Your distinguished colleagues don't have a clue about this one either," says Nina.

"I take it that all the people who carried out these crimes are now dead?" asks Shona

"Bill definitely is. He was sentenced, in true black hankie style, to hang by the neck until dead. He's buried here in the station and there's even a wee memorial to him."

"Is there? How come I never knew that?"

"It's no' something we talk about a lot. The new recruits get told about it but that's the extent."

"Only in Dundee could they have a notorious prisoner buried in the Police HQ and not a soul mentions it."

"Aye, but at least we know that neither Bill the

Ripper nor any of his descendants are recreationists. He didnae have any kids."

"Any others who might be out now and reliving the glory days of their youth?"

"Most o' them were never solved so we don't have a clue. They could be starting a new crime spree I suppose."

"Were *any* of them solved?"

"Aye. Sonny Mone went down for the murder o' the three women in No Man's Land. It wouldn't be him though as he was knifed in a prison brawl and that was the end of Her Majesty housing and feeding him."

"So you're saying we've nothing to go on at all?" Nina beats Shona to it by a heartbeat.

"Looks that way."

"You've all got faces like slapped bums. Get a grip. It's our job to discover what links these murders and to catch whoever is carrying them out. You're all in CID because you're meant to be the best we've got so get those supersized brains of yours working. I'm off to give the Chief the good news."

As Shona feared, the Chief isn't shaking her by the hand and offering her a congratulatory whisky.

"That's all well and good Shona but how do you plan on solving the cases? News of madmen recreating ancient murders in my city doesn't make me want to sing the *Hallelujah Chorus*. Find out what's going on and do it fast."

This time she consoles herself by thinking of stuffing the Chief's dead body in a packing case. She is feeling a bit sorry for snapping at the team now so goes back to see them.

"You're all off the hook for the night. I want you back here at 8 am with your faculties intact and brains fully functioning." Not that she thinks that will stop any of the youngsters having a night on the tiles.

Nina leads the charge to the pub. On her way out she says, "Our killer makes Beelzebub himself look like a stalwart of the community."

"You're not joking. I'm running out of energy and ideas. My get up and go has not only gone but chucked itself off the Law Hill. We need to go home and I might manage to find it somewhere along the way."

"You make me laugh Shona."

"I'm glad I'm good for something."

On the way home she rings Douglas.

"Hi Shona, my mum's got the kids. Do you fancy going to the pictures and for something to eat?"

She doesn't have to be asked twice. She picks him up and they settle on '*Lincoln*'

33

She sleeps through to the alarm in the morning. No early call out to a crime scene, so it would appear that the good citizens of Dundee have slept safely in their beds. The snow has also stopped, leaving blue skies and a sun displaying its brilliant yellow glory. It is the sort of winter's day that makes her glad to be alive - until she steps out on to sheet ice and nearly does an Olympic slalom down the hill. Torvill and Dean would have been proud of her sudden skating prowess. She vows never to mock Larry Baird again. Somehow, she gets to work without further incident. Traffic division is going to be busy today.

The team is heavy on the food side and light on the thinking side when she arrives. At least they are all here. Handing her a roll Peter says, with his mouth full, "Ye cnna mmm empty mmmch." She thinks it roughly translates as, you can't think on an empty stomach. She is inclined to agree and gratefully receives the proffered roll. Peter had got her the full Scottish - lorne sausage, bacon, egg, and black pudding. She's died and gone to heaven. Once she's eaten the heart attack on a roll she is ready to face the world of policing.

"Any bright ideas overnight?" There are no positive replies. "Me neither. I want you to go through every murder on the books and see if anyone has shown signs of doing this before. See if any unsolveds look like copycats."

The team turns to their task and she to her

computer, where she begins an intense search for copycats.

After a couple of hours, her eyes feel like they're full of budgie grit and she's no further forward. The team's had no eureka moments either.

"Has anyone got *any* ideas? Peter, you've been around the block a few times. You must have something you can draw on."

"Your average Dundee low life wouldn't be bright enough to think of this. The nearest they get to creativity is shooting each other with crossbows."

"I heard about that. Seems a bit strange."

"Never underestimate the population of Dundee, Ma'am. It doesn't surprise me at all that crossbows feature. Do you think it might be the reenactment groups that are doing it?" asks Roy.

"The only reenactment groups around here do World War 2 and Bannockburn. Not much scope for modern day murders," says Nina.

"Didn't the archaeological society put on something in the Howff last year?" asks Shona. Shona has learned that The Howff is a three hundred year old Graveyard gifted to the people of Dundee by Mary Queen of Scots. It's said there's a witch buried there. Yes, everyone knows that a witch wouldn't be in consecrated ground but why let facts get in the way of a good story.

"The archeologists did put on a show in the Howff. There are tourist walks that cover historic murders as well."

"That gives us something to work on. Get the tour guides, the archaeological groups and the reenactors in and see if we can dig anything up."

"As long as it's no' the dead bodies from the Howff we're digging up."

There is a collective groan.

"Peter, you're jokes are rubbish," says Nina.

"For a small city there doesn't half seem to be a lot of death tourism round here," says Abigail.

"Ach, there's nothing like a few dead bodies to bring the tourists flocking."

"At the rate we're going we'll be the murder tourism capital of the world," says Shona. "Go get the people."

"Blimey, even I didn't think we'd have this many live bodies to interview. Dundee really is obsessed with death and dying," says Shona.

"Aye. We're the murder capital of Scotland in more ways than one."

"What a claim to fame. We'd better get interviewing or we'll be here till midnight."

"Can we have some food first?"

"No you flaming well can't, Peter. We've only just finished breakfast.' His mouth opens. "Don't even think about complaining. You can have something when you've finished a few interviews. The sooner you get going the sooner you'll get your lunch." That gets him moving in the right direction.

"Interview with Sheena Andrews, DI Shona McKenzie and DS Nina Chakrabarti in attendance blah, blah, blah."

"Thank you for coming in to talk to us, Mrs Andrews, do you mind if I call you Sheena?"

"Please do. Mrs Andrews is my mother-in-law and she's a right harridan. I'd like to shove her in one of the graves in the Howff."

"Whilst I appreciate that you may not be BFF's with your husband's mother, this is perhaps not the place to talk about bumping her off."

"Sorry. It was a joke. I'm a bit nervous."

"For the record can you tell us what you do for a living?"

"I'm a tour guide. I do tours called the Dark Side of Dundee. Murders and the Howff and such like."

"What does that involve?"

"I take groups of tourists, and locals, around the sites and talk about the murders; make it interesting, put a unique spin on things, a bit of drama and a lot of embellishments."

"Would you say you know a lot about murders in Dundee?"

"Sure do. More than anyone else. I've done a lot of research."

The stupid sod is fast digging herself into a hole which might involve a jail cell. Shona slides a sheet of A4 across the table.

"Where were you at those dates and times?"

"I can tell you, without looking, I was home alone huddled under several blankets. Tour guides only get paid in the summer. I'm as poor as Pa Cratchit in the winter. Can't afford to go out."

"I'm asking you to look, not guess."

She looks and the answer doesn't change.

"Could anyone vouch for you at any of those times?"

"My mum was over a couple of times with groceries and some money for the meter. She cooked me a meal and then left. My husband works in a bar so he's out most nights. He might have been off on some of the nights. "

"Did you notice anyone strange hanging about your tours? Anyone who came on them more than once?"

"My last tour was September. I can barely remember what the weather was like never mind anyone strange. No one is jumping up and down in my brain saying me, me, so I suppose all was normal."

"I need you to write down the times and dates when you've got someone to vouch for your whereabouts. We'll check out your alibi. After that you're free to go. We'll be in touch if we need anything else."

"What? I haven't murdered anyone, I just talk about murders."

"Calm down and stop shouting. I'm talking about checking up on your whereabouts, not marching you to the gallows. If your alibis are tight then you have nothing to worry about."

The rest of the team tell much the same story. It is mainly summer work and none of them can remember anything.

"Get to work on checking out the alibis. If nothing else, it will keep us out of mischief."

A couple of hours later they have struck all the various tour guides and re-enactment geeks off their list of suspects. Everyone is squared away and accounted for on most of the dates. Unless they are all working together, to keep the tourists flocking, they don't have any grounds for questioning them further. Frustrated doesn't begin to cover it. Shona has an idea and goes to run it past the Chief.

"You want to do what? I know you're not quite right in the head, Shona, but why would we let the public know the only lead we have?"

"I agree it is off the wall, sir, but I thought it might let the killer know we're on to him, or her. It might stop them before the finish line." Shona has asked the Chief if they can hold a Press conference and let the good, and not so good, citizens of Tayside know they have a copycat killer in their midst.

"I'm going to stop *you* before the finish line. We'll have a riot on our hands. Leave me alone and I'll think about it."

She wanders down to the canteen, fantasizing about putting the Chief at the front of a riot without a shield or baton. Plotting revenge always cheers her up. As does food. Doreen willingly provides a plate of stodge and Shona sits down to devour it. Despite the killer littering the streets of Dundee with dead bodies, life is good.

Her astonishment knows no bounds.

"Shona, you can go ahead with your plan. I can't think of any other way to move forward and if it is a copycat killer then we just might have a chance of flushing him out this way. Call a Press conference for later today. You can head it up."

That roughly translates to 'if this goes wrong then I've had nothing to do with it'. Shona doesn't argue the toss and hurries to do his bidding.

Nina asks to go with her to the conference. She is dressed head to toe in designer expensive and Shona is wearing chino's and a shirt. Shona dolls herself up by putting her hair in a bun and applying makeup. That will have to do. Hopefully some of Nina's designer chic might shine on her and give the illusion she is equally chic - she hopes.

The world's Press has done them proud and many have turned up. When she says the World she of course means the Scottish newspapers are all here including the *Scotsman, Herald* and *The Times Scottish edition. The Courier* and the *Tele* are of course prominent and vocal. They are all over her like measles, and twice as irritating.

She steps up to the podium illuminated by a million

watts of flashbulb light.

"Over the past two weeks Police Scotland has been investigating a number of murders which have taken place in Dundee and the surrounding areas. It would appear from our findings that the killer is recreating historical murders from Tayside. Police Scotland is appealing for witnesses to any of these crimes. If anyone has any information, no matter how insignificant they may think it is, they are urged to contact the senior investigating officer, DI Shona McKenzie on 03005728761. The public can rest assured that the police are doing everything they can to bring the perpetrator of these crimes to justice."

Noise levels reach a crescendo as reporters vie to ask questions. She can't make out what most of them are saying but one voice rises above the rest. Her nemesis, John Laird, from *The Courier*.

"Do you think this could be linked to the previous Dundee spree killer?"

He is referencing a previous case, solved by Shona and her team, where a number of young women were murdered in the City.

"I can state categorically that is not the case." Given the conclusion of her previous case they'd be hard pushed to carry on.

"Harriet Logie, the *Scotsman*. What are the police doing to protect Scottish citizens?"

That old chestnut. "The best thing that the police can do is concentrate on catching the killer, or killers."

"Mark Smith, *The Herald*. Have the police got any leads?"

"We have told you everything we know at the moment. Now if you'll excuse us, we have a killer to catch."

A bemused Nina follows her from the room.

"I hate the Press," says Shona.

"I get that impression. What have the Press ever done to you to get you so riled up?"

"Never you mind. We haven't got time to dredge up my past."

Shaking her head, Nina, drops it and they return to the bosom of the team.

Roy is peering at a computer screen.

"Found anything useful?"

"Nothing about our murders. I've been printing out Press reports for all the other murders we've had in Dundee. It might give us a clue as to where the killer's going next. "

"Good idea. When you're finished, let me know."

Returning to her own piece of police station heaven she sits in the new leather chair. She has no clue where the investigation is going. Picking up the phone she decides to ring round the other forces to see if they've encountered anything similar. Most calls elicit nothing but sympathy and a general feeling she has a mare on her hands. However Shuggie McLafferty in Stirling is more forthcoming.

"Hi, Shona. I hear you're having a bit of fun up in Dundee."

"A bit of fun! That's not how I'd describe it. It looks like we've a copycat killer on our hands. I'm ringing round to find out if anyone else has something similar."

"We might have. A couple of years ago we had four unsolved murders. They're now on the cold case list. Let me look into it and I'll get back to you."

"Thanks Shuggie. Speak soon."

Her other enquiries turn up nothing so she decides to wait for Shuggie and hope he comes up trumps. She'll take anything she can get at this stage.

She is heading to rally the troops when she bangs

into Brian Gevers. He has a young girl in tow. Come to think of it she's seen other kids wandering about today. She wonders why her station is always awash with children?

"Morning, Brian. Who's this?" She smiles at the girl who grins back.

"Morning, Ma'am. Meet my sister Katie. It's bring your kids to work day. Not having any kids myself, Katie stepped into the breach."

"Nice to meet you, Katie. I've got to go and catch the bad guys so I'll see you soon."

"Bye Shona."

Shona grins as she hears Brian mutter, "You can't call the Inspector by her first name."

"Why not? I don't work for her."

When Roy has finished with the printouts, Shona calls the team into the briefing room.

"The floor's yours Roy. What have you got for us?"

"Probably more murders than you ever want to hear about," says Roy. "It's even depressing me."

She can tell by the thick wad of paper in his hand that he isn't joking. "Tell us anyway. Abigail, grab a pen, you're on the board."

"Jean Milne, aged sixty-five, Beaten with a poker and stabbed with a carving fork in November, 1912."

"Eliza Connelly, aged seventy-four. Bludgeoned to death in 1981. She was beaten so badly her blood covered the ceiling of her home."

"Dr Alexander Wood and his wife Dorothy. They were both aged seventy-eight. Battered to death in their home, May 1980."

"Nanette Hanson, aged twenty six. Shot to death by Robert Francis Mone while she was teaching in St John's High School, in November, 1967."

"Someone shot a teacher in the middle of a class? I

thought that sort of thing only happened more recently." Dundee never ceases to amaze Shona. Not only are they doing groundbreaking work in Computer Games but, also in murders. There's nothing like setting a grizzly trend.

"Gordon Dunbar, aged fifty-two. His body was found hacked to pieces and stuffed in bags. His head was missing and never found. This happened in December 1992."

"Gordon Johnston, aged fifty three. Hacked to death with an axe, forty eight blows to be precise, in Gows' Gun Shop."

"You can stop there, Roy. I get the picture. Dundee has a long and distinguished history of murders, leading to its macabre title of Murder Capital of Scotland. Could you get copies of everything you have and pass them out to the team. Jason, Iain and Burns, you can help him, or we'll be here all week."

"What do you mean we'll have to protect all the schools? Just where do you think we're going to get manpower for that?"

Shona knew the Chief would blow his stack at her news.

"Sir, our copycat might just decide to target a school."

"I appreciate that, but do you know how many schools there are in Dundee?"

"I know Sir, but..."

"It's not happening. Ask Uniform if they can lend you some manpower to swell the ranks. First thing tomorrow visit every school in Tayside and get them on high alert. They can screen all visitors."

"But Sir..."

It's a pity the killer wouldn't be targeting the station. She'd shove the Chief in front of the gun.

Back in the briefing room, silence reigns as they read the paperwork. Shona takes a sip of her aromatic French Roast blend. There isn't a cake in sight. That's a shame as the coffee is begging to be paired with a fresh pastry.

As they finish the list Shona thinks the silence will be shattered. Wrong. Not a word is spoken. They all look at each other.

Then, shoulders slumped, Peter says, "That's an affy lot of murders still tae copy."

"You're right. It is an awful lot of murders. Let's see if we can find a pattern to the ones already committed that will give us a clue as to where he's going next."

After about 50 minutes of checking, and rechecking they come up with nothing.

"The killer's all over the place. How would you usually deal with this?" asks Burns.

"Write all the ones he hasnae copied yet on a wee bits of paper and toss them all up in the air. Then pick one."

"Stop being so gloomy." Shona strives for positivity. "We need to catch the killer before he manages to get through his entire list and we need to come up with a plan that will help us do it."

More silence. This is depressing. No one seems capable of formulating a plan to write a shopping list at the moment. By this point the sun has set and everyone is tired. It is time for home and the solace of loved ones. Not that her loved one was available. He'd gone off to a conference leaving her with a case and no company. She decides to go and visit her uncle. An archeologist, he is between digs, and always good for some interesting food and even more interesting stories.

34

Low clouds and darkness offer cover, as the killer gets ever closer to his next victim. Although the snow is no longer falling the wind whips the snow from the ground into a maelstrom, which provides a cloak of invisibility and covers his tracks. He can see little in front of him but that does not matter. He has researched everything about this godforsaken area. Bleak on the brightest day, it is barren tonight. He knocks on the weather beaten door, which speaks of many hard winters and dreich summers. A screech fills the night as rusty hinges fight the wind.

"Aye,?."

No fear. A woman at home in her environment, trusting of all who come to her door.

"My car broke down. I'm lost."

"Come in fae the wild. You'll be warm in here."

He enters and walks towards the warm fire.

"I'll make you a nice hot cuppie."

As she turns towards the kitchen he pulls the short axe from his bag, grasps the sturdy handle and raises it.

35

Shakespeare wakes Shona by sitting on her face. This is her latest way of letting Shona know she isn't impressed with her performance. She hadn't returned from her uncle's until after midnight. By then, Shakespeare was complaining vociferously about starvation. This, despite Shona having rung her next door neighbour, Mrs Gordon, to go in and feed the cat. It turned out that Shakespeare now hated lamb, so had to wait until Shona returned to provide liver. As Shakespeare had a late night she was getting her own back by waking Shona at six am. Shona feels like chopping the cat up and putting her in cat food. Instead she shoves her off her face and tickles her under the chin, until she signifies, by purring, that Shona is forgiven. Between Shakespeare and the Chief Shona is firmly under the thumb.

Several extra strong cups of Brazilian blend, and a shower, later, she is wrapped up warm and out of the door. She might as well get an early start on the day. She stops off at the supermarket to buy fuel to get the salt mine workers through the day. Yes, that's right. She buys cakes. She also buys several newspapers. They all have variations of, '*Copycat Killer Digs up Dead Bodies*'. Not an original bunch the Press. At least they weren't slagging off the police in general and her department in particular. That is strange. Not that she's read the whole thing yet.

Peter is the first to arrive and is also early.

"Are you feeling okay? You're usually running in at the last minute."

"There's been a huge pile up on the main road through Fife so traffic's light on the bridge. Nobody's managed to get that far."

Shona throws him the papers and shoves the box of cakes in his direction.

"Get your molars round that lot. They'll supplement breakfast."

He helps himself to a humongous strawberry tart and brews a mug of builders brew tea to wash it down with. The rest of the team relieves her of the remaining cakes and she joins them in the briefing room. Brian Gevers also joins them along with several of his pals from uniform.

"Morning, Brian. You spend more time with us than in your day job. Does your sergeant not like you or something? Either that or you just need a cake."

"My sergeant thinks I'm the business. That's why he keeps lending me out. I'm his best asset." This is accompanied by a grin.

"Jolly glad I am too. Finish up the cakes boys and girls. We've a lot of schools to get round. I'm sure the sergeant will want his prize asset back quick as."

Six hours later they'd covered a very large area and return to Bell street. The schools, for good reason, are happy to oblige. They are going to keep a lookout and report any suspicious activity straight away. Myercroft Academy is particularly keen to help them, given their past experience with things that go bump in the night. The school had featured in a previous case. Add to that, a workman had, in the past, burnt down half the school, when replacing a roof. Unlucky doesn't begin to cover it.

"I'm worn out. How's a chap my age supposed to

keep up this sort of work with nothing to eat?"

Nothing to eat? He'd managed to take couple of pastries with him, and wolf them down, if the state of his tie is anything to go by. If moaning were an Olympic sport Scotland would win Gold with Peter as their star player.

"Stop whinging. You'll get fed soon enough. Did any of the schools have anything to report? Any strangers seen lurking around?" There's nothing to report so Shona sends them all to the canteen. The bats out of hell could have taken lessons from Peter as he dashes through the door. The others aren't far behind. Shona brings up the rear.

A plate of steak and chips restores Shona's grey cells and she's ready with a plan. "We need to speak to the relatives of each of our victims and see if they had any enemies whatsoever. Go right back to their schooldays. We're not leaving anything to chance. Ask about friends, boyfriends, girlfriends and acquaintances. Get them to come in and we'll interview them again."

Whilst the team is occupied, Shona catches up on a mountain of paperwork, which is threatening to bury her. About two thirds of the way through, the phone rings.

"Shona, it's Shuggie over in Stirling."

"I hope you've got good news for me."

"I've got news, but I'll leave it up to you to decide whether it's good or not. It turns out our cases could be copycat killings."

"Thanks Shuggie. I'm not sure where it gets us though."

"Me neither, but I'm off to reopen the cases. If anything turns up I'll ring you."

"Thanks. It's given me something to think about."

Now there's a turn up for the books. Shona is leaving to see how far the team has got, when the phone rings again.

"Ma'am, it's the duty sergeant. There's been another suspicious death."

Shona glances out the window, and despite her best efforts a sigh escapes. Darkness is falling and they've had a long day.

"You've got to be kidding me."

"Sorry, Ma'am."

"I'm not annoyed with you. Details?"

"An elderly woman's been found dead in a remote farmhouse in Forgandenny."

"Where?"

"Forgandenny. It's in Perthshire."

"Perthshire? Haven't they got their own team?"

"They asked for you specially, Ma'am."

"Of course they did. Anything closely resembling a suspicious death in Scotland and I'm the go to girl."

Hanging up, she grabs her coat and drags the team out into the freezing night.

"This is more wild than the Isle of Skye. I left there to get away from conditions like this," says Abigail.

"Sorry to disappoint you." They are plodding through deep snow, in a wind chill factor of about minus 10 degrees centigrade. It isn't a pleasant experience. Shona could fall on her knees and kiss the threshold when they reach the door of a ramshackle farmhouse.

"Can we go in?" she asks the frozen uniform at the door.

"Go right ahead, Ma'am. It's ready for you. You might want to take that coat off and leave it in the van though. The nephew found her. He's standing over beside that bush if you want to speak to him."

Shona does as instructed re the coat and then steps into a stifling living room. The temperature could give Hades a run for its money. A woman lies in a pool of blood next to a small axe. The heat intensifies the smell of blood to previously unknown levels.

"Switch the heating down. We're going to die of heatstroke in here."

"It's off Ma'am. We did it when we got here." Peter is mopping his brow with a huge handkerChief

"The DNA from our sweat's going to be all over this. Everyone out and leave Iain to it. Iain, I want every bit of evidence swabbed, bagged and tagged. Wear a full body suit."

"Jings, Ma'am, are you trying to kill me?"

"We'll leave the door open a crack that should let a bit of the hot air out. I'd open the doors and windows but with this wind the place would be covered in snow."

"Iain's full of hot air. It's probably him heating the room."

"Roy, why are you still here? I thought I ordered you to leave. Move or you'll be roasting in hell."

"I already am"

Shona speaks to the young man who is standing as far away from the house as he can get without disappearing. He looks dreadful and his teeth chatter like bongo drums. "I'm Detective Inspector McKenzie. Did you find the body?" The boy nods and then vomits.

"What's your name?" Shona's tone is gentle. The man is obviously in shock.

"Ji... J.... Jim...La...la.." He can't get it out.

"It's okay. We'll get someone to take a look at you. Come over to our van and sit down." He willingly follows.

"Jason, get an ambulance up here. Then I want you to go with Jim to the hospital."

Jason whips out his phone. He gets a signal, which is a minor miracle around these parts. Sometimes Shona can barely get a signal in Dundee.

Iain hollers for them to come back in.

Things have cooled down in the cottage so they are able to take the scene in without covering it in liquid DNA. A woman, of about seventy, is very definitely dead. This is evidenced by the fact her skull is caved in and it looks like there are brains mixed with the blood. Either that or the killer has taken time to throw sausage meat around. Shona notices Burns and Jason are looking a bit peely wally.

"Out now, before I use the axe to recreate the murder on you."

They rush to do her bidding and she can hear them taking deep breaths. These young coppers aren't what they used to be. You'd think Jason would be a bit hardier given his Army background. As she turns back to the body a young woman rushes in followed by a waft of DKNY perfume. Mixed with the smell of blood it's a bit sickening.

"Who the heck are you and why are you running round my crime scene?" Then she notices the blue overshoes. She must be something to do with the investigation.

"I'm Whitney Williams, the police surgeon." Shona is stunned.

"Sorry. You don't look old enough to be at a crime scene."

Whitney takes it in good spirit. "If I had a pound for everyone that said that, I'd be a millionaire and would be living the life in a villa in the Bahamas." She steps towards the body, does a few tests and says, "Yep. She's deader than dead, to misquote Dr Seuss." With that she, and her perfumed cloud, fly through the door.

"She's a bit more lively than Larry," says Nina.

"She certainly is. Iain, what did you find?"

"Nothing obvious, but I've dusted for prints and we'll get the axe into evidence now. I'm off outside to take a look. Now the snow's stopped there might be something."

"Thanks Iain. Once that's done you're all going to do a sweep of the area. Apart from you, Peter. You're coming with me to canvass the neighbours. Given the location you're the only one who might know where the neighbours are." Peter is happy to oblige.

There is chorus of groans from the others that could have been put on as a show at the Caird Hall.

"Stop moaning. You're a right bunch of whingers. A stint back on the street might remind you how good you've got it in CID."

That gets them moving. The search is prolonged and thorough.

Once in the briefing room Shona says "What have we got? Iain you're on first."

"A couple of lovely footprints, Ma'am. Mostly everything was swept over by drifting snow. The prints are a size 10 man's shoe. Whoever wore them has an unusual gait. They might have a pimp."

"A pimp? This is a murder not the Ruskie investigation." Shona can barely be heard over the gales of laughter.

"A limp. I mean a limp." Iain's face is as red as the victim's blood.

"Aye right."

"That's some faux pas," says Roy.

"That's enough from you lot. Leave the poor lad alone. Anything else."

"We found small red areas of snow near the footprints. Iain took specimens," says Nina.

"It could be anyones including an animal but more

than likely the victims. I'll get it analysed and let you know."

"Go and start on that. Our victim's name is Annie Pettry. Peter and I spoke to the neighbours in three farms nearby. I use the term nearby in its widest sense. They all said, she was pleasant, helpful and always friendly. They didn't see each other often as they were all busy but she would always lend a hand when needed. The owner of the village shop said she came in once a month and got a few things. She was more or less self-sufficient. The farm isn't large anymore but it can support her. No one else in the village knew much about her as she wasn't seen much."

"Not much of a legacy to leave is it," says Abigail.

"I suppose not. We'll have to see what her nephew has to say. Roy, as far as I can tell this isn't in your list of old murders."

"It doesn't ring a bell with me either Ma'am."

"When we're done get on it and see what you can find. In the meantime we'll need to interview her relatives. She may have been killed for the farm. Peter, and Nina, see what you can get on property values around the area. They're going up at the moment and might just be worth killing for."

Shona leaves them to it and briefs the Chief. He is his usual charming self but just tells her to get on with it. Preferably without any more murders being committed. Maybe she should take an ad out in *The Courier*. Could everyone in Dundee please stop murdering people, as the Chief doesn't like it? Stupid old sod, she thinks.

She is interrupted by Jason. "Jim Laurence is in an interview room with a cup of tea. He's much better and ready to be interviewed."

"Thanks Jason, you can come with me. The others are all gainfully employed."

The preliminaries over, she starts. "Thank you for coming in Jim. I know this must be difficult for you but it is important that we ask some questions."

"No bother. I'm happy to answer. I'm feeling better."

"I'm told that Annie was your aunt."

"She was my great aunt. My grandad was her brother."

"What time did you arrive?"

"About 5 o'clock. I'm doing work on the house. I'm doing general maintenance at college."

"Did you notice anything different?"

"No. The door wasn't locked but it never is. No one bothers round here."

"Did you see anyone in the area, even if you know them?"

"No. No one would be stupid enough to be out in this weather."

Well somebody was, thinks Shona.

"Was there anything different inside the house?"

"I don't think so. I don't pay much attention."

"Did your aunt have any close friends?"

"I don't know. My mum might be able to help you."

Shona takes the contact details for his mother and lets the lad go. It is obvious he doesn't know anything and from the way he looked at the scene, he'd be hard pushed to kill a midge.

She sends Jason to ring Annie's niece and ask her to come in. It is going to be a long night.

By the time she's interviewed Jim's mum, Sheila, it is after 9 pm. It turns out Sheila knows nothing either. She is comfortably off with a husband who works on the oilrigs. She had a good relationship with her aunt and seems distraught at her death. She doesn't know if anything is missing but says she will think about it and get back to them.

Peter and Nina have found out that a housing development company wants to buy Annie's land to build high-end houses. Sheila says her aunt had turned down a more than generous offer. Annie loved the farm and wouldn't give it up for anyone. Shona makes a note to follow this up in the morning.

As she is passing the main office on her way out Roy barrels into her.

"Glad I caught you, Ma'am. This one's a copycat killing as well."

She follows him to his computer.

"One Janet Henderson aged fifty. She was found bludgeoned to death. A heavy axe lay next to her on the kitchen floor. The reason it wasn't in my original search is that it happened in 1866. I didn't go back that far."

The news leaves Shona reeling. "Good grief. Is our killer going to go back to the Jacobite rebellions? We've no chance of getting a handle on this."

"Do you want me to widen my search?" "Leave it for tonight and go home. I'll think about it."

Shakespeare and a nice Laphroaig single malt are calling her.

36

The next morning all thoughts of chasing builders fly from Shona's head when she arrives at the office. For once Peter is there before her and says, "You'll want to read this Ma'am." He pushes a copy of *The Courier* across to her. The headlines scream:
"Killer's Letter: I am not a Copycat. I am a Craftsman"
  "What the..." She has to stop to calm herself down.
  "You might want tae sit down before you read the rest."
  She ignores him and carries on.

> 'In a strange twist, last night *The Courier* received a letter from Dundee's serial killer. The letter can be read below.'

> So the police think I'm a Copycat Killer. How wrong can they be? I am a craftsman. I am showing the original killers how it can still be done, even with today's forensic techniques. I am following in a long line of Scottish Craftsmen who are proud of their trade. Nothing will stop me until I am the best that Scotland has ever seen. The best is yet to come.'

Shona throws the paper across the room, picks it up again, and says, "Grab your coat. We're going to *The*

Courier."

"Are we no' waiting for the others? We could have a cup of tea."

"Never mind the others or your tea. Move." White-hot anger propels her forward, Peter racing behind. They meet Nina at the door of the station.

"What's up?"

"Dinnae ask. Just look at *The Courier*."

Shona drives in silence with her knuckles white against the steering wheel. Her first word is spoken at the reception of the newspaper office. Flashing her badge, "Get me the reporter who wrote this?"

"There's no need to be rude." The receptionist obviously feels that staying alive is overrated.

Shona moves closer and says, "If you don't get me this reporter I'll show you just how rude I can be. It will involve handcuffs and a cell."

The receptionist scurries off and comes back with a man.

"Did you write this?"

"No, but I am the editor, Benjamin Blacklaw. Would you like to come through to my office?"

Deciding a public slanging match in reception might not be the best way forward Shona complies.

"Would you like a tea or a coffee?"

"No we wouldn't." Her gaze falls on Peter and he snaps his mouth shut. "We would like the reporter who wrote this." She waves the paper in front of him "We need to ask him some questions."

"I'm afraid that won't be possible. We cannot give out any sources."

"This is a murder investigation and that letter is evidence. Why weren't the police told?"

"You were told. In my newspaper."

"So was the rest of Dundee. How am I meant to

catch the killer with you plastering evidence over the front of *The Courier?*"

"Freedom..."

Shona stands up. "Don't give me that rubbish. I'll be back with a warrant and that reporter had better be available. If he, or she, isn't then I will be crawling over your offices with such intensity that you won't get a paper out for months." She walks out Peter still tagging behind.

Shona calms down somewhat on the drive to the Sheriff's office.

"How can you say the Press are only doing their job when they pull a stunt like this?" she asks Peter.

"Even I'm not defending them today. This is bad."

The Sheriff is happy to oblige in the issuing of a warrant. "I hope you get some answers, Shona."

Shona phones Iain on the way to *The Courier* Office and asks him to meet her there. "Bring a fingerprint kit."

This time the editor coughs up the reporter's name. It is her nemesis John Laird. As usual he looks like a bag of rags. She's never seen such a scruffy oink in all her life. If he went down to the Salvation Army reject shop he'd get better clothes. Mind you they are probably designer ripped and cost a fortune.

"Can we have a quiet office to talk?"

"You can use my office," says the editor.

"Thank you, but I will have to ask you to leave."

"Not a..."

"It's non-negotiable." The stern voice gives no room for argument so he leaves muttering about police persecution. That will probably appear in the papers tomorrow but Shona doesn't give a hoot. She turns her gaze to John Laird.

"Why was this not handed in to the police the

minute it arrived?"

"The Killer trusted us with it. It wasn't meant for the police."

"Wasn't meant for the police? Of course it was meant for the police. When did it arrive?"

"Yesterday afternoon."

"And you didn't think to let us know?"

"It was a scoop. I am a reporter. Why would I hand it to you."

"So we can solve the bally case. Is this a joke to you, you cocky little git? More people can die while you're playing games. In fact one woman did."

She turns to Iain, "Get this letter into evidence and fingerprint this joker."

"Who else could have touched this and where's the envelope?"

"I touched it, and my editor. I think that was it. The envelope went into the recycling bin."

"You have got to be kidding me. You've thrown vital evidence in the bin?"

She turns to Peter. "Arrest him."

"What for, I haven't done anything?"

"For perverting the course of justice and withholding evidence."

"I've not got any handcuffs, Ma'am."

"Shame, read him his rights. If he doesn't come easily I'll get a couple of squad cars down here."

As they leave the office a camera flash goes off, blinding them all. Shona doesn't care. She strides towards her car and throws the reporter in. "Buckle up and shut up until we get to the station." The prisoner obliges.

Once they return to the station he isn't a prisoner for long. Shona is called into the Chiefs office.

"Shona, why do you cause havoc wherever you go?

I've had the editor of *The Courier* on the phone. Why have you arrested one of his reporters?"

"He withheld evidence."

"Have you got the evidence now?"

"Yes Sir."

"So he hasn't withheld evidence. Let him go."

"But he threw the envelope in the bin and it's gone."

"So he's a prat. When I did my training there wasn't a law against that in Scotland. Maybe it's different in England."

"Sir, he kept the evidence until this morning."

"As I say he's a prat. Now let him go. I know you think that he's low on the food chain, and I may agree, but we can't arrest people for that. When we've got something concrete to arrest him for, you'll have my full backing."

"Thank you, Sir." There isn't much more to say.

Before putting the reporter out of his misery she asks Peter to take him to an interview room.

"Interview with John Laird blah, blah blah. I have to tell you, you are free to go. However, I would like to ask you a few questions as a witness."

"Anything to help the police."

"You say you threw the envelope in the bin. Can you remember anything about it?"

"Brown, could have come from anywhere, probably Poundland."

"Size?"

"A5."

"Did it have a stamp on it?"

"No. It was handed in by a courier as far as I know."

"What company?"

"How the frick do I know. Do I look like someone who deals with incoming mail? It was marked urgent and sent straight up. The 'girls' on reception would know."

After she sends him packing Shona and Peter break the news to the rest of the team.

"You've got to be kidding, Ma'am," says Roy.

"How'd he manage that little trick?" Nina, for once, is taken aback.

"They certainly seem to do things in a strange way in Dundee. We'd have kept him for weeks on Skye."

"I'm sure that's not true Abigail."

"It's true Ma'am. We didn't arrest many people up there so when we got hold of them we kept them."

"Abigail, you could only have kept him for the customary 48 hours."

"Well it felt like weeks."

"Remind me never to get in to bother in Skye. That doesn't change the fact that we've had to let him go. I need grease and stodge to dissolve my disappointment." Shona leads the charge to the canteen.

Once refueled, she sends Nina and Abigail to talk to the receptionists at *The Courier*. They draw a blank. She can't remember. The courier still had his helmet on and visor down. He was fit and dressed all in black, tall and with a sexy voice. As to the firm, who cared? She doesn't think he'd been in before. She just noted the name and the word 'urgent' and sent the letter straight up. Shona doesn't think this particular 'girl' is ever going to move up the corporate ladder of publishing.

"Roy, go with Jason, Nina, take Burns, and Peter, you work with Abigail. Speak to all the courier firms in Dundee. See if they delivered anything to *The Courier* last night."

Shona goes to get a cup of the sludge that masquerades as coffee in the station. How can a day, which starts out badly, continue to go downhill? She takes her coffee to Iain's little fiefdom.

"How's it going? Have you found anything useful?"

"As you can see, it's printed from a computer. Standard grade paper, 80 gsm, which is used in loads of places. Libraries and offices for a start. No signature. I'll send a portion off for analysis. That will tell us which brand of paper and ink it is. That could take a few days though unless we expedite it."

"Get it done. Don't worry about how much we'll have to pay for it to be rushed through." Sod the expense, she thinks. It's the boss's budget and he'll just have to put up with it. They have nothing else to move the case forward.

"What about fingerprints?"

"As we suspected, just John Laird and his boss. I'm sure our killer's bright and he would use a clean sheet of paper and wear gloves."

There is no moving on from that.

The remainder of the team return footsore and empty handed.

"How can there be so many Courier firms in one wee city?. You'd think this was Auld Reekie, no' Dundee."

"Auld what?"

"Auld Reekie, Edinburgh. It got that name from all the smoke that used to hang over it."

"Thanks for the Scottish history lesson. Did you find anything?"

They shake their heads. No one had delivered anything to *The Courier*. In fact most of them hadn't delivered anything at all as they were closed for the night.

"So it looks like our killer delivered it himself?"

"It would seem so, Ma'am. He's a brazen one. Walks right up to the front door as bold as you like."

"He's got confidence. I'll give him that. Confidence or not we're going to get him. I'll bet my granny on that."

"You don't have a granny, Shona," says Nina.

"Yes I do. She's currently in Ecuador. I think it's Ecuador. It could be Paraguay. South America anyway. She's touring the world. What's this got to do with anything? We've multiple murders on our hands and we're talking about my grandmother."

"Where are we going with the case, Ma'am? I'm a bit lost," says Abigail.

"You and me both. I don't think I could find my way back to it with a map. Look into Sienna Laing's murder again. I'm not convinced her death has anything to do with this case."

Shona thinks about the case. She runs her hands through her hair and compiles a mental checklist of what is happening. So far the dead include three nuns, two prostitutes, a publican, a drunk, a trophy wife, a gay man and a farmer. Items missing are, three crucifixes, a locket, a wedding ring, a tap, a pair of boxer shorts, and a watch. They have to figure out if there is one person they all have in common. She picks up the phone to dial Sheila Laurence.

"Mrs Laurence, it's DI McKenzie. Can I ask did your aunt wear any specific item of jewellery?"

"She always wore an antique rose gold cross. It is a family heirloom and is passed down to the oldest girl in each generation. I will get it next and then my daughter after that. It... it's mine now, I suppose. Am I able to get it?"

"I'll see what I can do." Actually she doesn't have a hope unless we catch the killer thinks Shona. Next she phones Mary. "Afternoon Mary."

"Is it? With the amount of bodies you're throwing

my way I don't have time to notice. I've more bodies in my mortuary than they had during the Battle of Culloden. Are you English always like this?"

"I'm Scottish, Mary, born if not bred. Ninewells Hospital is where I made my debut."

Mary laughs and says, "What can I do for you?"

"Did Annie Pettry have a cross on when she arrived at your place?"

"Not that I'm aware of. I'll take a look." A couple of minutes later she is back. "No, just an old Timex watch."

"Thanks Mary. See you soon."

"No disrespect, Shona but I hope it's not too soon. Your enviable ability to attract bodies is wearing thin."

"I'll do my best to keep the body count down."

Putting down the phone Shona hurries down to evidence.

"Sgt McPhearson. How are you?"

"Grand, Ma'am. We don't often see you down here."

"Could you check the evidence from our latest murder for me? Is there a rose gold cross?"

"Come with me and we'll take a look." He opens the door and Shona enters the inner sanctum. It does her no good. Not a cross to be seen.

Shona thinks the day is going nowhere, but Roy comes into the office and cheers her right up.

"I've found something, Ma'am. Not about the copycat but I've been looking into Fergus Laing's accounts."

"Roy, is that legal?"

"As far as I know, Ma'am."

It sounds a bit suspicious to her but she'll have to run with it.

"A large sum of money, £145,000 pounds to be precise, has been routed through a million different branches to a bank account in the Caymans. The route it took makes spaghetti junction look like a Roman road "

"Roy, I think I love you. Fergus either paid to have his wife killed or he's money laundering. He doesn't know Stephan and Gregor Alexeyev by any chance?"

"I could look into it."

"Good plan. Before you do could you go and bring Fergus in for questioning."

Shona knows Fergus has arrived the minute he steps through the door. In fact the whole station does.

"How dare you treat me like this. I am a respected businessman in this city and have been for many years. I will not tolerate being arrested."

"You haven't been arrested. I've explained several times we just need to ask you a few questions. Have you heard me read you your rights?" Roy has had enough.

"You put me in a police car in front of all my neighbours."

"It's not a police car. It's my own personal BMW."

Shona interrupts their witty repartee. "Mr Laing would you like to come with me? DC MacGregor, can you please get Mr Laing a cup of coffee and meet us in the interview room."

Fergus opens his mouth, but Shona interjects. "Mr. Laing, if you have anything to say please save it for the interview room."

The usual preliminaries then, "Thank you for coming in Mr. Laing. As my DC explained you have not been arrested, we just need to ask you a few questions."

"Do I need my lawyer?"

"That's up to you." All Shona needs is Margaret McCluskey cluttering the place up.

"I won't bother at the moment, but if I don't like

the direction your questions are taking, it will be a different matter."

"You can ask for a lawyer at any time should you choose to do so. Can I ask you to tell me a bit more about your business?"

"What's this got to do with my wife's murder?"

"We're tying up a few loose ends. Now could you please tell me a bit more about your business?"

"It's an import and export business. I import goods from abroad and sell them locally. I also export Scottish goods internationally."

"What countries do you deal with?"

"As I said, many countries, internationally."

"Can you be more specific?"

"Why do you need to know all this?"

"If I didn't need to know I wouldn't be asking the questions. Now could you please answer?"

"I want my lawyer."

"Interview terminated as the witness requests that his lawyer is present. DC MacGregor, take Mr. Laing to ring his lawyer."

An hour and a cream cake later they are back in the interview room. The battleship McCluskey has joined them.

"Where are you going with this line of questioning Inspector? My client's business has nothing to do with his wife's murder."

"If that's the case then he won't mind answering my questions. I am trying to rule out another line of enquiry."

"Why don't you tell us what this line of enquiry might be?"

"Why don't I just tell you everything I know about this and every other case in my files. For heaven's sake, will you let me ask my questions or we'll be here all night. You might be getting paid four hundred pounds an hour but the rest of us aren't."

Margaret's beady eyes glare at Shona but she keeps her mouth shut.

"Where were we? Of course, what specific countries do you do business in?"

"The Far and Middle East, Europe, the States, Canada, Australia, New Zealand, South America and Russia."

Shona's ears prick up at that.

"Do you know Gregor and Stephan Alexeyev?"

"They are local businessmen. Of course, I know them."

"Have you had any business deals with them?"

"No. I've met them at local business dinners. That's about it."

"Have you done any business in the Cayman Islands?"

Fergus's face drains of colour so fast Shona thinks he is going to faint.

"Please answer the question Mr Laing."

"Why does my client have to answer this?"

"I'm not asking him to sign a confession in blood. It's a simple question with a yes or no answer."

You can almost see the cogs whirring in Fergus's head as he works out what to say and where they are going with this. Shona rides the silence out. Fergus will fill it eventually.

"No. I've never had any business deals in the Cayman Islands."

Bingo. Pull the trap shut. Shona pushes a piece of paper across the table. "So how do you explain this?"

Margaret bends close to Fergus and reads the document.

"How did you get this?" the lawyer asks.

"I'm asking the questions." Shona sends up a prayer that Roy came across it legally. "Why is your client transferring large sums to the Cayman Islands?"

"I would like to speak to my client alone."

"Absolutely. Before you do. Fergus Laing I am arresting you for incitement to commit murder. You do not have to say anything, but it may harm your defence..."

"You can't do that," Margaret is on her feet.

"I just did. Now as I was saying Mr Laing. It may harm your defence if you do not mention when questioned something, which you later rely on in court. Anything you do say may be given in evidence. DC MacGregor, get the prisoner processed and then he can speak to his lawyer."

Fergus slumps to the floor.

By the time an ambulance has arrived to take Fergus and a couple of constables to the hospital, the Chief has long gone home. Shona phones him.

"What do you want now Shona?" The Chief sounds more weary than annoyed.

"I was in the middle of arresting Fergus Laing when he collapsed."

"Why were you arresting Fergus Laing?"

Shona explains the situation.

"It sounds like you had grounds, but why can't you arrest someone without drama."

"Sorry, Sir."

"For once I believe you. Try and get through the night without any more deaths."

She is left listening to the dialing tone. She would like to wrap a telephone wire, tight, round the Chief's very dead neck. Another one for the book.

"Roy, we're the only idiots here. Go home and I'll see you in the morning. Good work today."

"Thanks, Ma'am." Roy is off like a whippet.

37

A ringing phone wakes Shona from a deep sleep. "DI McKenzie."

"Ma'am ye need tae get haud o' *The Courier* and read it afore ye' get in."

"Peter, it's too early for me to be translating. Speak English."

"Sorry. You need to buy a copy of *The Courier* and get here as soon as you can."

"Tell me."

"The killer's at it again. You need to get in."

"I'm on my way. Meet me there."

Shona phones the station and asks the duty sergeant to call the rest of the team. She travels via the corner shop to buy a newspaper. One glance and she knows why Peter is rattled.

'Killer Website'

'The Craftsman has revealed exclusively to *The Courier* the URL for his website. In a surprising twist, the Killer will be keeping the public up to date with his murders via this site. *Courier* readers can access the site at:

www.thecraftsmankills.com'

By the time she reaches the station the local, national and international Press are swarming around the front door. They are like a pack of hyenas only more noisy. She takes her frustration out on the Duty Sergeant.

"Get that lot off my doorstep. Put them in cells if they won't move. They won't be cluttering the place up then."

"All right Ma'am. Anything you want."

When she reaches the office John Laird is sitting on a chair, hands behind his back, and one scruffy leg propped on the other.

"What are you doing here?"

"I thought I'd save you the trip down to *The Courier* and bring your evidence up here."

"Very kind I'm sure. You didn't think to bring the evidence in before you published it?"

"Not for a minute. The public has a right to cutting edge news."

"At the expense of a murder investigation? How will you sleep at night if anyone else is killed?"

"Like a baby. It's not my fault if the police can't do their job."

"Can't do their job! The only thing stopping us doing our job are bottom feeders like you."

"Now now. There's no need to get mad."

Shona stops herself from rearranging his teeth. "I don't have time for this. Where's the evidence?"

He pulls an envelope from his pocket.

"You're contaminating it. Iain, get it in a bag. Laird, don't move a muscle until my DC gets back. How did it arrive?"

"By courier again."

"Who's handled it?"

"The courier, me, the editor and the receptionist I suppose."

Once the evidence is safely in a bag and off to be registered Shona sends the reporter packing.

"I can't stomach him for another minute, the supercilious git."

"Why sit on the fence? Come out and say what you really mean." Nina laughs and even Shona has to crack a smile.

"Let's look at this website."

The website is worse than she imagined. The killer has displayed, and numbered, his 'trophies', the items missing from the victims. On a background of black velvet the Mickey Mouse boxer shorts look incongruous - a splash of colour amongst the brown and gold. Underneath is written

'A Craftsman Displays his Wares'

Blood drips from the letters.

"Can you trace this Roy?"

"I'll do my best. It's probably well hidden."

"Get it taken down."

"I will, Ma'am, but not until I've tried to trace it."

"You mean this is going to be on view to the public until you've finished investigating?"

"Sorry, Ma'am, but that's right."

"For heaven's sake. Get on with it now. I want this down the minute you're finished."

Shona fears the day will not go well and she is right. The Chief tears her off a strip and she has distraught relatives camping on her doorstep.

The first one is there by ten am. It is Rosie Adamczac who has hotfooted it from Blairgowrie in record time given the snow and the state she is in. Through sobs she manages to say, "My Stan's boxer shorts are on display for the whole world to see."

"I know Rosie, and I promise you we will remove

the pictures as soon as we can."

Shona can hear choking sounds and she turns to Nina. "Sgt Chakrabarti, could you please ask one of the DC's to bring in a cup of tea for Rosie. I'm sure she would like one."

Turning back to Mrs. Adamczac she says, "Rosie. I appreciate this must be distressing for you. I can assure you the police are doing everything they can to catch your husband's killer. We need to keep the website open at the moment as part of the investigation, but the minute we can we will close it down. You have my word on that."

"Thank you. You're a kind lassie. I wouldn't want your job."

This scenario is repeated with several other distressed relatives. By the time she's spoken to them all, she's thinking she doesn't want her job either. She doesn't get paid enough for any of this.

She finds Roy head down and hard at work. "Have you managed to trace it yet?"

"Nowhere near it. Whoever set up this website knows exactly what they are doing. I'd be better trying to get into the computers of the North Korean Army."

"Keep at it, Roy. Let me know the minute you have anything."

He turns back without saying a word and continues tapping keys. Shona heads towards Iain's cubbyhole.

"Have you heard back from the lab yet?"

"Yep. It came about an hour ago but you were busy. It is Hewlett Packard paper and Hewlett Packard ink. Pretty standard in most homes."

Sighing. "So we're no further forward?"

"At the moment no, but it might just be what we need to nail a suspect when we have one."

"Thanks, Iain."

Back in her office Shona kicks the waste paper bin. It is either that or the first person she sees. Patience is not her strongest virtue; in fact she doesn't have that particular virtue at all.

She is stopped from lobbing the nearest object out of the window, by the arrival of the procurator fiscal, who has returned from his course.

She kisses him. "Douglas. I've never been so glad to see anyone in my life."

"I've missed you as well. Good to see you. How many dead bodies have you managed to accumulate in my absence?"

"Only a couple." She outlines everything that has happened.

"Blimey, Shona, this is a new level of weird, even for you."

"I have to agree with you. Have you got any ideas as to why this is happening or who might be doing it?"

"I'm afraid not. We had a lot of murders before you arrived, but not as many as this. I've not had huge amounts of experience with serial and copycat killers."

Roy interrupts them with a frenzied knocking on the door. "Ma'am, you've got to see this. You too, Sir."

They follow Roy as he rushes from the room. One look at his top of the range iMac screen tells them why he is so rattled. There, filling the screen, in glorious high resolution technicolour, is a photo of the three dead nuns. Underneath are the words

'A Masterpiece by The Craftsman'

Shona fetches the Chief. He joins the open mouthed throng around the computer. There is a silence so thick it would need a saw to cut through it.

"Get This Website Down Now," says the Chief.

"Sir, this may be the only way to catch the killer."

"Now." The Chief turns and walks towards his office, back ramrod straight.

"Douglas can you ask the Chief to relent?"

"No. I agree with him." He Follows the Chief

"Roy, are you anywhere close to finding who owns this site?"

"No, Ma'am."

"Then take it down. The rest of you back to work."

Shona takes a coffee back to her desk, praying it will turn into the finest malt. It isn't to be. It doesn't even resemble coffee never mind malt. This day is going from worse to hell.

Just how hellish it is about to get Shona soon finds out. The desk sergeant appears in her office.

"Sorry, Ma'am, it's not good news."

"Spit it out sergeant."

"There's been another suspicious death."

"Where?"

"Broughty Ferry. An elderly man and his wife. Dunalistair Gardens."

"Thanks." Shona picks up her coat and grabs the team. "Looks like we've another copycat on our hands. A ringer for the Doctor and his wife." She then grabs Douglas, this time with not a shred of romance involved.

The crime scene is not a pretty sight. Worse than usual that is. The man is in the hallway and the woman lying against the kitchen door. Copious amounts of sprayed blood and their badly beaten bodies show what has happened in the final minutes of this elderly couple' life.

"Iain, get photos. From the pattern of blood smears I'd say they tried to get away. Catalogue everything inside and out."

"I'm not sure how well outside photos will do in this blizzard."

"Do your best."

The bodies having been taken off to the tender ministrations of Mary, the team is back in the briefing room and on the case.

Canvassing the neighbours has elicited that the dead couple were Ernie Smith and his wife Elsie. A sociable couple they were friendly with everyone. Shona and Peter have already been to their daughter's house to break the news of her parent's death.

Iain has taken several cracking photos, which are now up on the board.

"The blood patterns suggest they tried to defend themselves. I think the husband stayed in the hallway to allow the wife to get away."

"Why didn't she make it?" asks Abigail. "It must have taken some time for the husband to die."

"Looks like the killer laid into the husband leaving him to bleed out. The wife might have been upstairs and by the time she realised what was happening it was too late." Iain knows blood patterns like no one else in Scotland. Shona is thankful to have him on the team.

Iain continues, "The wife tried to get out. I found blood on the handle of the kitchen door, and smeared down the door."

"Poor woman," says Abigail.

"Indeed. So how are we going to find her killer?" says Shona.

"We might be able to catch the courier if one of us stands in for the receptionist," says Nina.

"Good idea. Who's going to volunteer?"

"We might need to do shifts."

"Okay. Nina and Abigail off you go and get changed into your most vampish clothes fit to trap Mr

Sexy Voice. I'll speak to the editor and get it squared. With a warrant if necessary."

After a spirited discussion about freedom of speech the editor agrees. The receptionists get a couple of buckshee days off and the female sergeants get a change of scene.

38

A couple of days later the case is still stalled and the Chief's temper has deteriorated rapidly.

"Why are two of my sergeants still loafing around providing free employees for the Press? Bring them back."

"I agree, sir. This seems to be getting us nowhere. Have you any ideas where we can go from here?" Shona is desperate.

"None, but you need to come up with something fast. The Lord Provost's coming in to see me. He's not impressed."

"I'll do my best, Sir but I seem to be fresh out of inspiration."

Nina and Abigail are pleased to be back in harness.

"I'm never going to moan about my job again. That's the most mind numbingly boring few days I've ever spent," says Nina.

"I never thought I'd be glad to see Roy and Jason in the same room." Abigail laughs and the aforementioned coppers join in. Goodness knows why the team is so cheerful but Shona is happy to see it.

"I'm not a praying woman but even I was praying that Mr Sexy Drawers would turn up to relieve the boredom. Anybody sexy would have been an improvement on a bunch of grieving Dundonians putting death notices in the paper."

The game of deadly chess continues with the Killer

taking control of the board. At least no more pawns are sacrificed in the process. The death toll in Dundee remains static.

A few days later, Shona arrives at the office to be met by Peter and a copy of the paper.
"We're on Ma'am. *The Courier*'s at it again."

'The Craftsman's Bloody Reign Continues'

'In another world exclusive *The Courier* brings you the latest letter from the Dundee Craftsman.

You think you have stopped me. Wrong. A Craftsman never stops. He is always learning, always developing his technique. My latest handiwork can be seen at

www.thecraftsmanneverstops.com'

"Here's the website."
The screen fills with a photo of Archie's beaten body, stark against the white snow, blood the only splash of colour.
Roy clicks and an updated photo of the trophies appears. It now contains two matching wedding rings. His latest victims', Shona assumes.
"Get it down again, and get that letter from John Laird or whatever scum has their hands on it."

The letter is safely in Iain's hands for analysis, when he calls her through to his den.
"Ma'am, I think I might have something."
He shows her the faint imprint of some letters on

the paper.

"They look like a signature Ma'am."

"I can't read what they say."

"It looks like an L rd."

Adrenaline slams through Shona like one of Harry Lawson's trucks.

"Laird, John Laird. Our killer's the journalist."

"Could be, Ma'am, but remember he's had the letter in his possession so this could happen naturally."

"It was him. I know it. Now I know why the Press was all over this like botulism. They knew about if before we did. Call the team together."

Shona informs the Chief.

"You need to make sure that everything's in place before you arrest him. Check everything out about the man. If you get it wrong he'll disappear into whatever sewer he crawled from and we'll never get him."

"Of course, Sir."

The team is jubilant.

"Hold the champagne. We're not there quite yet. We've a ton of research to do before we march in with handcuffs."

"It's still the first lead we've had," says Nina.

"Aye. it is. So we can be a wee bit cheerful."

"We can. First things first. Handwriting analysis. How long does it take Iain?"

"We could get it done in 24 hours but they might speed it up for us."

"Explain the situation and see what can be done."

"Nina, get on to *The Courier* and see what type of printers they use and printer paper. Be discreet, we don't want to warn him. Find out how long he's worked there as well."

Shona rings Shuggie in Stirling and he says he will make enquiries for her. Something else is puzzling her.

Whoever committed the murders at the convent knew the place inside out. Why would an oink of a reporter know anything about a convent? Picking up the phone she dials the number.

"St Winfred's Convent"

"It's DI Shona McKenzie. May I speak to the Mother Superior please?"

"I'll just get her for you."

There is a wait of about five minutes, during which time Shona's head is spinning.

"Mother Superior. What can I help you with this time, Inspector?" Shona thinks her tone is surprisingly cordial given their recent encounter.

"Reverend Mother, does the name John Laird mean anything to you?"

"I can't say it does."

"Please could you ask the others if they know of him, and if so, in what capacity?"

"I will, Inspector. We are praying for you and this case."

"Thank you." There isn't much else she can say to that.

Shona is back to playing hurry up and wait.

A few nail biting, coffee and adrenaline fuelled, hours later the answers start coming in.

"John Laird's been at *The Courier* for about eighteen months. They use a variety of printers and HP paper. The printer in John Laird's office is HP."

"Shona, it's Shuggie. John Laird worked at *The Stirling News* for a couple of years. He left about eighteen months ago, so that would fit in with our unsolveds."

"Ma'am, we've got the results back from the Electro Static Detection Analysis of the letter. The imprint definitely says Laird. The handwriting analysis will take longer and they'll need a sample of John Laird's handwriting for comparison."

"It looks like we've got our man, chaps. Good work. All we have to do now is arrest him."

"Given the amount of dead bodies he's left in his wake, I cannae see that being very easy."

"Exactly my thoughts. We're going to be armed. Get pistols. I don't want to take any chances. I'll follow you down to complete the paperwork. Jason, you do know the meaning of pistol don't you? It looks nothing like a rifle."

"Yes, Ma'am." Jason doesn't have the look of a man who is going to behave. He manages to slip rifles past her at every opportunity.

"Soldier boy, you're not in the Army now you know," says Roy.

"You could be doing with a stint in the Army, it might make you a better human being."

"Boys this is no time to be bickering. We're all on the same side here."

She turns back to the rest of the team.

"Put stab vests on as well. I don't want anyone getting injured. Jason, I know that might be impossible for you. Try to stay in one piece."

Shona briefs the Chief.

"I will need extra manpower to guard all the entrances to the building sir."

"Ask Uniform, they might have extra officers to give you."

"Thank you, Sir." She turns to leave.

"Shona."

"Yes, Sir." She turns back.

"Well done, but try to bring everyone back without a visit to Ninewells Hospital this time. You can't seem to arrest people without chaos ensuing."

"Of course, Sir." Stupid old coot is what she is

really thinking. Does he think she wants all the drama that exists in her orbit?

While they are getting ready the phone rings.

"Inspector, it's the Mother Superior at the convent."

"Thank you for getting back to me."

"One of the older nuns recognises the name. He is the great nephew of Sister Mary Agnes who died many years ago. He used to come and visit her in the convent."

"Thank you, that's helpful."

"You're welcome."

Another nail in John Laird's coffin.

39

As they get out of the van, Shona says, "All those from Uniform get the area secured. I want every exit covered no matter how insignificant it looks. Keep your guns at the ready and shoot if necessary."

"Is that an order, Ma'am?" asks one of the coppers.

"It is. Shoot only to keep yourself or your buddies safe. No wild west heroics. It's Dundee not the Alamo."

She turns to her own team. "Follow me."

They enter through the front door and rush through reception flashing their badges.

Miss Not too Bright, the receptionist, says, "You can't go through there."

Shona shows her badge again and says, "This says we can. Now, if I were you I'd sit down and keep out of the way."

The receptionist, looking like she is about to burst into tears, complies. They are now familiar with the route to John Laird's office. He isn't there.

The only other occupant of the room says, "If you're looking for John he had a phone call and left at warp speed." He waves towards a door at the other end of the office.

Miss Not too Bright, must have warned him. That will be her in handcuffs as well, thinks Shona.

They barrel through the door to which the journalist has pointed. The best thing would be to empty the building, but they don't want Laird slipping out undetected. It's a close call, but it is late and there are few people left in the building anyway.

They creep along quiet corridors check countless dark rooms. Adrenaline coursing through their veins has them all jittery. Shona stops.

"Take some deep breaths. Widen the search. Peter, you're with Jason, Nina, with Roy, Abigail, you take Burns. I'm with Iain. Split up. We'll take a floor each. Meet back in reception."

Shona and Iain move at a crawl, searching every nook and cranny. They open every cupboard, no matter how small. John Laird is wiry and Shona wouldn't put it past him to squeeze into a miniscule space. They freeze as they see movement. A cat brushes past them.

"Who would have thought there would be a cat in a newspaper office?" whispers Iain.

"It'll be here to catch mice."

An hour later they have searched the building from top to bottom, and not one one dust mote is left unturned. The only thing they haven't found is their suspect. John Laird is nowhere to be seen.

Shona turns to Miss Not too Bright, whose name, according to her badge, is Cheryl.

"Did you phone John Laird and let him know we were coming?"

"Of course. It's my job."

God spare me from idiots Shona thinks.

"Is there a basement in this building?"

"Yes. It's huge."

"What's it used for?"

"Storage mainly. It's full of junk."

"Show us how to get in."

Cheryl, who has got over her unwillingness to help the police, shows them the way. Her compliance is probably aided by the gun Shona now has in her hand.

The basement is dim and, as Cheryl said, full of junk.

"Split up again," Shona whispers. She points each

pair in a different direction.

She moves forwards, closely followed by Iain. What is that faint rustle? A mouse darts out running across Shona's feet. Shona bites her lip hard, drawing blood. They stop dead and catch their breath. Shona, licks her bleeding lip and signals they should move. The basement is overheated and sweat is dripping in her eyes. She wipes it away and creeps forward.

After, what seems like hours, but is only about ten minutes, they step into a small dimly lit passageway. John Laird is facing them and pointing a gun at Abigail. Burns is lying on the floor, blood dripping from a head wound. His breathing is laboured and his face has a deathly pallor. Shona's heart screams into her mouth. Please God let Burns be okay.

Outwardly calm she says, "John, put the gun down."

His eyes are darting everywhere, his hand shaking with adrenaline-fuelled nerves. It is plain to see that the reporter isn't so strong and calm when confronted by live opponents.

How can someone so scruffy be responsible for all these murders? thinks Shona. Everything about him is frayed, from his ratty jumper to the holes in his jeans. Something is nibbling at Shona's brain cells. She can't quite place it.

She says again, "Put the gun down." Peter and Jason dash up the corridor and stop as they take in the scene.

"No. You are going to let me go and I'm going to take Susie Wong here with me." Despite his nervousness his voice is strong and calm.

"You're never going to get out of here, John. Why make it worse? You don't want another death on your conscience."

"What does another one matter?" He moves the

gun to point at Shona.

The awful thing is, he is right. However, Shona isn't going to lose a team member. There is movement and, edgy, the journalist pulls the trigger. At the first sound the team dives to the floor. The bullet goes wide and ricochets of the walls, landing safely in a corner. No one is hit.

Laird throws Abigail to the ground. The crack of bone hitting concrete tells them she's battered her head. Laird hightails it up the corridor.

"Move. He's getting away. Peter and Jason stay with Burns and Abigail."

By the time they get to their feet, and bolt in pursuit, he has disappeared. The sound of pounding feet bounces off the cracked concrete walls of the corridor. Speed takes priority over silence as they give chase.

Shona stops dead as she enters a cavernous room full of equipment shrouded in dustsheets. Iain bangs into her back.

"Watch where you're going."

They scan the room, taking in every visible cranny.

"Iain you go right, and I'll take the left."

Shona creeps forward, her eyes darting in every direction, including upwards at a few overhead walkways. The minutes tick by and she sees or hears nothing. The only sound is that of her heart pounding. She stands for a few moments her ears straining into the silence. She hears a shout and runs in its general direction. Dashing around a huge machine she sees Iain pinned to the floor with John Laird on top of him. John has Iain's gun which is now pointed at the imprisoned copper.

"You're making things worse. Put the gun down. Now."

"You should double as a stand-up comedian. How can things be worse? One more dead body isn't going to

293

make a difference."

She can see a shadow moving behind John Laird. Just as John notices it as well, a foot shoots out and knocks the gun from his hand. Roy has come to the rescue. Before John can take it in, Shona has a gun to his head.

"Move and I will shoot." He tries, and Shona rams the gun harder into his temple. "Just give me an excuse to pull the trigger. Don't even think about twitching."

Nina snaps handcuffs on the journalist and Shona drags him to his feet.

"John Laird, I am arresting you for the murders of Sister Mary Claire, Sister Mary Elizabeth, Sister Mary Josephine, Archie Green, Tilly Methven, Stanislaus Adamczac, Dylan Masters, Annie Pettry, Ernie Smith, Elsie Smith and one unknown female. You do not have to say anything, but it may harm your defence if you do not mention when questioned something, which you later rely on in court. Anything you do say may be given in evidence."

Having said all this, Shona feels a lot better. She only hopes she's got all the Sister Marys right or his lawyer will get him off on a technicality.

"Nina, and Iain get this lunatic in a cell. I'm going to go to the hospital with Abigail and Burns."

40

As they travel to Ninewells Hospital in an ambulance,
Abigail looks pale, but apart from a horrific bump on
her head, says she is fine. Burns, on the other hand is in
a serious way. The paramedics work on him all the way
to the hospital. His breathing deteriorates and they
intubate him. On arrival at the hospital he is whisked
off and Shona is left standing in a crowded waiting
room. She gives the receptionist all the details she
knows about Burns and tells her who she is. She then
leans against a wall and waits. Half an hour later
Abigail appears.

"How is Burns Ma'am?"

"No one's told me anything. How are you?"

"They say I'm fine. Someone needs to keep an eye
on me overnight though."

"You can come home with me."

"Thanks."

A nurse enters the room and shouts, "DI
McKenzie."

Shona pushes herself from the wall and walks over.

"DC MacIntosh is on his way to theatre. We have
informed his next of kin and they are on their way. If
you leave your number we will let you know how he is
once he is out of surgery."

"Is he going to be all right?"

"There's nothing more I can tell you at the
moment."

Back in the office Shona slumps into her chair. John

Laird is safely in a cell but this does not make her feel any better.

She informs the Chief, who is, both concerned and condescending.

"Keep me up to date. Also get me a car. I will go to the hospital and see his parents. Every time you complete a case someone is seriously injured? I thought you might have started improving by now."

She is thinking, improving, I'm improving all right. Her aim to shoot the Chief.

In the middle of typing up notes, Shona has a eureka moment. She finds Iain. "Did we take a black fibre from one of the first murders? I seem to remember thinking it came from one of the nun's habits."

"We did."

"Check it against the fibre from John Laird's scruffy jumper. I bet we have a match."

"Good catch, Ma'am. I'll go and do it now."

Once John Laird is in an interview room he is more than happy to tell them all about his exploits. He seems almost proud in fact. Shona takes down the whole sorry statement and then asks, "Why did you do it?"

"I have known since the minute I could breath that my life would matter. I knew that the world would be changed because I was in it. My mother always said I would be famous one day. She believed in me. She told me every day that I was special. That I would do something extraordinary. Everyone has 15 minutes of fame and this was going to be mine. I wanted to write a prize winning book."

"All this for a book. You killed all those people for a book? Even you can't think that is extraordinary. It is depraved."

"A craftsman needs to perfect his craft. Sometimes

there is collateral damage."

Shona leaps to her feet. Peter drags her back saying, "He's no' worth it Ma'am."

For once in her life, Shona listens to the voice of reason.

She has just about finished her paperwork and ready to take Abigail home for tea and TLC, when the phone rings.

"DI McKenzie."

"It's Dr Muir, in A&E at Ninewells. I am sorry to inform you that DC MacIntosh did not make it through surgery. He died forty minutes ago. His next of kin requested that I let you know."

As Shona replaces the phone, tears roll silently down her cheeks. She prepares to tell the team.

John Laird was wrong. One more dead body does make a difference. It makes a difference to her.

WENDY H. JONES

Wendy H. Jones lives in Dundee, Scotland, and her police procedural series featuring Detective Inspector Shona McKenzie, is set in Dundee.

Wendy, who is a committed Christian, has led a varied and adventurous life. Her love for adventure led to her joining the Royal Navy to undertake nurse training. After six years in the Navy she joined the Army where she served as an Officer for a further 17 years. This took her all over the world including the Middle East and the Far East. Much of her spare time is now spent travelling around the UK, and lands much further afield.

As well as nursing Wendy also worked for many years in Academia. This led to publication in academic textbooks and journals. Killer's Craft is the second book in the Shona McKenzie series.

THE DI SHONA McKENZIE MYSTERIES

Killer's Countdown
Killer's Craft

FIND OUT MORE

Website: http://www.wendyhjones.com

Full list of links: http://about.me/WendyHJones

Twitter: https://twitter.com/WendyHJones

Photographs of the places mentioned in the book can be found at: http://www.pinterest.com/wjones64/my-dundee/